PILGRIMAGE

Kirk House Publishers

CHINA
Jixi
Vladivostok
Nakhodka
Chongjin
NORTH KOREA
Songjin
Shenyang
Fushun
Dandong
Haedung
Dalian
Pyongyang
Seoul
Inchon
Qingdao
SOUTH
KOREA
Kwangju
Taegu
Ulsan
Pusan
CHINA
Qingdao
Fukue-
shima
Kitakyushu
Fukuoka
Oita
Uwajima
Nagasaki
Shikoku
Kyushu
Shanghai
Kiire
East
China
Sea
Yellow
Sea
Tokara-
retto
Osumi-shoto
Ryukyu Islands
Amami-
shoto
Senkaku-
shoto
Okinawa-
shoto
Naha
Saito-
shoto
RUSSIA
Sakhalin
Wakkanai
Hokkaido
Sapporo
Nemuro
Hakodate
Aomori
Akita
Morioka
Sendai
Niigata
Iwaki
Sea of
Japan
Sado-
shima
Kanazawa
Nagano
Honshu
Tottori
Gifu
Yokohama
Tokyo
Kyoto
Nagoya
Hiroshima
Kobe
Osaka
Hamamatsu
Philippine
Sea
North
Pacific
Ocean
Iwo-jima
Torishima
Bonin
Islands
Volcano
Iwo Islands
45°N
40°N
35°N
30°N
25°N
125°E
130°E
135°E
140°E
145°E
0   200   400 mi
0   250   500 km

J A P A N

PILGRIMAGE

Daniel O'Brien

First Edition
Printed in the United States of America

Paperback ISBN: 978-1-959681-82-3
Hardcover ISBN: 978-1-959681-83-0
eBook ISBN: 978-1-959681-84-7
LCCN: 2025903965

Cover design and interior design by Ann Aubitz
Cover Photo: Red and Blue Laced Suit of Armor from the Kii Tokuawa Family, Mid-Seventeenth Century from the Minneapolis Institute of Art
Permission granted, Minneapolis Institute of Art
Red and Blue Laced Suit of Armor from the Kii Tokuawa Family, Mid-Seventeenth Century
Suit by Unknown Japanese Artist
Helmet by Saotome Iechika
Materials: Iron, leather, lacquer, silk, wood, gold leaf and powder, bear fur
The Ethel Morrison Van Derlip Fund 2009
On View in Gallery 219 at the Minneapolis Institute of Art

Published by
Kirk House Publishers
1250 E 115th Street
Burnsville, MN 55337
612-781-2815
Kirkhousepublishers.com

DEDICATION

*This book is dedicated to the recently deceased spiritual guide,
Qapel-Doug Duncan.*

May it benefit all beings.

ACKNOWLEDGMENTS

I would like to give appreciation and gratitude to my meditation teachers (Sensei et al.) and community who help me to become an engaged, aware person more and more each year.

Also, I am indebted to the beta readers with experience in Japan, my editor, Connie Anderson of www.WordsandDeedsInc.com, as well as the Kirk House Publishers for the professionalism of this piece of work. Gratitude to Mr. N. Matsushita for his generosity in sharing about the pilgrimage route prior to my visit of March 2024.

Significantly, my wife who, having spent many hours wondering what I am doing glued to the computer, and for helping us live a healthy life in many ways, deserves appreciation for her steadfast support. Further, she is clearly on her own journey to explore life, which inspires me in my journey.

Lastly, the many students who have inspired me to be a better teacher, not only in high school but also in the meditation classroom.

Finally, our dogs: first Fuku (means good fortune) and Kazu (means harmony), who taught me compassion in many ways, as well as the meaning of being a good team member.

Chapter 1
JIMMY'S DILEMMA

Jimmy sat at his oak desk in his well-lit classroom at the World Academy upper school. He imagined *Wa-rudo Akademi* was the right pronunciation because of his ten-year stint in Japan some years before. His total and complete sense of euphoria and peace after helping Saori—the mysterious ghost from the Heian Period of Japan, integrate her soul—had lasted for several months in his moonlit house. Then he had been side-swiped.

When it hit him in his gut, he felt weak, remembering his meditation teachers had said, "The ego is incredibly slippery." Jimmy had not gotten over all his conditioned patterns around relationships, clinging to the good feelings he had that resulted from the visits by the ghost that certainly went beyond a simple *friendship* as he had wrongly come to believe about their relationship. So, even if much healing had happened, he realized that because of his shyness around women, he avoided intimacy—and as a result, had clung to the idea of Saori showing up. This filled the void in him in a way that he welcomed because it felt safe. Saori was a ghost, so she couldn't do anything funny, couldn't mess it up. Yes, he was clinging to the sense of their relationship being safe.

In his youth in a small town in Minnesota, no one had ever encouraged him to care about others in a way that had showed him how to do it. His family all got together in the evenings for a formal family meal of chicken and potatoes almost every weekend. Being kind was assumed, not taught.

The beautiful, small-town church was welcoming, but it served as more of a routine formality than as a teacher who gave him tools to help others beyond simply praying for them.

These things were why he missed Saori so much. He keenly felt that something was missing, and her absence only confirmed that. She was his first opportunity to really care about another, and he felt that he'd truly accomplished that, helping her to integrate her karma, healing her past deeds and returning to her Heian time period in Japan. What he hadn't realized is that being true to her was limited in that she obviously wasn't a living, breathing woman in the modern period. And furthermore, she was always wearing a kimono each time she appeared. Knowing her created a double burden: despite having helped her, what remained was for him to try to be in a relationship.

His need to figure this out was Jimmy's response to people who saw him as distant, even when he cared deeply about them. And…he had no idea how to sensibly approach and date women. This was only too obvious as Janelle, one of the teachers at his school, found out at the ski resort. He regretted being so standoffish with her, a woman who was obviously interested in *him*. For now, that path was closed to them as they emotionally went their separate ways when all Jimmy could think about was the ghost. Janelle lost interest when she was left completely out of the loop—even when they were alone in the teacher's lounge at school.

Jimmy looked around his classroom at the world maps and paraphernalia—bells, a *noh* mask from Japan and another mask from Venice, Italy—reviewing the assortment of items that he'd gathered on trips around the world. He recalled his home life, growing up with four siblings where it had been "fend for yourself." He was glad that he'd learned so much about *friendship* from Saori, the beautiful 800-year-old ghost. While he'd learned through that journey to care about others, he still had a feeling of awkwardness about just that—being *related*, especially with women. It was obvious that he lacked experience dating women because he hated the risks involved.

Conditioned patterns around relationships were certainly still a hurdle for him, although he wasn't naïve about this. What surprised and frustrated him was how much he clung to the patterns. He was exasperated by how hard it was to go beyond those patterns and simply reach out to women and be "related."

Jimmy wondered: *How the hell can a ghost still have me in her grasp, and she's not even around?* The question was rhetorical. He knew from his many lessons and conversations with his teachers, McDougal and Sensei, and through his own experience, that conditioned patterns liberate a little at a time. Meditation was no silver bullet. It took time, experience, and determination to heal the pain of karmic-conditioned tendencies of one's patterns that cause a feeling of separation, discomfort, and so on. He was up for it, but long from being over it. He took a deep breath like the meditation teachers had taught him, breathed out while relaxing, and paused till he was back under control. Looking around the room again at the world map and other images of important figures on the walls, such as prominent Americans, Frederick Douglass and Phyllis Wheatley, and hearing the loudspeaker announce the important points of the day, he sorted the papers on his desk and began once more to prepare the day's lessons.

Mid-morning, and the sun was coming in the classroom's lone window. Jimmy stopped what he was doing and carelessly dropped his round, wire-rimmed glasses on his desk out of frustration. Although it was the middle of the lesson, he was too distraught to continue. His students took notice of his sighing and tried to make sense of this odd behavior as a nervous Jimmy worked to pull himself together. Murmuring began at the back of the room, then moved throughout. The students in their blue-and-gray uniforms were trying to be polite but also grew concerned.

Yes, he missed the ghost, Saori. The summer trip to Open Breeze, the meditation center he called home with the Tibetan initiation called *wong kur*—though an empowering and joyful occasion, did not change this fact. The smell of incense at the ceremony, and especially the bell and *vajra,* only brought the image of her more clearly to his mind than ever as he reflected upon the altar with the various hues of red in the Vajra Yogini celebration, the deity of the day. Saori had integrated her 800-year journey, but he was left trying to pull himself together, intensely feeling the loss of her. Their bond had only been tightened, in his mind, with her integration back into the Heian Period of Japan, a period that traversed the dates 794-1185 CE.

The blissful feelings he felt upon helping her had been real; however, his humanness remained intact, and at present he realized an impediment to moving on. He felt he needed more. He wanted the connection with her in real time, in person. Noticing his rapid breathing, he took several moments at his desk to use his meditation practice to intentionally calm down.

Jimmy gave the students a reading assignment, which made them visibly relieved he was back. Then he went over the meditation practice—feeling himself sitting on the chair…feeling his feet on the floor, and his hands on his thighs, he brought his awareness into the body. Naturally his breathing slowed down. He was able to go back to the day's lesson, although the unease remained as the bell to end the school day chimed. Instinctively everyone looked at the clock, but several students looked at him seemingly concerned, and in leaving, they exchanged looks. A student named Mahmoud even stayed back to ask him how he was doing, but he urged her to catch her bus as he tried to convince both her and himself that he was fine.

Why is this happening? he thought. After all, Jimmy was in his early thirties and was a seasoned meditator who easily dealt with student concerns, as well as the angry outburst of students and so on. He thought, *This isn't normal for me. I'm normally fully in control and not concerned with such mundane things. What gives?*

It was very true that Jimmy cared for another and wanted a real connection with another person. He realized that it wasn't an odd concern. He was only being human; however, this did little to assuage either his need for human connection, being with someone who would bring joy in companionship—or his frustration at the fact that these conditioned patterns remained so strong after all these years. He'd had the help of meditation teachers for years, so he thought that these patterns should no longer bother him. He understood even more clearly now that the help of such a teacher, someone with more experience, was essential. He would contact his teachers when the chance arose, but what could he do for himself? This was something they'd been encouraging in him for a while.

Relax, he told himself. He'd have to practice relaxing. That was for sure. *Be natural*, he told himself, another of his teacher's instructions.

Jimmy taught the semester, and as the first half of the school year drew to a close, he realized this empty spot in him, the void left by Saori integrating and leaving, had to be filled by something. He knew this would only be filled by him becoming somehow more whole himself. He needed a purpose, but how could he find out what that was? *…Maybe graduate school, study in Japan*? He was surprised that this realization to seek out a deeper understanding of himself—his purpose— came from meditation.

The realization arose in the meditation room, a room with a desk, shelves filled with books from his Asian studies courses, American Government course, and his social studies lessons, a truly eclectic bunch. He came to believe that his karma was to become an expert at something…he'd give it more thought, but he believed he needed to take action soon. His restlessness was pushing him to move, to not be too settled in, too comfortable at the school in Minnesota. But where to begin?

Several weeks later, while meditating, Jimmy realized what this meant for him. *That's it.* After a weekend-long series of meditation sessions, his mind was quickly drawing up plans to help people understand the importance of cultures coming together in the world. First, however, he'd have to go through the journey and become a master of himself through more fully studying Japanese culture. He'd have to go back to Japan, so he made plans and didn't renew his contract at World Academy for the next school year, taking a leave of absence instead.

Several days later, Jimmy had an undecipherable dream.

All those years of ancient teachings were finally paying off for what really mattered—the securing of what is truly beautiful about Japan. His master had taught him well the ways of Japan and its ancient traditions. What he needed to do was burned in his heart.

The events of the last few centuries revealed that through the underground, Christian sects began by the Spanish and Portuguese Jesuits, had been eliminated in Shikoku. This only resulted in an even-more worrisome influence—that of Buddhism—something that, Shinto, native and more suited to Japan could not stand to bear. As a result, he desperately needed to create a separation between Shinto and Buddhism, cleave them from each other so to speak, and because of the diluting of the culture, he said to himself, "We are committed to driving Buddhism from our native Japan."

Thankfully, his teacher had shown him the importance of ridding the homeland of this scourge. His master came from a long line of Shinto priests dedicated to nature, the gods, and the wonder that is Japan. Their heritage went back to the time of the Kojiki, the founding of Japan.

There was no more obvious influence of Buddhism in Japan than in its subversion of Shinto in the realm of burial and funerals, which, of course, resulted in forgetting the traditions of the past, something that particularly irked this man and his master. He found Buddhism, in addition to being foreign, to be totally unforgiveable in its usurpation—in this way. If there was no ceremony, no native rite of honoring the ancients, then what was left?

Finally, the man mused that Ieyasu, the Tokugawa Shogun or military general, had established a policy of sakoku, whereby foreigners and foreign influence were kept out of Japan for around 250 years, and the foreign trade that happened was only with permission from the Shogun and was carried out exclusively by the Dutch.

At least Ieyasu got all the damn foreigners out of Japan, the samurai said to himself. If we work with diligence, we can get rid of foreign influences in the nineteenth century. All of us will make sure of it. Samurai blood flows through enough families around Japan to remove this menace.

Jimmy awoke from his dream, sweating and confused. *What is the meaning of this?* After a few minutes of making no sense out of the dream because of no context, he fell asleep. The dream slipped away into oblivion.

Chapter 2
TO JAPAN

One night in his meditation room, with the light of the moon bouncing off the shrine, illuminating the vajra, bell, and offering bowls, Jimmy continued to ponder what his newfound approach would bring. To Japan he would go to delve deeper into…*deeper into what?* He was pestered by, yet often glad that the spiritual side of his nature would not leave him be. In this case there was no getting around it.

He'd heard about pilgrimages on social media—and out of interest, had joined various groups that talked about the pilgrimages in Japan: Kumano and the Shikoku 88-temple route. When he lived there years earlier, he'd already walked to the Kumano Grand Shrine in Wakayama Prefecture. It was a stop after visiting Mount Kōya in the same region of the peninsula. But the Shikoku pilgrimage was something new to him. Social media and the internet told him that 88 Buddhist Temples were established on Shikoku—one of the four largest islands of the Japanese archipelago. It is south of Honshu, the largest island, and located just west of south-central Japan.

Try as he might—and he had tried—he could not let go of the urge to begin a pilgrimage. Now that he'd heard about the 88-temple Shikoku pilgrimage, it was a full-fledged feeling in him that he couldn't ignore. He thought: *Is this how I will heal myself?* He read that pilgrims make promises such as: not lying, being greedy or exaggerating

(*Shikoku Japan 88 Route Guide*). Jimmy felt that he wanted to undergo this kind of practice. It fit in with his vows of generosity and loving kindness. He wanted to be explicit about his path in life. He hoped the pilgrimage would make that obvious beyond simply—may I awaken speedily for the sake of all beings, which is the Boddhisattva vow he'd taken at Open Breeze. Healing would come from being certain about what he needed to do in life.

Jimmy had no clear-cut answer as to why he was called specifically to a pilgrimage of walking the Shikoku route in Japan, as opposed to any other. He chalked it up to the universe *giving him another nudge as it had done all his life*. After all, he'd been left to wonder about the appearances of Saori for so long prior to their friendship and emerging loving relationship across time. Clearly the universe had its own timeframe for things, and it didn't seem too concerned with Jimmy's individual wishes and thoughts. Then again, that didn't seem strange, since he was only one of billions of humans on the planet. *His* dharma learning, *his* needs did not come before the needs of others. Any realization would take the necessary route to be understood if ever it could be. Jimmy was coming to understand more each year that what happened to him wasn't personal. He'd have to trust in the universe.

He became determined. He'd go on the pilgrimage come what may. He wondered whether he'd get out of it what the common person would: increased confidence in life, spiritual understanding, or perhaps a sense of what to do next. He realized that it didn't really matter what he thought might happen. All that was important was that he made the decision *to go*. He'd find out what he was meant to, whatever that was.

The lightning speed with which Jimmy put his job on hold for a sabbatical, and then made arrangements, was dizzying but completely necessary. As the spring blossoms and sprouts came out, he continued making plans, travel plans as well as finding a home base in his beloved Kyoto, the Heian capital of Japan. He would become a master teacher of Japanese culture and history after the pilgrimage, if the pilgrimage didn't change these initial plans. He hoped these actions would provide him with a platform to continue his life-long journey to awaken to what is *truly beautiful*, what is inherently *good*. He prayed that this would happen in this lifetime.

Jimmy started preparing immediately by studying through an online course — Becoming an Expert on Things Japanese. He'd deeply imbed himself in the ways of Japanese culture once more and explore historical concepts that have influenced Japan throughout its history and perhaps up until this day: life of the samurai, Zen, the tea ceremony and various arts such as *ikebana*, flower arrangement, and so on.

The complex latticed wooden ceiling of a tea ceremony house, the flash of light reflecting off a samurai sword, and the austere ambiance of a Zen temple like the one he'd stayed at in his earlier time in Japan, with all smooth wooden walls and tatami reed mats, all this flashed in his memory from his time in Japan.

These studies, he realized, would help him better understand the deep life teachings he continued to receive from the master teachers at Open Breeze. These thoughts brought him back to the stunning tea ceremony with one of his co-workers in Japan. She didn't seem to fit the bill but was transformed once in a kimono — and more deeply while preparing to whisk the tea; she was a natural. His friend in Wakayama city was into ikebana, so Jimmy had been introduced to many presentations of flowers. He felt blessed to have learned more about the way of flower arrangement. And still, there was so much more to learn. What adventures were still to be had? This was taking his mind off Saori, if only temporarily.

Jimmy had already been introduced to life in Heian Kyō, the ancient Heian capital of Japan, thanks to his interactions with Saori, since she was from that period of Japanese history. He felt like there would be value in expanding his knowledge of the *Sengoku Jidai,* the Warring States Period lasting for nearly two centuries and ending in the early 1600s because it could help him to historically understand life in Japan. He'd continue studying about the coming to Japan of the concepts and practices of Buddhism, Zen Buddhism in particular. He remembered back to when the idea to return to Japan came to him. He wondered where the ideas all came from. *The universe clearly holds more than I or anyone can understand.*

Jimmy felt determined to find out about life. After all, why did he have such a feeling of loss with Saori being gone? It was gratifying to become friends with her, regardless that what was left was to learn about being intimate with another. So, this would be the purpose of going on the pilgrimage. For now, he'd have to stay focused, another thing he wished to be better at—even as an experienced meditator. These would be things he'd focus on for himself while walking as much of the pilgrimage as he could. Fortunately, the courses would eventually lead to a master's degree in Japanese studies.

So, the ways of the samurai would be the best form of study for him to continue. It would take him into the modern period, up through the end of the influence of the samurai early in the Meiji Period. He thought about the order as he knew it. Heian Japan, then several hundred tumultuous years, followed by the full-blown Warring States Period, which literally bled into the Tokugawa Shogun period, a period of stability beginning in the early 1600s—and the exclusion of foreigners he suddenly recalled mentioned in his dream about the master and samurai. This made him pause, though not being a clear memory, he continued. Then in the 1800s with Admiral Perry's bold and obnoxious move, the modern world collided with Japan once more with a treaty in 1854 establishing trade leading to the modernization of Japan in the Meiji Period.

Excitedly, Jimmy registered that night and began the course of online study the next day the first session of the series of courses in the—Becoming an Expert on Things Japanese course.

Several weeks later, after the familiar twelve-hour flight, Jimmy was back in his adopted home again. *Home?* This statement came from a feeling of familiarity, yes familiar, and somehow, he still felt daunted, if not a sense of foreboding this time. He wasn't sure what he would learn, but it was becoming understood that he was drawn once more to Japan to learn about life. The first time, he went from college student to adult. What would this time bring? He breathed in the humid air and started unpacking and planning the journey on Shikoku.

Arriving in Japan was something he was used to. He became acclimated quite easily, having already become accustomed to the inevitable bouts of jetlag. He settled in his temporary housing at a university in Kyoto. Since it was the capital that seemed continually in conflict in the early part of the Kamakura Period right after the Heian Period, and then almost forgotten during the turbulent times of the Warring States Period, it was a good place to begin his studies.

Kyoto had everything: cultural treasures, temples, shrines, modern-as-well-as traditional performances, and of course the Minamiza Kabuki theater. It marked where he had stopped running from the Yasaka Shrine—while in Kyoto to help Saori integrate her soul.

He ran out of the shrine all the way to in front of the theater after a harrowing experience with flashbacks to Saori's Heian experience—from her own time.

After going on this pilgrimage, he planned to finish his studies and move to Tokyo, the place called Edo in the Edo Period, when the Tokugawa Clan united the entire country to enforce a lasting peace after the Warring States Period of Japanese history. The samurai caught the collective imagination of people all over the world. Something clearly resonated: the vows of loyalty to their *daimyo* (the regional lords who ruled on behalf of the Shogun). Samurai were unique in world history in that they'd take their own lives if their loyalty was not complete, or they were dishonored in some way in battle, or had the misfortune of being on the losing side. True, the knights of medieval Europe vowed to not back down from a fight, but the samurai seemed to execute this kind of courage to the extreme—cutting themselves in half in the *hara kiri* or belly-slicing ceremonial suicide. Jimmy was to find out in his course that this was only later in the Edo period and not from an earlier time when the Samurai began. Prior to the changes that came about in the Warring States period, the samurai fought primarily on horseback with bows and arrows and for rewards of land, money, and prestige for their families. The cult of the sword was real but a relatively modern development after fighting was no longer the mainstay of the samurai.

The pilgrimage would begin just as his two-week course, "The Impact of Zen on the Arts in Japan" finished. He was already enthralled with the course, learning about artistic influences that had emerged from the combination of the Japanese aesthetic and Zen. So many were artistic imports originally from China: simple and refined, "one-corner," often called "thrifty brush" because of the use of few brush strokes; *wabi-sabi*, finding beauty in imperfection, something that impacts especially modern Japanese ceramics, and so on. He wondered how often he'd be able to find traces of these along the route, perhaps an austere tea ceremony house.

So finally, after weeks of planning, Jimmy was at Temple Number One. It had all the markings of a temple in Japan: a large wooden gate, a main wooden building with a bronze statue of a buddha, a bell, and incense wafting in the summer air. The sun had crested the moderate-sized mountains several hours earlier.

After walking out of the pilgrim supply shop, Jimmy crossed the path made of pebbles. He had just bought his round, conical hat, white garments, *wagesa* or golden sash, orange *juzu* or rosary of 108 beads, and an 88-temple *shuincho* or book for collecting stamps at each of the temples along the way—the trappings of a pilgrim.

Wandering around a bit aimlessly, he was filled with trepidation about finding out what he still had to learn about being intimate with others. He stopped and centered himself. Well, there was no way around it, intimacy—*with women*—he told himself with finality. He was okay with men, could talk the talk, but now simply considering a warm talk with a woman, in close proximity, caused him to break out in a nervous sweat. It was a typical hot, sunny day in humid late July. As he wiped the sweat out of his eyes, his eyes fell upon a placard. The temple was named Ryozenji – Vulture Peak, after a vision by Koboda-ishi of the historical Buddha, Shakyamuni, teaching at Vulture Peak.

The first temple of the route had many items for purchase, not only in the pilgrim supply shop but also in the temple proper. Jimmy bought the bracelet of beads that corresponded with the eastern zodiac sign of his birth, the year of the snake. It had the image of *Fugen Bosatsu* or Fugen Bodhisattva. Bodhisattvas are beings who forego or give up on enlightenment to be of service in helping others achieve enlightenment. Jimmy put the bracelet on his wrist right away as a reminder to live in the present moment. He also planned to stay present, thinking about Manjushri, the Buddha of wisdom. He practiced the Manjushri mantra for several rounds of the mala or rosary and then prepared to leave the temple, which was itself dedicated to Shakyamuni, the historical Buddha, the founder of Buddhism some 2,500 years ago.

So, this is where it all begins, Jimmy thought. According to an online suggestion, he'd gone to Osahiko Shrine, with its red-orange *torii* or gateway to the shrine. He learned that hemp has been tied to the life of the Japanese since prehistoric times, according to the temple signs and a documentary he'd watched. Along the route, accessible within a day's walk, were several temples and shrines. He'd stop at each of the temples numbers two to six on the pilgrimage and pray for a successful pilgrimage, to find what he could about being peaceful in the world, and especially the cultivation of wisdom through being present, and ultimately his purpose in life. The shadows of the trees told him the sun was still rising. The intermittent morning breeze gave a pleasant break in the humidity.

Jimmy had his pilgrimage book stamped, which he imagined was the first of many stamps. The professional brush-stroked the name of the temple and the date of his visit in brilliant calligraphy into his book, complete with sections for all 88 temples along the route. Jimmy paid the 300 yen and looked around, taking in the various statues such as Kannon the Buddha of Mercy or Compassion and the scent of incense. As he prepared to leave, an old woman came running up to him.

The woman offered Jimmy a bandana to put under his hat. She told him that while this is not required for the journey, it would make a big difference as to how the straw hat sat on his head. It would prevent the skin from being irritated before it toughens up. He was grateful. It was obvious that the scratchy hat could use this buffer, especially since he didn't wear hats very often. He thought, *The incredible kindness of strangers.*

"*Arigatō gozaimasu,*" he thanked her politely.

Care for others was often the rule of thumb rather than the exception in Japan. He'd experienced this countless times in train stations, museums, bus rides, and the like. It was part of what made him love Japan, as giving care to those in need was the standard. The time to depart had arrived; he'd take the proverbial first step.

Finally at the start of the pilgrimage, Jimmy found that he was unable to take that next step, the first trek of the 88 temples on the pilgrimage route called *o-henro. The moment of truth has come. Why am I going on the pilgrimage?* he wondered, and the answer came, although it was quite general. Beyond his quest for intimacy, any other learning would be revealed on the route. Once more, he'd have to trust that the universe was sending him on the right journey. Would he be able to complete the whole route? What did he have to learn? Only time would tell. He was to explore his purpose in life.

He had a renewed sense of foreboding that he'd felt on sleepless nights after dreaming about a person falling off a cliff in Japan. The dream recurred and was anything but certain or obvious; it was just…foreboding. And now he was about to walk along what he believed was the course, the route that included that cliff. As he finally moved his foot forward, he instinctively asked himself for the hundredth time, *who fell*?

To get past his sense of unease, he reestablished a determination to better understand life and the purpose of going on the pilgrimage for spiritual growth. Having come to terms with the urge to go, and moving his second foot forward, he was on his way.

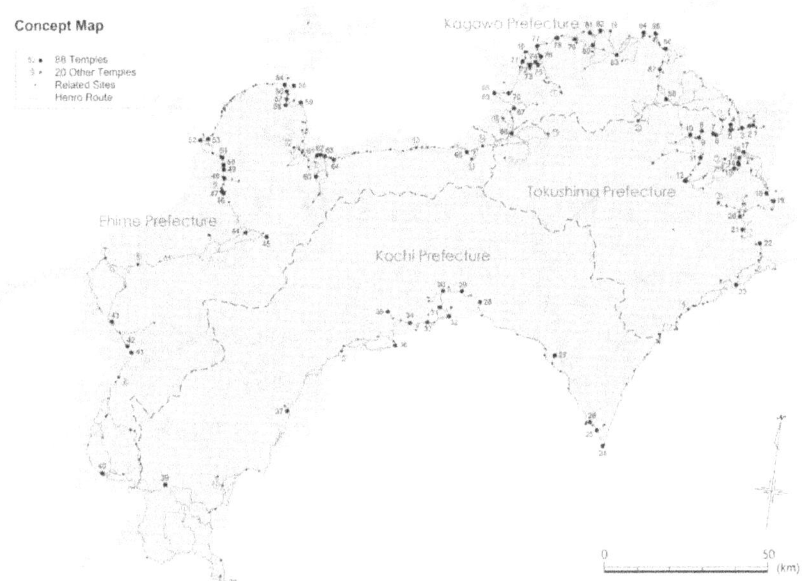

Concept Map
88 Temples
20 Other Temples
Related Sites
Henro Route
Kagawa Prefecture
Ehime Prefecture
Tokushima Prefecture
Kochi Prefecture
0
50
(km)

Chapter 3
ANOTHER RETURN

Jimmy walked along the sidewalks and paved ways marked sporadically with arrows to show the way. It was lined with small farm fields from time to time and sometimes gave Jimmy the opportunity to overlook a small valley or a winding mountain path. He stayed at a Japanese *ryokan* or inn the first night.

On the second day, he walked for about half a day, and then stopped but only briefly, to have some *sanuki udon* or local udon wheat noodles. He walked into the early afternoon. It went on like this as Jimmy grew accustomed to his stride and the arrows pointing the way along the route, sometimes formally on signs denoting the pilgrimage route, and at times, drawn with spray paint, probably by a helpful local resident. On the second day, he walked from Temple Number Ten to nearby Number Eleven and stayed at a pilgrim hostel called Oyado 11.

As he progressed into the third day, the changing elevations on this tree-lined mountainous route from Temple Eleven, Fujidera, to Temple Number Twelve, Shosanji, gave him energy and striking views. He joked to himself that he was experiencing all four seasons as the rain, sun, clouds, and cold wind took turns that day. He was thoroughly soaked by the time he sat down to have lunch about halfway between the two temples. After eating a lunch he'd purchased at a food market the day before, he continued along the trail.

He had donned the traditional attire for the pilgrimage and insisted on wearing the *geta* or wooden clogs, which helped to create his current *karmic* dilemma.

One misstep and his right foot slipped and down he fell, his body rolling, sliding and racing at a high speed through the bushes, branches, and underbrush. Moments ago, as he'd looked up, he had slipped and was tossed over the side of a cliff, his backpack getting caught on a tree branch. Jimmy took a breath, and the tree branch snapped. As he fell, he grabbed the root from which he currently hung a few feet farther down the hillside. Dust and small rocks fell around him. With one hand, Jimmy continued to hold onto the root of a tree 30 feet down the hillside. He struggled to get his second hand onto it to secure his hold, realizing *that was lucky*. Stunned and sweating profusely, he wasn't able to catch his breath. His heart raced as he surveyed a ravine far below, between two slopes along the 88-temple pilgrimage route of Shikoku, Japan.

What in the world am I doing here? Jimmy's answers followed directly. The simple answer was his propensity to explore. The more pressing, if not distressing answer was that he'd lost conscious attention to what he was doing, resulting in the 30-foot fall off the side of a steep slope. Amazed and bothered by the cause of the fall, he recalled in an instant what happened.

Remembering the cedar trees he'd seen while hiking the Kumano trail of the Kii Peninsula, he'd looked up, while still walking, at the overhang of pines along the route. The combination of a small rock under wooden clog footwear, a scraping noise and a slip on the stones sent him over the side of a particularly steep section of the trail, causing him to vault, then roll over the edge. It was not reassuring as he remembered having seen a sign that said "Careful: Pilgrims have fallen off of the cliff in this area."

Hanging on the side of the slope, all at once thoughts from nine months earlier came back to him in his heightened state of alert: Saori's integration, his bliss from having helped her, and the reality setting in that he'd have to get on with his life without her, went through his mind. Even in his predicament, the long months since her healing roared through his mind, signifying the importance she had held for him. He prayed for her as a true friend, resulting in her karma healing and her going back to her time, the Heian Period. Just like that she was gone. His prayer, against his wishes to stay with her, allowed her to leave him. It was a sacrifice he was proud of but now also regretted.

Although his second hand grasped the root, he breathed only a little easier. While this gave him a chance to assess his predicament, he was far from out of danger. Both hands held on, sweat flowed down the side of his face, and ignoring the developing ache in his forearms, Jimmy looked around, wondering whether there was a chance to escape alive. The opposite side of the ravine was dotted with pines and thick with brush. Below him, he realized it would be a fall of about 150 feet to a rocky base. The smell of leafy vegetation comingled with the sound of the breeze flowing through the leaves of the trees. The root creaked and then moved. Perspiration dripped down his face, and he thought, *it won't hold much longer*.

Jimmy looked to both his right and to his left. He saw a bulge sticking out of the side of what was an otherwise grass-covered, sandy slope. To the right, about nine feet over and fifteen feet below him, was the ledge of a rock. He had one chance. Holding tight to the root, he pushed off the slope and swung to the left. The root squeaked and groaned as he arched a hard swing to the right, let go, and fell with a thud of the slippery wooden sandals and the crunch of his backpack. He landed half on and half beside the backpack, bruising his right hip on the bulging rocky platform. A bruised hip was a bummer—but also a small price to pay for securing his life. Jimmy laughed out loud when he considered how many times his teacher, Duncan McDougal, implored him to simply, "Let go." *Seems he was right*, Jimmy laughed, a relieved-and-nervous laugh; then he winced in pain.

Taking a moment to settle down and assess the situation, Jimmy pulled his water bottle from his backpack's side pouch, miraculously intact after the impact. After a drink and several calming breaths, it dawned on him that he was in only a slightly better situation than before. While he was no longer in immediate danger of falling, he could see no way off that cliff. He looked along the side of the steep slope, hoping to see a stairway or other branches, but there were none. Perhaps no human had even been where he currently stood. It was still a dramatic drop into the ravine, and the pilgrimage route was now more than forty feet above him.

Trees and rocks stuck out of the side of the steep slope along the way up. If only he'd brought a rope. It was four o'clock in the afternoon, according to his cell phone—which in this remote part of the course was unable to connect to a network and was also running out of charge. The rustic nature of this leg of the journey was what had appealed to him originally; it was touted as the region where one could "Get away from it all." *Shikata ga nai*—or there was nothing else that could be done, he thought. He'd have to try climbing from rock to tree to rock, working his way up the cliff.

Pulling himself up to the first protruding rock, he reached for the next tree and slipped, catching himself on the first rock, pain shooting through his hip. He needed more rest and more nerve. He backed down to the ledge and lay down. After meditating for twenty minutes, he moved to stand up but found that he couldn't put weight on his right hip, and worse, it was growing stiff, making getting to his feet painful now that the adrenaline rush had receded. In his condition, he wouldn't be able to make the climb, especially with his antiquated footwear.

Jimmy took out his sleeping bag and free-standing tent he'd brought along for the trek. He had no idea how long it would take till he was ready to try again; regardless, he needed rest. Jimmy rolled out his sleeping bag to take a nap and fell asleep.

Thinking that he had slept only a short while, he woke to find that he was thirsty—and it was the next day. He met the day with only half of a bottle of water and a growling stomach. He leaned out farther onto the ledge and looked up, just in time to see the conical hat of a pilgrim walking away. He called out. The person looked around, certainly amazed to hear another voice, especially since no one was in view. Recognizing that the raspy voice was coming from the ravine, the shocked, elderly man called down "*Daijōbu ka*? or Are you okay?" Jimmy said, "So, so" pointing to his hip.

"Wait here" the old man's voice echoed down. "I'll get help at the next site." The man proudly told Jimmy that he was on his tenth time traveling the pilgrimage, gleefully mentioning that he was *only* 90 years old, which made Jimmy chuckle and wince. Then, the man was gone. In the guidebook, Jimmy discovered that the next stop was about an hour's hike farther down the path. Having the man come along at all made Jimmy think, *I must have at least some good karma*. Reading on, he found warnings that along this area of the route between Fujidera, Temple Number Eleven and Shosanji, Number Twelve, indeed, pilgrims have fallen down the side of the mountain. *It's a bit too late*, he told himself sardonically.

Jimmy had some time to think while the elder continued down the path. In classic Japanese style that he'd grown accustomed to in his second home, the man had been willing to help someone younger or with less experience and didn't dwell on the details with Jimmy. The man's conical hat merely nodded, and he was off. No need to confer more. While waiting, Jimmy recalled his friends back in what used to be his home, Minnesota.

Leaving Minnesota hadn't been easy. Besides the memory of Saori's encounter, that ghostly friend from the Heian Period of Japan, there was the relationship to the guys and gals at his former school who called themselves the Motley Crew, especially Janelle. Even that relationship cut both ways. He was growing increasingly more comfortable around women, and really liked Janelle's warmth and humor, but were they actually suited for each other? Only time would tell. He did have his doubts but couldn't say whether they were caused by his fear of intimacy or that they genuinely weren't a good match. He chalked it up to lack of experience with women.

He had told her of his trip to Open Breeze, his adopted meditation center in Canada and remembered she totally missed the point of spiritual exploration. Still, she was serious about being healthy herself and practiced yoga, which is certainly compatible with meditation. He had known deep in his soul that for him there had always been an attraction to the spiritual life…*I wonder, could a relationship with her work out?*

Jimmy had grown up Catholic and so, of course, he'd also considered, even for some years, the call to become a priest. He'd wanted to explore life and seek out some meaning in it. He knew this about himself. After Saori was gone, that part became crystal clear. He'd have to continue his search, wherever that would lead him. He couldn't let the Motley Crew and Janelle hold him back from this restless longing for significance. Also, there was his trip to Open Breeze not long ago. Both teachers at the center, Katarina Pauline and Duncan MacDougal, encouraged him to explore—they always had. When he got the itch to walk the pilgrimage route in Japan, they urged him to go, although he was not sure just why. Perhaps they recognized a sense of wonder, an awe along the way that had something to do with it. It would be a challenging but important task to complete a pilgrimage. Perhaps it was also that he'd be on his own, and as such would plan, decide, and create the trip by himself. It would be another avenue of growth.

Exploring the world, balancing personal competence, developing a personal vision, and living in community were important parts of the process of training at Open Breeze. Jimmy thought: *I love their approach. I'm so energized by exploring, and being aware of community needs and not only my own seems more important every year.*

These things merged for him. It became his duty to continue his life's purpose, to awaken the full potential of what it means to be human, and with that knowledge, to do his best to help others live lives of meaning and purpose. How that would manifest was yet to be told. Sitting on a rock jutted out over trees, with a long possible fall, he suddenly felt a deep security in his enthusiasm and direction.

Chapter 4

CONTINUING THE JOURNEY

Jimmy looked up again and again as his water bottle emptied little by little. One hour. Another hour. He drew in long breaths to attain meditative ease but found only short-term relief this way. As the sun continued to cross the sky and it grew hot, he was getting worried, and his hip was better only in that it didn't hurt all the time as it did the previous day, provided he didn't move it. His tent and sleeping bag were long packed, and he was growing increasingly impatient, worrying, *I'm not practicing patience well—one of the six key Buddhist tenets, the virtues called parami* or *paramita*.

By the time he'd rechecked the tent and repacked, a breeze wafted across his face, and the sun slowly continued its ascent in the sky. He looked up again hoping to see a rope, some source of help.

Jimmy cursed himself for losing awareness so easily. After all, the whole point of the pilgrimage was to gain deeper insight, not to become more dull and stupid. *Wow, am I stupid.*

"Guilt is useless." One of his teacher's words came back to him. The other, Katarina Pauline, would often note how all one can do is to get better by training oneself based on the current circumstances. If one's best wasn't good enough, it pointed to what even now needed to be learned. Jimmy picked up a small rock and threw it in frustration, but all that accomplished was he realized how far below him the bottom was as he watched the rock fall in front of him. The grassy cliffside remained on both sides of the valley, and the plethora of pine trees spruced up the scene—but didn't assuage his feelings of being stuck. *Stuck here, I am. I must figure this out. This pilgrimage must come to something. May it benefit all beings.* He was pleased that the vow to awaken on behalf of the planet came to mind.

The trip up until now hasn't all been wasted. In fact, I've been practicing meditation long enough to understand that even advanced students, even awakened beings, have things to learn.

While meditating at Temple Number Three, Konsenji, on the first day of the journey, he'd recalled swinging at a park in his youth in Minnesota. He had jumped off the swing and bumped into a girl who was running by. He hadn't seen her. He realized sometimes bad things happen; they just do. It hadn't been either his or the girl's fault on that autumn day. While this didn't excuse his current lapse in awareness resulting in his own fall, it calmed him down. Sometimes things just happen. It's what people do about it that matters. That girl was hurt a little but got up, and after rubbing her leg, smiled at him and ran along as though nothing had happened. She was a kind of a guardian angel for him in the present moment. He relaxed a little. Thinking of the temple, he recalled that it had many legends, such as Kobodaishi bringing forth water by striking the ground with his staff, which he was rumored to have done various places around Japan.

This interlude gave him hope for the rest of the pilgrimage. *Perhaps I really can find what my purpose in life is. That would make the whole experience seem worthwhile.* He relaxed once more and spent some time in contemplation.

After several minutes, he heard "cha-ching," the ring of a bell, what would be a very nostalgic if-not-strange sound were he still in Minnesota. While it was barely audible, it was a welcome sound. He realized immediately it was a common bell on a bicycle, in Japan used by young and old for shopping, school, recreation, or errands.

When the old man waved his arms wildly over the edge of the mountain, Jimmy was too thirsty to call out but waved weakly in return. The Japanese gentleman smiled, happy to help another, a fellow citizen. The old man had informed the temple manager of Jimmy's location, and they'd shared the bicycle to get to him. Following the greeting, a rope came sailing over the side of the slope and landed at Jimmy's feet. Next, Jimmy realized that the man was not alone; a young man called Yuichi was there also. Yuichi waved, but then for some reason abruptly disappeared.

Yuichi Murano was the manager of the next temple on the route, Shosanji. He normally was busy checking registrations and making sure that his assistant was getting the rooms ready. He even guessed, that the one foreigner who had registered but not shown up the previous day was Jimmy. Yuichi was tying the rope to the nearest tree across the path so that they could bring Jimmy up the slope by leveraging themselves against a large rock along the side of the path not far from where Jimmy had fallen.

The two men, young and old, first brought up Jimmy's backpack and tent and then Jimmy. It was quite an effort to pull up someone who could hardly use one side, his hip hurting still, but somehow, they managed. Saying the normal profuse thank you statements and warm goodbyes, Yuichi and Jimmy parted with the old man who was happy to continue his tenth pilgrimage.

Yuichi peddled while Jimmy held on for dear life. It was bumpy, causing his hip to hurt, but it was also very lucky that this stretch of the journey was one of the areas not far from Shosanji where a bicycle could be used.

In a short while, they arrived at the next temple, and Jimmy was relieved that they had a room for him for the night. He looked around at the wooden and plaster structures, the wall hangings in the lobby. The one in the lobby read *ichi-go; ichi-e* meaning "each meeting is a once-in-a-lifetime meeting." It was a saying commonly used in Japan, but Jimmy took it to heart. In his room, another scroll included the characters for the four seasons, something venerated in Japan, especially in art and the famous haiku poetry style of 5-7-5 syllables.

Jimmy's arrival signaled everyone to spring into action. His luggage was placed in his room. Snacks were brought, along with cool *mugicha* tea made from roasted barley. After reviving, he ordered some food at the onsite restaurant before taking a bath to soothe his hip.

Later in the day, he was able to walk for a little bit with less pain, but the going was slow. He joined other guests for dinner in the communal dining room. On the *tatami* mats were placed various low tables with dishes of pickled vegetables, ceramic soy sauce vessels, cylindrical tubes filled with chopsticks and the like, a typical cafeteria setting in Japan for overnight stays. Servers brought trays with dishes made from foods that were in season. The meal included a large lacquerware-covered bowl of rice and a *chawan* bowl, a ceramic bowl for putting the rice into for eating. Jimmy served himself as much rice as he could eat.

"You been in Japan long?" Yuichi asked in English, but eventually they began speaking in Japanese since it was easier to communicate that way for all concerned.

"Only on the pilgrimage a few days, but in Japan for several months. On the way, I visited some friends and went to a taiko concert in Kobe, before entering Shikoku from Awaji Island."

"How do you like the pilgrimage? Of course, I mean aside from your fall?" Jimmy silently acknowledged Yuichi's kindness as he sat beside Jimmy asking if he was all right for the sixth time.

"Well, I am quite excited. I wasn't sure if I could continue, but the bath worked wonders for this sore hip," he said.

"You can stay an extra day at no charge," Yuichi offered. Jimmy said he needed to think about it, which was true since he needed to stay on a schedule to resume classes after completing the entire 88-temple route. Little did Jimmy know that this was not going to happen, even if his hip had already been fully restored.

Jimmy did stay the extra night and found that the bath and rest allowed him to move out on his own, although much more slowly than previously. He smiled inside. He was being forced to be deliberate. Just like something one might learn on a pilgrimage, he thought. It became apparent that there was no way to rush the pilgrimage. Eighty-eight temples would take time to visit—whether he stayed at them or simply dropped in to have his pilgrimage book stamped. It seemed the teaching that universal natural laws must be followed was to be experienced time and time again. *Ow*, he thought, as he walked, feeling a twinge of pain in his right hip every so often juxtaposed with small farm fields, trees, and mountainous skylines.

Several temples were fairly close along this part of the journey he realized as he passed Temple Thirteen. He had to travel up and down some hills and meditated at times to get calm enough to push through the pain and move on. In a few days, he was feeling better. His step quickened, and he became hopeful.

He came to a temple that had been established by Kobodaishi. He realized for the first time that the last few temples had not only been established by Kobodaishi, but also that they were administered by the same monk, a man of the late Tokugawa and early Meiji periods. *It must have been quite a chore. The monk must have been an amazing, industrious man.* Jimmy had read at one of the temples that this man found a way to get the temples to communicate with with each other via a system of runners.

Jimmy lodged at one of the temples for the night. After a light meal, he turned in and enjoyed a *futon*, the covered mattress pad and thick, fluffy top covering. He always felt so cozy snuggled in their comfort. The moon shone through a crack in the *shoji* paper barrier on the inside of the window, and he relished both the moonlight and memories of Saori. He reached out and waved his hand through the moonbeam before turning on the light in the room to read. The air was not cool, but the summer night in Japan was cooler than during the day, giving a comfortable repose.

After reading more about *Shingon*, the Buddhist sect started by Kobodaishi, and its impact on Shikoku, he turned out the light. He was very present right then, feeling a sense of emptiness that was calming and not disturbing as it was the first time he *had felt* it, which was really an experience more than a feeling. Sleep overtook him, and he began to dream:

"There's no time to lose, Jiro," the abbot addressed his lead student, calling him away from the meditation sit. "They'll be here any moment. We must either hide or run." Jiro knew what this meant. After coming by earlier to threaten the monastery, the group hadn't given up as hoped. It was dusk. The setting sun shone off the walls of the temple that were otherwise bare to encourage bare attention, not too much extra to cloud the consciousness.

"Then run we must. They may try to burn the place down to smoke us out," Jiro said.

"They wouldn't dare!"

"It depends on how desperate they are."

"They have seemed desperate as of late," the abbot acknowledged, trying to calm himself as is possible in meditation though so far, he'd not been able to have the breakthrough experience that allows one to be calm in all conditions—proof of how hard it was to obtain that state. He had to admit that in spite of his long and arduous efforts, he was not fully enlightened.

An arrow flew by their heads. "Go out the back and hide. They'll think we made a run for it."

"Yes, Sensei," Jiro replied. They made it out the back, but Jiro was hit by an arrow as soon as he exited the building. As the other ran

away, Jiro was taken into custody but died from his wounds as they were dragging him out of the temple complex. The invading group expressed relief that "one more" was out of the way.

Jimmy awoke startled. It was the middle of the night. *Where was that? What is going on? First a samurai rants in my earlier dreams, and now I have two monks in my dreams under siege, and one killed. And there is the recurring dream of someone falling off a cliff…, like I did.*

The next day, he shrugged off the dream as he continued walking along the path that led first up and then down along bamboo forests. Jimmy was accompanied by the smell of cedars and rocky climbs. It was a beautiful day to be present and alive.

Chapter 5

PERSISTENT DREAMS

A few nights later, and several temples further along the route, Jimmy dreamed again, and when he woke, his pajamas were drenched with sweat. It was the middle of the night. As his heart raced, he wondered: *What did I just see?* It was the all-too-familiar dream of someone falling off a cliff in what looked to be a mountainous region of, of…now he was sure it was the Shikoku pilgrimage route. His renewed understanding came from the scenery of the hills, trees, and the now-familiar shrubbery, though he remained stumped as to why it was a recurring dream for him since he'd never been to Shikoku before. Wide awake, he now recalled the mountain trails he'd witnessed on his journey so far. None were the same as his dream, even if the vegetation was similar. A dream from his harrowing experience would have been set at the protruding rock ledge, but that wasn't the case. The pilgrimage route seemed to be where the dream took place, but he believed it wasn't anywhere he'd already been.

A new understanding came to mind. *It's not me that has fallen in the dream.* He'd assumed the dreams had been a bad omen for his trip; however, the person in the dream was wearing an old-styled *samue* or two-piece garment with various layers, now visible for the first time. *It's not me but someone from long ago.*

Why am I having these dreams? Why is this dream, especially, recurring for me? He had no way of knowing that the monk—Jimmy assumed the man was a monk because of the *samue*—was associated with *Shingon*, the Buddhist school affiliated with Kobodaishi, the man who'd established many temples along the route. Jimmy eventually found out that indeed, the monk was Kobodaishi's successor as manager of the route, though much later in Japanese history.

Walking along the path muttering to himself about the dreams he had about samurai, monks, and someone falling, he realized *This trip is way beyond being only about myself. I must be called to carry out the journey for some purpose still to be revealed.* He could hear his meditation teachers reciting, "May I awaken speedily for the sake of all beings," after talking about bodhisattvas, the awakening beings who remain with people on earth to teach about moment-to-moment awareness and point those seeking direction toward awakening. *Awakening is a kind of understanding the universe—or turning to God more fully—whatever that means for each being on planet earth.*

Jimmy recalled the "Dharma for the Planet" website he'd come across and how there was a group of beings working to help the planet realize its human potential. He was encouraged that there was a magnificent bunch of beings working together rather than each only for themselves. *I hope my work helps with that someday.* Purposefulness entered his step. His hip felt better just thinking of this. He hoped he could make some difference in the world, however small.

Jimmy continued walking, alternately rearranging the cloth under his hat and pausing to rest under the shade of trees from time to time. He was encouraged once more to work to understand himself in the hope of assisting other beings. He began to focus on the energy it took to make each step. His hip bone wasn't an issue, but he was still getting all his muscles back to strength after having favored his right hip. His breathing was smooth despite the natural exertion being put forth to keep moving along. The beauty of the sun coming through the trees and hitting the pine needles and slopes once again refreshed in him a sense of awe. He loved being in Japan. He was amazed by the natural beauty found in so many places around the country: temples in the mountains of Hiroshima Prefecture, the Mountains of Nagano and Yamanashi Prefectures, and, of course, the northeastern region of Japan that included places such as Towadako, a beautiful lake in Aoyama Prefecture, northern Japan.

Several birds took flight, surprising and pleasing him at the same time. What must it have felt like to walk along the trek centuries ago with no cell phones and no way to rely on motorized vehicles? His mind loved to think about these things. This propensity must be attributed to his love for learning history and for the calling to be a high school teacher or perhaps his love and need to be in natural settings. It was an added benefit that his students engaged with the topics demonstrating wit, wisdom, and youthful exuberance. He looked forward to returning to the classroom after his sabbatical, armed with new information for his students.

Jimmy was glad that he'd brought back to Minnesota various trappings from previous visits: a small portable tea ceremony kit, *samue* or meditation clothing suitable for either martial arts or Zen practice, etc. On this visit, he'd brought along his makeshift altar, being sure to set it up each night before going to bed, and he also brought the walking stick from Mount Kōya. In fact, one night he earnestly set the altar up before doing anything else. He laughed to himself about the need to take himself less seriously, the need to lighten up. He'd almost been in a panic since he didn't set up the altar before drinking water after having swung from the tree to the protruding rock after his fall. Of course, in loving memory of Saori, he took along the *Vajra,* his most treasured item, honoring the vow he'd made to keep it with him always.

Easy, Jimmy. While this demonstrated his intensity, it also represented growth as he chuckled about it rather than chiding himself, bringing a relaxed smile to his face and a warm feeling to his whole being. This was something new. He had usually been so harsh with himself.

Thinking of his students got him wondering how the Motley Crew, his teacher friends in Minnesota, were doing. He made himself a to-do list, noting that he'd send an email to them later and laughed about the urge to do so.

The man sitting on a rock admiring the sunny day looked to be about Jimmy's age. Hmmm. He took a practiced measure of the mountain with his eyes as he walked up to the sitting man.

"Hey," Jimmy offered a cheery greeting.

"Hallo," came the response with somewhat of an accent, but Jimmy wasn't sure of its source. In the modern period, it was certain that there'd be international travelers, unlike in Tokugawa times when the country was off-limits to foreigners for 250 years. The man offered a follow-up comment while Jimmy continued standing, which allowed him to take weight off his right hip. The breeze coming up from the cedar-lined valley was refreshing.

"Seems like the trees in this area are newer, a bit younger than in the last region I came from."

"Oh, and which direction did you come from?" Jimmy asked, looking at the trees even more closely. Jimmy could see this man was the epitome of the modern scientist in his skillful observation as Jimmy took in the scent of pine needles amidst views of cedars.

"I came by that way," the man said, indicating that Jimmy and he were traveling the same way, heading westward along the route.

"I see what you mean by the trees. You have a keen eye for detail. I am interested in developing that skill more in myself. I am Jimmy Swenson," he said, while offering his hand.

"Bernd Munich is my name. As you can guess from my last name, I am from Germany," he said, smiling underneath a set of heavy glasses and wavy brown hair.

"And you're here conducting scientific experiments?" Jimmy inquired.

"Well, sort of. I teach at Tokyo University."

"Wow, that's cool. I teach in Minnesota in the U.S. at a small high school called World Academy. Or at least I did until not long ago. The future is uncertain for now." Even in this brief exchange, Jimmy was getting the sense that he was really going to like this man. *His energy is good,* he thought. *He seems very open.* The man continued to look at Jimmy seeming to wonder about Jimmy's clothing. It seemed that Jimmy's intuition was right on. They fell into talking quite easily.

After a few minutes, Bernd asked him, "Do you think it's necessary to wear the traditional pilgrimage garb? I chose not to, but I guess it was more that I hadn't realized it was a thing. My decision to go on the trip was rather sudden. You see, I…" he said, then hesitated, realizing how the next thing might sound.

Jimmy's interest was piqued. After all, his decision to be where they now were was made only months ago and seemed to run counter to all he'd been building over the past couple of years—a home in Minnesota.

"Go on," Jimmy urged. "It might be that I have something similar to tell you, too."

"Well, I started having dreams, and one dream especially brought me here. This was after Yuri and I went to Mount Kōya. Do you know where that is?"

"Yes, I've been to Mount Kōya in Wakayama Prefecture. Wait a minute, did you say, *dreams*? And, if you don't mind me asking, who's Yuri?" Jimmy asked.

"Yes, dreams, and Yuri is my wife. Why do you find my dreams so interesting?"

"Well, I've been having some myself, but you go first."

"I think it's probably nothing, but still, the dream related to what seems to be a fateful turn of events or about someone in the past on *this* island, the smallest island of the four major islands of Japan. The dream made me feel like using some of my summer vacation to explore this pilgrimage route. I have come to think, when something like that happens, it's a good idea to follow up on it, to trust that there's a reason for it. Unfortunately, Yuri cannot get much time off from work, so she didn't come. You married?"

"Ah, well, um, no, I'm not," Jimmy was taken aback by the question.

"Sorry. Is that a bad question to ask?"

"No, not really," he replied, having recovered, thanks to a deep breath and his meditation practice. Jimmy noticed the wholesome, what many might think of as the positive side to something, as Katarina Pauline, who everyone calls "Sensei," had urged him to do—he was getting quicker at dropping the small stuff. He told himself, *Good job, Jimmy,* as she had instructed. He'd thought about relationships and being married so many times but was only recently able to commit to any kind of relationship, and the ghost was gone, leaving him to start all over again, making this momentarily awkward. Aside from his connections with Janelle and the Motley Crew, he had little intimacy with anyone. Eventually Jimmy forced out these words, "It's just that I guess, I'd like to be married, but it hasn't happened so far."

"Not to worry, right?" Bernd said encouragingly.

"Right," Jimmy said, a little surprised at the strength of his initial reaction. He thought he didn't care that much about being married but obviously did in some ways. He was hoping—but clearly not there yet—that he didn't care either way. Not being overly concerned would leave room for his search for awakening, something, according to the teachers, that required one's complete and total effort. Didn't the teachers say the path required *Complete Effort* among the other approaches of the Eight-Fold Path, a teaching that had been around since the time of historical Buddha in India?

Complete aspiration, complete livelihood…Bring yourself back, Jimmy. Be with Bernd, not your automatic thoughts.

"As for your dreams, I've been having some pretty fantastic dreams, too. What is it that you are following up on?" Jimmy asked.

"I wondered if the sights I saw in my dreams on Mount Kōya were of Mount Kōya, but when I explained them to a Mr. Fujimoto, a local researcher to whom I had been introduced by a connection I have at the University, he told me that it sounded like either something on the Kumano Route, the 33 temple pilgrimage on the Kii Peninsula or perhaps," he mused while slowly rubbing his chin, "something along the 88-temple pilgrimage route of Shikoku. For some reason, I kept coming back to this route in my mind, so here I am."

"Here we are." They shared a smile.

Bernd started by explaining what Mr. Fujimoto told him of the Kumano Route, in his ancestral backyard, but then suddenly stopped and mentioned his trip to the Shikoku Route as a young man. Jimmy got a little queasy upon hearing this and with thoughts swimming in his head, sat down on the rock next to Bernd.

Recovering, he asked, "You mean you talked to Mr. Fujimoto? I met him myself not so long ago. These two coincidences are almost beyond belief."

"What do you mean, these *two* coincidences? Bernd asked, also seeming amazed at the connection that was unveiling before his eyes. "I used to not believe in coincidences, and then, with the events of a few years ago…. It was a strange ride." Bernd told Jimmy how he was slowly becoming accustomed to strange things. He recalled that he and Yuri had met so many different people while looking for Star Points several years earlier. That search brought them into contact with danger and mystery in many unexpected ways. He hoped he could tell Jimmy more sometime, but it was too soon for that.

"Um, not only have we met the same person on Mount Kōya, but we have also had dreams since visiting there." Jimmy wondered if Bernd, too, had visited Fukuchiin, where the Christian motifs displayed on samurai armor gave him a chill. He'd bought the walking stick, currently in use, at Okunoin, the huge graveyard which also houses Kobodaishi's mausoleum.

"I stayed at Fukuchiin, a temple suggested to me by a visiting Taiko player from Kobe, whom I came across after a concert in Tokyo. He kept mentioning the importance of bringing our world together through music. I was impressed by his presence of mind and his passion for what he does, so I booked my stay on Mount Kōya that night," Bernd said.

"You're kidding," Jimmy thought, and then realized the truth of the situation as he looked from his walking stick to the one Bernd used, and realized they'd come from the same place, somewhere on Mount Kōya. One had to stay at Fukuchiin to even visit the inside of the temple and see its treasures. He knew this since he'd seen another man turned away while he himself was staying there. *We'd both stayed at Fukuchiin.* Amazed, Jimmy finished with, "This has to be more than a coincidence; there must be a reason for us connecting here. It doesn't strike me as only luck."

"I guess not, although like I said, I am coming to trust the universe more and more each year, and I'm a scientist," Bernd said with a smile. "Considering my dream, well, it was about someone being in trouble, I think, but the image was unclear as was the problem involved. And, well, here I am. This is as far as I've gotten in my search. I was about to give up, not having any leads, and then you walked up."

"Well, I asked about your dream because I had one, too. In fact, it keeps recurring. Someone keeps falling off a cliff, I believe, somewhere along this route."

"That makes a lot of sense. You see I had a tumbling sensation in my dream—but the dream didn't repeat. Weird, huh?" Bernd asked while supporting himself with the walking stick that he'd bought on Mount Kōya.

"And Bernd, until the other day, I thought it might have been me who fell. In fact..."

"You, what do you mean?"

"Well, since the dream kept recurring, and I fell down a slope about a week ago—"

"You what?"

"I fell off the side of a hill between temples eleven and twelve. In fact, since then, the dreams have gotten both more vivid and scarier."

"Scarier, how? I'm intrigued."

"I noticed not only the person falling. Another dream started to happen. Wait a minute. Let's walk and talk." Bernd nodded. They picked up their backpacks while they talked and started off together with ease. It was late morning, and they had to move along to get something for lunch. Jimmy continued. "In the various dreams..."

"You had two, right?" Bernd chimed in.

"I'll get to the reasons as soon as I can; however, something is not clear, but I am unsure what. For now, the most recent dream included two monks at a temple, eerily like some place from around here, though in what time in history, I have no idea. And Bernd, one of them was killed by an arrow, at a temple!"

"That's pretty strange, I'll have to admit," Bernd said, at first shocked, and then deep in thought. Jimmy could imagine his scientific brain trying to figure something out.

"Why at a temple?" Bernd asked.

"I have no idea. It's puzzling, isn't it? I can't believe anyone would be shot by an arrow *at a temple*, though the warring states period of Japan, the *Sengoku* Period, is famous for both the level of chaos it brought and for the Buddhist warrior monks at, for example, Tendai Sect temples. So, it wouldn't be a sole occurrence."

Jimmy continued explaining his dreams. "You know, the other monk was running away from the temple when my dream ended. I have absolutely no idea what happened to him."

A pause in the conversation allowed both of them to process the described scene. "So, Bernd, what convinced you to go on this pilgrimage, instead of the Kumano pilgrimage?"

Bernd reviewed his experiences since entering the pilgrimage route. He'd been deep in thought any number of times. "I wonder if it has something to do with the connection to Shingon Buddhism. I, like you, seem to have some kind of odd, but undiscovered, connection, with Shingon, the sect of Buddhism began on Mount Kōya."

"I see."

"But that's the simple version. Several years ago, when Yuri and I were on a journey together, we began meditating in earnest. I fell off my meditation practice for more than a year now…I am glad you asked, Jimmy. I miss the calming nature of meditation. I miss taking time out to not be busy. I miss meditation. Therefore, I'm on this pilgrimage to reinstate the spiritual life for myself, I guess. And when I return to Tokyo, I will take up meditation again. I doubt it is an accident that I met you. Bro, we're in this together, aren't we?"

"You got it, bro," Jimmy replied. They gave each other a high five and planned to meditate together sometime.

"Unfortunately, what remains unclear to me is how I might help or find out something about someone from such an amorphous dream—without much shape or clarity—especially a dream I had only once, unlike you, Jimmy."

Chapter 6
WORKING TOGETHER

After walking in silence for a while, the conversation started up again as these two men continued to synchronize. "And arrows would suggest an earlier time, not the twentieth century but a time earlier, like the Sengoku Period," Jimmy said, reviving talk of the dream. Bernd was no stranger to Japanese history, having talked about it not only with Yuri but also with his colleagues at the university.

By and by they came to a place that served *sanuki udon*, a kind of thick, wheat-noodle dish famous in Shikoku, that Bernd had yet to try. Sitting down for lunch, Jimmy got an ill feeling and wondered what was up, while Bernd munched on noodles. Jimmy felt like he couldn't even look at the ceramic bowl filled with a flavorful broth and thick white noodles that normally he loved. He looked around for some clue, while Bernd seemed not to notice anything wrong. Something was a little off, but Jimmy couldn't tell what it was. However, the foreboding soon passed. Upon consultation, Bernd, ever the scientist, told Jimmy not to worry about it and that it was likely the result of their talking about their dreams, the heat, being hungry, and so on.

Jimmy went to the restroom, and along the way he noticed the view that spread out before the restaurant, which was more like a small hut with *tatami* or woven reed mat floors for the guests to sit on next to low tables. He began to feel a little faint again, though he persisted in exploring the view before him. Hills and trees, and small, rounded mountains spilled out across a vast distance; bamboo forests filled the sides of slopes that alternated between very steep and gradual slopes. It was abundantly green, pleasing, and peaceful to the eye. There were various samples of a type of tropical tree that he didn't know the name of but reminded him of palm trees. He'd seen them in various places around Japan. From that elevation, the view was amazing.

Jimmy drew in a slow, deep breath and relaxed further, feeling exhilarated each moment he exhaled and breathed in that clean mountain air and let it out again. The ill feeling passed, and he noted to himself how he loved being there right then. A few moments later, he returned to find Bernd calculating the steepness of the slope across the valley from them. Bernd thought this area included unusually steep sections of the pilgrimage route.

Their stomachs full, they ambled out and began the five-kilometer hike to the next temple and its nearby lodgings. Jimmy loved that there were so many kinds of plants and, he imagined, animals, too, such as rabbits or pheasants. He hoped that they wouldn't run into any of the wild boars that may be lurking around at night. The mountain boars of Wakayama on the Kii Peninsula were scary—he wondered if they were on Shikoku, too.

They walked for about half an hour with little variation in the view. Eventually, the two rounded a corner that veered to the right, and both fell silent.

"What is it?" Jimmy asked, even though he sensed the reason for Bernd's silence. As it sank in, he remained still, drew in a deep breath, and looked across the valley and back again.

"This is the view from my dream," they said almost in unison. They looked at each other and first smiled, then grew serious. Jimmy's intuition about the vegetation and landscape making this the route in his dream had been correct.

"That means that someone was in trouble around here," Jimmy said solemnly. This was the place he'd seen time and time again in his dream, several trees along the edge of a steep slope dropping off precipitously. *But who was it who was harmed? And more importantly, why? What did that person do to end up falling over the cliff in front of where they stood?* Like Jimmy, did he slip off the side, or did he fall for some other reason? And, while he was used to unusual happenings after his time with the ghost, Jimmy noticed with wonder that Bernd seemed at ease with what was going on.

Bernd responded to Jimmy's surprise at him taking this in stride saying that after all, he and Yuri belonged to an international aid organization, something like Doctors Without Borders.

"That's very interesting," Jimmy said with a tone of inquisitiveness but didn't know Bernd well enough to push him further.

"Ah, well...it's a bit of a, eh, long story." Bernd obviously didn't want to divulge more. It would have to wait. Jimmy noticed that Bernd exuded a sense of calm regarding this matter, which Jimmy took to mean that he had nothing to hide—and there was some other reason for the hesitation. Jimmy was calm, even though his sense of compassion had awakened his interest in what had happened here for the person who fell. They took pictures of the area from any and every angle they could imagine before moving on.

"I think it is important to get to know others and to help. I mean about the person who fell," Jimmy said.

"Definitely. So many of us are into ourselves—when the world needs us to collaborate and work together. It is becoming more logical and more necessary each year," Bernd added.

"No kidding. I have been training to *get over myself*, so to speak."

"Not easy, is it, Jimmy?"

"An understatement. This friendship is growing into something deeper, a chance to learn more deeply what it means to care about others," Jimmy said.

"Yes, it is."

Later in a shared room at the hotel, they compared photos and stories. Instinctively, they kept their voices low. Jimmy and Bernd continued swapping stories after a dinner of local seasonal fare: fresh roasted fish, a selection of local pickles, steamed rice, and various other delectable foods.

Jimmy related the dreams he'd been having in detail, hoping that together they could figure out what happened, what the dreams meant, and why they both had had the same one. This last question might be answered by a hunch Jimmy had.

"Could it be that we have something in common, some information or something we both encountered? Can you think of anything? What did you talk to Mr. Fujimoto about on Mount Kōya?"

"I looked at various pictures of historical time periods and several objects, that's all," Bernd dismissed the idea, not finding any logical connection in it. Realizing that they both needed to know more to understand what was unfolding before them, Bernd paused, then continued.

"Mr. Fujimoto and I walked around the Koya University library for a while discussing the dream, but mostly we talked of the Kumano pilgrimage route of the Kii Peninsula until he mentioned this 88-temple route in Shikoku, and then I felt something inside, a warmth in my heart. It was getting late, so we parted. I went back to the place I was staying for the night, thinking nothing of it at first. The next morning, I walked with this stick, purchased at Fukuchiin, to Okunoin, but nothing else of significance seemed to relate to the dream I had." Bernd continued. "It took me weeks to recall Mr. Fujimoto's last comment about the 88-temple pilgrimage route, and then it kept turning up wherever

I went; my colleagues talked of the pilgrimage, it was in the news. There was even a newspaper article showing people wearing the traditional garb you're wearing. It seemed I couldn't get away from it, so yes, that was enough to get me here. And what convinced you?"

"Our visits with Fujimoto at the University seem related, that's for sure." Jimmy wondered, *Bernd went to Okunoin…is that significant?*

"But the dream is too similar to be insignificant. I had it only once, but you said that for you, it continues to recur. You said the last time in the dream, you saw the clothing the person falling was wearing, is that right?" Bernd put his logical mind to use. "And by the way, I think we are going to have to get you some change of clothes. You will be much more comfortable in the long run with easier-going clothing. It's not important to be too formal. For me, I hope to learn to pay attention, and not only evaluate everything according to what seems logical to me."

"Yah, I guess you're right." With some small changes, Jimmy became his regular self in comfortable clothing, opting for hiking pants he'd brought along and he removed the white overshirt of pilgrims. He did keep the walking stick for the time being and the golden *wagesa* or pilgrim sash. He was glad that Bernd pointed out the walking of the route was priority, not what one looked like while going on the route. They arrived at Onzanji, Temple Number 18, a temple that Kukai had to perform rites for 17 days to allow women, his mother in particular, to enter the temple, previously forbidden, and later that night, they returned to the story.

"Right, the person who fell over the side of the steep incline was wearing some kind of traditional clothing, I think."

"What kind? An outfit for performing funeral ceremonies?" Bernd asked, having been to several of those while teaching at the university. Jimmy looked around the room, located his backpack and took out his own *samue* that he used while meditating.

"Not exactly. This outfit, albeit a modern version, one wears to either work at a Zen temple or meditate at one. In the modern world, this is often the white garment worn at a martial arts class, though they don't have to be only white. As you can see, mine is indigo with white stitching. I like to wear one simply because they are comfortable, no matter what you're doing," Jimmy finished, pleased to be of help in this way. He continued, "That is why I think that he, the person in the dream, was a monk. He must have been some kind of meditation practitioner or something like that."

"You said there were two monks, and one was called away from meditating, right?"

"That's right."

Bernd continued. "One was shot by an arrow, and the other ran away. Do you think the monk who fell was the same one who got shot by the arrow? Was he the other monk from your dream or someone totally unrelated to the first two?" Bernd asked with his quick mind.

"Okay. I see what you're getting at. Dreams can be a mix of happenings. The falling could have been the monk falling after being shot. But wait, that doesn't make sense. I remember now that the second monk looked pretty much dead and was dragged away by the attackers. Further, why would you have had a dream about someone falling? And what about the cliff in the background? It was a serious fall, as we both saw after lunch that day."

"There is no guarantee that our dreams are even related," Bernd mentioned with a nervous smile that conveyed concern. "However, I hope they are," he added quickly, trying to reassure Jimmy who took a deep breath. He'd hoped they were getting closer, but they appeared to be heading away from understanding the dilemma better.

It was getting late, so they decided to sleep for the night and talk more the next day. Before bed, Jimmy prayed, as he always did before sleeping. He prayed to become awakened himself and for all beings to have happiness joining the practices of *metta* or loving kindness and hoping to make good on his Bodhisattva vow to *awaken speedily for the sake of all beings*. Sleep took both men quickly after the eventful day. Another dream entered Jimmy's slumber:

My, how things have changed…I can't believe this is the same country I was born in. I value the beauty of the change of seasons, the wonder and awe from so many scenes filled with the beauty that afforded a fecund, green land of hills, mountains, forests, clearly gifts of the gods as told in the Kojiki, the ancient story of the gods and the creation of Japan. We must save Nippon, OUR homeland. We must save it while it still remains beautiful; we must get rid of all detrimental foreign influences and by all means any foreigners who remain against the Shogun's orders.

Jimmy snapped awake at this last statement about *Nippon*, the name for Japan in Japanese. This man's sentiment recalled the Tokugawa Shogun, the one who had called for *sakoku*, the exclusion of foreigners with the aim of removing unwanted, foreign influence. Jimmy would inform Bernd, since this likely meant the dreams, at least some of them, were related to the Tokugawa Period of Japanese history, also called the Edo Period that lasted from 1603 to 1868.

Who was the man in the dream? He had a deep resonant voice and some followers; however, Jimmy couldn't tell how many were there, and it was apparent that the speaker had their rapt attention. He was tall and strong, advanced in age, but not weak. He wore, as far as Jimmy could tell after an internet search, an outfit fitting for someone of samurai status.

Over breakfast, they connected. Bernd had slept well; nothing special happened overnight as far as he was concerned. Not true for Jimmy.

"That's interesting, Jimmy. It seems like you're on the right track to think the dreams have something to do with the Tokugawa Period.

I am amazed that the scene we both saw yesterday, despite the modernization of Japan, looked so much like it does now, if indeed, it was a scene from the Tokugawa period or sometime in the last two to three hundred years."

"No kidding." Jimmy mused. There was no way of knowing exactly the time frame, but at least they had something to go on with this new dream. And then it all came back to him: the dream while in Minnesota of a samurai claiming to have gladly approved the exclusion of foreigners in the Tokugawa Period. Jimmy had forgotten it after going back to sleep.

"Bernd, this is what I meant when we were first talking about the dreams. I knew there was more but couldn't remember until now. You see, the dream of falling being so vivid overtook this memory. And my own fall, too, had been on my mind."

Jimmy revealed a fresh insight to Bernd, that the samurai dream was also recurring in his subconscious mind but not something he was fully aware of until the present. "The dream went something like this, Bernd. There was a man, who I have come to believe was a samurai, and now believe to be of the later part of the second half of the nineteenth century. That is when there was an intense influx of foreign influence in Japan. He was ostensibly a sword master who was all for the exclusion of foreigners from Japan." As Jimmy recalled this part, he paused to take it in. He realized that everyone around this man in the dreams was wearing swords and cursing foreign influence in Japan. Then he informed Bernd of his new understanding. Bernd realized the importance as well. Jimmy continued. "He was angry at any foreign influence, which included Buddhism, in Japan."

"Wow." Bernd said thoughtfully.

"You see, this man completely held his followers' attention. He preached aggressively, but I could not make out all the antiquated language nor do I remember it all."

"Right. That makes sense, the particular use of terms related to the time," Bernd said.

"And it may be that they were meeting in secret, making it even harder to discern, though this is only my intuition. It was a brief dream."

"Understood." Bernd went into his own thoughts for a moment, recalling the Secret Society he'd met while searching for the final Star Point, an episode from several years earlier. *Would Jimmy be someone they could ask to join*? He came back to the present. That was for another time and way too soon to decide. "Why was the samurai against things foreign, and of all things Buddhism, which has obviously flourished in Japan?"

"It may be that he was for Shinto or the traditionally existing beliefs of Japan, of which, it seems, he was a student. The Japanese "Are Shinto" according to a text I picked up at Kasuga Grand Shrine in Nara City. Indeed, this man seemed to be worried about losing the soul of Japan, at least I think that is what he said. The more I recall the dream, the more I think he was worried that if one version of influence came from outside, then another and another—until there would be nothing left of the original Japan, the culturally significant and superior Japan that he knew in his time, that would be a tragedy."

"Ironically, those kinds of changes did take place in the Meiji period, resulting in the end to the samurai. This man was prescient," Bernd said revealing his studies of recent Japanese history.

"He seemed to see both forward and backward in time. The man was worried that if Buddhism was allowed to flourish, as it had in the past—or some new foreign influence or both—that they would overpower the culturally rich Japanese traditions, and this was something to be prevented. That much was certain from his speech, the parts I could understand. The point about the Meiji Restoration is relevant, I imagine. It places the speech in the late nineteenth or early twentieth century," Jimmy said.

"Hmmm." Bernd was familiar with fanaticism, having been carefully taught about that in his own culture under Hitler. He went on. "This is stunning, Jimmy."

"You're telling me," Jimmy said. "In addition, I had these experiences last year that, ah—" He'd stopped short, having almost told Bernd of the ghostly visits of Saori. He'd almost blurted it out. He figured, Bernd, like everyone else wouldn't believe him, but he still wondered…

"Go on, Jimmy. Any clues would be helpful." Jimmy realized, having started down this corridor, that the samurai dream may have to wait.

"Oh, it's nothing," he responded, not willing to go into more detail about the ghost, at least not at the present. And Jimmy realized Bernd had also been guarded about something in his past. "It's just that 'unusual' is what I continue to experience about Japan. While living here for ten years total in high school, and again in my twenties, I met so many warm and wonderful people, had so many great experiences, and I was able to visit again not long ago, making connections with many new and, well, *old* friends." He realized that he still missed her, his ghostly friend who'd gone away—permanently.

Jimmy hoped Saori was well, back in Heian Japan, heaven, or wherever she was now. His heart warmed just thinking of her and the friendship they'd shared.

Coming back to the present, he experienced a spontaneous mental pause. He wondered if this was his body's reaction to holding back from Bernd. Other than this instance, he found an easiness being around him. Perhaps he'd get to meet Yuri, Bernd's wife, some day. He was already growing fond of Bernd. Hopefully they would come to trust each other. *Trust and being able to share all with another are what I seek most in life* he was slowly coming to realize. *Will Bernd and I get there? Only time will tell.*

As he dozed off, he witnessed in a new dream…*"That's right. Exclude foreigners." A samurai was to cut down his opponents in battle after battle. "I'll make a lineage of people who only follow Shinto, who will rid the country of foreigners and enforce Sakoku — the exclusion of foreigners and foreign influence from Japan. From Shinto priest to Shinto priest, we'll spread the glory of Japan."*

Jimmy came to his senses feeling befuddled. He imagined that he had just seen the founder of the samurai's master's lineage, which seemed sometime in the Tokugawa Period. He'd need more clues to see if his intuition was correct.

Chapter 7
GROWING FRIENDSHIP

Bernd and Jimmy walked the route together for some time, having already traveled nearly one-fourth of the pilgrimage. They stayed overnight at Temple Number Twenty-Two, *Byodoji* or Equanimity Temple. Both thought their achievement was significant being one-fourth of the way along the route and doing it together. Journeying together sped up the pace, and they were continually in awe of the natural beauty of the route, the many mountainous views, steps of small fields for planting crops carved out of the mountains to produce food, and the beautiful vegetation of Shikoku: flowers, moss, and trees. Jimmy imagined that the ten promises or benefits of the pilgrimage, posted at the temple he embarked from at the beginning of the route, must have been true. The first three were: living a long life, gaining the ability to be direct, and speaking compassionately. Jimmy thought, *I wish to speak compassionately, be direct, and not phony with others. Would that help with being related to another?* Without a doubt. He remembered that the teachers at Open Breeze spoke often of compassion, even of it being a measuring stick for whether to follow a teacher or not.

"I'd like to have those characteristics," Jimmy continued, having said them out loud, recalling the promises of the pilgrimage.

"Me, too, of course," Bernd replied while they walked around the temple grounds. Spontaneously, they gave each other a high five. Bernd paused afterwards, noting that it was the kind of thing he'd gotten used to with Yuri but had not experienced that level of spontaneity with others before. For Jimmy, Saori came to mind—and he was suddenly ready to take a risk.

"You know, Bernd, I am not normally very forward with people. I am very glad that I met you. I am glad to not be taking this journey alone. That is sort of what happened the last time I was in Japan."

"What do you mean, *sort of*?" Bernd quickly noted the point.

"That's not easy to explain. It has to do with me. I am only now as an adult learning to trust others."

"Unfortunately, many humans give us reasons to not trust others, but to be sure, we're not all like that."

"Yah, I think so, too. For example, there is a group of teachers in Minnesota that kind of adopted me right away at World Academy. We even have a group name, the Motley Crew, if they still consider me one of their ilk."

"Wasn't that a band in the 1980s?"

"Yes, but we don't share much in common with the band. We're pretty low-key, and we don't spell it the same way."

"Of course," Bernd responded, following up with jovial laughter. He told Jimmy how he'd been to not only a Motley Crüe cover band but also a Bryan Adams concert in Germany.

"I miss the Motley Crew, I guess, Jimmy said. I'm kind of interested in one of the teachers, but I'm not sure what'll come of it."

"You'll know when the time is right. Trust me," Bernd reassured him. "That's how it was for Yuri and me. It was simple, mutual, no stress." Jimmy realized that married people had been telling him that for years, so there must be something to it. He smiled. It wasn't worry so much as an ongoing niggling feeling. He was fascinated with so many things in life that he didn't spend *all* his time worrying about having a relationship. It seemed only a natural consideration rather than a concern, or was it? Certainly, subconsciously he'd been avoiding intimacy. This last thought stayed with him a while—although it was time to leave.

They got their books stamped and left Temple Twenty-Two, moving on. Jimmy continued pondering his subconscious and intimacy and thought of the two men's easy connection. *What's the difference with Bernd? Is it me?* Jimmy wondered. They were both on a pilgrimage, ostensibly each for themselves, but most certainly in it together, at least for the time being. Bernd was also musing over their connection, happy to be on the route with Jimmy's intuitive nature to balance his logical tendency.

Jimmy was really enjoying himself despite the rankling within caused by the dreams, and he was happy to have this evolving friendship and chance at intimacy. Still, a part of the mix of emotions running through him was the growing realization that a relationship, with a real, live woman was something he fervently desired.

Chapter 8
TEMPLE TWENTY-THREE

Seven hours later they were nearing Temple Twenty-Three, Yakuoji, one of the temples on the route not founded by Kobodaishi. Jimmy told Bernd that he was getting excited as each temple brought them closer to Temple Seventy-Five, Zentsuji, the birthplace of Kobodaishi. "It is one of the unique facts that I have learned about in exploring this path prior to beginning. What's something you learned?"

"I appreciate how Kobodaishi established so many temples throughout Japan," Bernd said.

"I read that of the pilgrimage routes in Japan, either the Kumano Route or the Kannon Route on the Kii Peninsula is the oldest pilgrimage route; however, the one we are on is the most popular both within Japan and internationally," Jimmy said.

"Yes, it's the first thing that comes up in an internet search for pilgrimage routes in Japan," Bernd said.

Jimmy continued, "As part of my history courses, I learned that Kobodaishi established the Sect of Shingon Buddhism on Mount Kōya in 816 CE, gaining the approval of the emperor, and then later established this 88-temple pilgrimage route in Shikoku. I wonder if it was because Shikoku is the place of his birth, his *furusato* or hometown and the deeply held belief that where one was from mattered dearly. It was where one belonged. The Japanese really take stock in their place of birth, don't they?"

"As do the Germans, but less intensely than the Japanese, it seems. Yuri loves to go home every chance she gets. Her family is important both to her and to those on the small, Japanese island she is from."

"Wow. That sounds interesting. I have only really been on the four main islands of Japan. I have no idea about the thousands of islands around Japan. Come to think of it, it seems that all people around the world make a big deal about where they were born."

"Agreed. You know, if we get a chance, perhaps we can visit her small, Japanese island village together sometime," Bernd said warmly. "But for now, I'm hungry. Let's get some lunch."

At a restaurant along the way, they each had a *teishoku*, a set meal including rice, pickled vegetables, and meat or fish for lunch. Jimmy had the *tonkatsu teishoku*, his favorite, deep-fried breaded pork cut into narrow pieces dipped in a rich sauce the consistency of ketchup, but with a flavor all its own. Bernd had *okonomiyaki*, a favorite of his often called a Japanese pancake, which was nothing like what one would expect in Minnesota, starting with the filling of cabbage and ending with a unique sauce.

At this restaurant as in others, the owner shouted *"irasshaimase"* as they walked in, the greeting of welcome. Jimmy's meal was served with rice and miso soup, a salty broth made of fermented soybeans.

Both were eager to continue walking after the meal break. They hoisted their backpacks and entered the homestretch toward Temple Twenty-Three, the one famous for not only the pilgrimage route but also for the luck it was supposed to bring for those said to be in their *yakudoshi* or unlucky year, according to Jimmy's guidebook and *Japan-visitor.com*. When they stopped for a break, Jimmy unfolded a wrinkled page in a book that showed damage from his risky landing on the side of the slope near Temple Twelve Shosanji. He'd never forget that mountainous region as long as he lived. He was lucky already, he thought, since he was still on the pilgrimage and not at the bottom of that ravine. The whole route map showed them that they were probably about one kilometer from Number Twenty-Three, Yakuoji. They continued walking.

After a while, noticing his silence and distant look, Bernd asked, "You okay, Jimmy?"

"Yes. I'm all right. I was just having a flashback to the fall that I experienced near Temple Number Twelve."

"That must have been scary. I'm glad you're all right."

"That's more than can be said for the person in my dream, I fear."

"What makes you say that?" Bernd asked.

"Well, it's nothing certain, but a headfirst fall like that seems deadly, doesn't it?"

"I only had the dream once, and it was several months ago. I hadn't figured out whether the person was falling headfirst or otherwise, but what you're saying does make sense." He paused and asked, "What the heck does it mean, Jimmy? It's not just weird that we both had the dream; it's weird that we've had the dream at all."

Concurring, Jimmy nodded. An uneasy silence ensued for a few moments. Could be their common interest in Japanese history or some kind of connection to a previous life, but Jimmy said that he had no explicit recollection of any past life.

"Neither do I," Bernd said.

"The persistence of it is a bit tiring sometimes, waking and not knowing why the dream continues to recur."

"I can't imagine," Bernd said. "I don't remember my dreams very often. I didn't used to put much stock in dreams, but I'm wondering a lot about this shared dream. I've been a science guy for so long that this is in a way intriguing and also a bit discomforting.

As they finished the remaining kilometer, Jimmy's mind was cranking out possible scenarios, working on this problem so that he could bounce his ideas off Bernd's logical, scientific mind. "You know, Bernd, every time we get near or are in a temple, it's like my dreams or the recollection of them becomes more intense. I didn't have any dreams while I was walking one of the long stretches between Temples Twelve and Thirteen and slept in the tent. I am glad that I brought that along."

"Thank you for sharing, Jimmy," Bernd said in obvious appreciation.

"Gladly," and Jimmy meant it. It was so nice having Bernd along. Jimmy could see that Bernd had something else to share.

"Do you think each temple has a clue as to the reason for the monk's fall?" Bernd asked.

"That seems unlikely. No one can be related to all the temples."

"I guess that makes sense, though obviously, Kobodaishi, the man called Kukai in life, has been associated with most if not all of the route," Bernd confirmed.

"True. But he wasn't around during the period of exclusion called *sakoku*," Jimmy responded. Then something dawned on him. "Hey, Bernd, I saw a plaque back near Temple Twelve and one of the temples near where we both think the fall happened, the place we believe we'd seen in our shared dream experience."

"What did it say?"

"Well, I couldn't read all the characters, but it mentioned that he was…wait a minute! Let's compare guidebooks, and we may have to do an internet search. Let's get to the next lodging place. I have something I want to check out." They picked up the pace.

When they rounded the next corner, Temple Twenty-Three was in sight. After checking in, they made plans to rest, bathe, eat, and explore Jimmy's idea.

Chapter 9
THE MANAGER

Hungry and tired, Bernd and Jimmy took baths, ate dinner, and explored possibilities. Both were interested in figuring out what happened. They sat down with tea and a laptop and began to discuss what was on Jimmy's mind.

"You see, the plaque disclosed information about a man, a Buddhist monk named Tsuruya, who was celebrated for having done so much in his short life. I would like to find out more about what he did. So, let's look. Let's see if my guidebook has anything about someone memorialized at Temple…Oh, which one to begin with? There were several. How about Temple Twelve?—though I get queasy each time I think of it. It's the temple known for being high up in the mountains." Jimmy pointed to a page in the early part of his book, *Shikoku Japan 88 Route Guide*. He continued. "Oh, that's right. I remember now. I was winded, having arrived there with a sore hip. Since I fell somewhere between there and Temple Eleven. I was so exhausted after the climb and subsequent fall, that I got my *shuinchō* or memorial book stamped and written in, and I hardly remember that day because of the pain in my hip. The plaque, as I am remembering it now, was posted prominently just inside the entrance to the temple."

"What did it say? Can you find it? My book has the guy's name, but not what it said about him," Bernd replied, matching Jimmy's excitement.

"Sorry, Bernd. No go for mine either. It looks like an internet search is in order." Bernd maneuvered the laptop in front of him. Jimmy began his own search on his phone.

"Find anything?" Jimmy asked after a few minutes.

"Seems like he was some kind of, can you read this character?"

"Yes, it is an antiquated term for manager or something like *seneschal*, the medieval, European term for estate manager. I guess perhaps it means for the temple or group of temples. He was a kind of super-abbot or something like that," Jimmy said.

"Or the head monk of the entire region, however much area that covered at the time."

"Right. The character has that implication. Holy cow, he must have been very important. How could someone in his position have fallen?" Jimmy replied incredulously.

"What do you mean? Nobody said it was him that fell," Bernd asked in disbelief.

"Um, I don't know. It's just a feeling I got. It came out of nowhere. It reminds me of something from last year."

"Yes?" Bernd said.

"I was on Mount Kōya and, well, ah, I…"

"Go on Jimmy, this has to be important."

"It's kind of strange."

"It won't be the first time that I've heard of something strange. Trust me. I can't tell you about it now. Our current search is more important, but I am no stranger to strange things."

Here goes nothing. Jimmy began. "I was on Mount Kōya, and as I was leaving, I picked up a book in the kiosk in the train station that ended up helping me and another make a great connection, and fulfill our purpose for being in Japan, I guess you could say."

"I thought you said you were in Japan alone, and that's not so strange." Bernd's astute mind hadn't missed this important detail.

"True, but the details will have to wait till later." Jimmy hoped this would satisfy Bernd for the time being. "I hope we can find out what happened to this man and why we both had a dream about him. It's just my intuition that he is the one who was murdered, I mean fell. I can feel it in my heart, as odd as that might sound. My spine tingles just thinking about it, but it's nothing that's certain." They exchanged blank looks, noting that Jimmy had just said *murdered*.

"I believe you. Like I said, I am no stranger to odd happenings. Yuri and I went on a journey several years ago. I think the universe or God looks out for all of us. At least I hope that is right. I need all the help I can get," Bernd finished with a smile. It was getting late, and because they were very tired from thinking so hard, they decided to give up for the night.

Bernd didn't seem to mind Jimmy's insistence on meditating each night. Jimmy wondered if Bernd would be open to being invited to meditate, so he finally asked.

"Yes, of course, I'd love to. I wasn't sure if I should ask to join you, so I meditated on my own all this time. I realized some days ago that waiting to return to Tokyo was only me resisting looking within. Still, I didn't want to bother you." Both broke out in laughter at the hesitation each had shown, as unnecessary as it was.

I really must be more engaged, open, and direct if I am to relate to others, Jimmy mused. From that point on, they meditated together with the result of deeper meditation for both. It always seemed easier together, Jimmy realized, as was taught at Open Breeze.

After meditating, they went down to the front desk where each bought a can of beer.

"Jimmy, I am learning to be more natural, not so rigid in my logical mind."

"Me, too, but it is because I have always been on edge. Duncan McDougal has been saying this for years. Perhaps this pilgrimage will help," Jimmy said, settling into a chair. Sipping beer, they relaxed into the evening. The search and journey would resume the next day.

The next morning after breakfast, they were set to be on their way. All they could find from the internet was that the man was both a monk and the regional abbot, like a bishop would be for Christians, a leader of more than one church in a region or diocese, in this case a group of temples. Jimmy wasn't surprised that humans had come up with similar ways of organizing themselves. Humans seemed more and more similar each year that Jimmy lived—having likes and dislikes, cares, concerns but also love. Further queries remained. What had happened to the abbot, as they had started to refer to him? The guidebook related that he died at forty, a relatively young age for someone of his status. He would have had enough food to eat and certainly plenty of exercise going back and forth from temple to temple, which made the youthful death seem even more unusual.

As Jimmy awoke the next morning, he wondered whether the monk had traversed the entire 88-temple route? He had died in the late nineteenth century. Was there any reason for his death besides disease or injury? It seemed like the universe was trying to tell them something, but mostly he and Bernd were drawing a blank.

"The answer might never be found." Jimmy was being realistic.

They were about to leave when a calligrapher, a man brush-writing characters in pilgrims' memorial books, overheard Bernd mention the abbot to Jimmy. He then said, "What'd you say? That man is famous for having walked the entire pilgrimage four times. One time for body, one time for speech, and one time for mind." The fourth time he called "integration." After the calligrapher wrote in English for them as he had for visitors over the years, he wrote in Japanese *kokoro wo iyasareta*" for "integration," recognizing Jimmy's level of understanding of characters which became obvious after a few moments. Jimmy was thankful for the courses he'd attended; they refreshed the characters for him and taught him even more of the antiquated ones, which made him miss Saori even more.

Jimmy nearly fell over when he saw the term *iyasareta* or integration, a term he associated with Saori's healing of her karma—any of her past actions that had kept her around for so long as a ghost. The healing or integration sent her back to her time in Heian Japan. Fortunately, he was able to lean against the post behind him to catch his breath. He was stunned to observe the term in this context again so soon. Saori had been gone for less than a year. "God, I miss her," he said loud enough for Bernd to hear.

"Bernd, you got this. I don't feel so well right now." Bernd looked supportive and confused.

"You okay? the calligrapher asked."

"Yes, I just need a moment. It's the heat." Jimmy sat down near the counter so he could listen but also breathe to relax. Bernd asked for more details about how the man died so young. Jimmy listened for any details he could tell them.

The calligrapher told them the man had been in between temples when he'd fallen off of the side of a cliff at a place they both figured was about where they had stopped to take pictures earlier on the journey. They exchanged a quick glance while the calligrapher continued.

"It was considered unfortunate, since he was young and still full of promise. He'd even made some of the Buddhist temples along the route more famous than the existing shrines because of his work, something he was apparently proud of," the man said and briefly looked away. The calligrapher excused himself to go on an errand, and the two moved away from the memorial book-signing stand as someone showed up to replace him.

"The 88-temple route was settled in the sixteenth and seventeenth centuries, however, the route is associated with Kobodaishi from the ninth century according to Tourism Shikoku."

"Gotcha," Bernd said.

"You know, many things must have been in flux until the modern period," Jimmy concluded. He looked around, feeling better. Bernd got them each a cold green tea from the vending machine, and they sat down to strategize before leaving. Bernd saw on Jimmy's face what was becoming a familiar look of deep thought. As much as he wanted to know what Jimmy's utterance was about, he gave Jimmy space to think.

"You know, this is kind of starting to make sense."

"What is?" Bernd had no idea what he was talking about.

"Well, we are on an 88-temple pilgrimage route in Japan, right?"

"Check."

"And, we have gone about one-fourth of the way. No, that's not what's important now. The man was the leader of perhaps the entire, if not at least a large section of what had by the nineteenth century become an established *Buddhist* pilgrimage route." He stopped there, letting it sink in for Bernd.

"So far so good, but can you get to the point? Why did you emphasize *Buddhist* route? Everyone knows the route is a Buddhist pilgrimage route."

"I wonder if anyone was around in the nineteenth century who would have been angered by there being an established *Buddhist* pilgrimage? Jimmy asked in a spirit of inquiry.

"According to the man at the pilgrim book-signing office, the monk advanced the significance of temples over Shinto shrines as recently as the nineteenth century" Bernd said.

Jimmy continued, "If the routes bothered someone, then that person really would have been angry about the prominence of Buddhist temples over Shinto shrines as they are on this route. Also, if Shinto and things native to Japan were even what the person preferred then, yes, it's only logical," he finished his explanation, making them both laugh out loud since Jimmy was supposed to be the introspective one and Bernd the scientific logician.

They set out walking again, discussing what they'd discovered so far.

"So why does this matter?" Bernd asked. "What do we need to know about this to understand it better?"

"Well, for starters, we could think about who it was who would care whether the route was Buddhist or Shinto. I mean, modern Japanese don't seem to care which is which, using Shinto shrines for blessings for young children and relying on Buddhist priests for funeral ceremonies. Everyone in Japan seems used to these practices now."

"Do you think that was practiced before the modern period as well?" Bernd resumed his scientific questioning.

"I have no idea, although my friend told me that there was no word for "religion" in the Japanese language until the Meiji Period, again the period of foreign influence in Japan."

"Do you think that matters?"

"No idea. Really." Jimmy was beginning to wonder whether it wasn't a little later rather than earlier in the Tokugawa Period that the monk was killed or whether it was in the early Meiji Period. That is *if* he was the one who'd been killed. *If* anyone had been killed at all. He was beginning to place whatever it was that happened confidently in the early Meiji Period as foreigners flooded into Japan.

"Was that what the first samurai dream was about?" Bernd said out loud—but he hadn't seen another pilgrim walking closely behind them. Jimmy nodded agreement, having been thinking the same thing.

"Recently, I had another dream about some kind of master, but the first dream, the one with the samurai was…" The woman pilgrim tuned in upon hearing the only word she understood in the sentence: *samurai*. "Bernd, the samurai in my dream, praised the Tokugawa Shogun for *sakoku*, the term for exclusion of foreigners. I'm not sure what time he was living in, but he was against the foreign influence, so I guess…" Again, the other pilgrim's ears perked up.

"Go on." Bernd was listening and had his own thinking look on his face now.

"Well, if someone were to be angry about the *damn foreigners* in Japan and wanting them to leave, wouldn't it make sense that they were thinking back to the period of exclusion in the Tokugawa period as stated in the dream? And it would make sense that they were living either not long before the end of the Tokugawa Period in 1868 or perhaps during the time of extreme foreign impact during the Meiji Period that came just after the Tokugawa Period, right?" Jimmy said, "A time in which Nationalists would have believed that there was a need to rid Japan of meddling foreigners."

"It could have even been later after the impact of foreign ideas and inventions that may have seemed to be a corrupting influence in Japan," Bernd affirmed, following up with, "And wouldn't the samurai be envious of foreigners as they began to lose status themselves during the Meiji Period, while foreigners gained in status because of their advanced technology, which Japan had only begun to adopt at that time?" Bernd had studied how German innovation came to Japan in the Meiji Period.

"This must be of key importance. A monk who had changed the importance of native Shinto shrines toward the advancing of Buddhist Temples would have aroused the ire of those who were angered about any kind of foreign influence!" Jimmy said.

"It's starting to make sense, Jimmy. Some kind of vigilante, perhaps a disgruntled samurai, killed the foreign religion-loving Buddhist monk.

"And made it look like it was an accident. At least that is what it seems. It may even be that if this was murder, the intent was to kill the leader, this influential monk, in hopes of separating the flock or something around the area of his influence."

"Jimmy, I think you are on to something," Bernd said.

They were in agreement—and so was the woman only a few paces behind them. They were getting too close to being *on the right track*, the pilgrim concluded; however she only understood some of what had been said—and the rest from intuition and the note she'd received minutes earlier from the man at the pilgrim book-signing office of the temple. Her rudimentary English was coming in handy, even though she hated it when forced to learn it in school.

The woman pilgrim understood the term "foreigners," and even bristled upon hearing it. And the two putting together sentences that included: *samurai*, "foreigners," *Shinto*, and Buddhist terms, terms she'd been trained to look for, caused her antennae to go up. On high alert, she carefully began to allow more space between them, then sized them up as best she could while purposefully covering her face with her pilgrimage conical hat. She remembered, as she'd been trained to do, every detail of what they were wearing, the color of their hair, the way each of them walked, and any other details she could.

At the next bend in the road, she just disappeared. Jimmy and Bernd hadn't even noticed that she'd been tracking them. Jimmy's heart center warmed, making him increase his alertness, but a quick look around found nothing out of place. Bernd looked back, but the path was empty other than the trees. As far as they knew, they were alone as they headed toward Temple Twenty-Four. They wouldn't make it there that night—but not only because it was more than a day's walk, seventy-five kilometers away.

Chapter 10

SURPRISING ENCOUNTER

After stopping beside the trail in what seemed like the middle of nowhere, they began to set up Jimmy's tent and the small camp stove Bernd had brought. Jimmy was glad that they were travelling together. The view across the valley would be breathtaking in the morning while they drank freshly brewed coffee, thanks to Bernd's stove. On the other side of the tent was the backdrop of a mountainous slope filled with shrubs and wildflowers. It was one of Japan's picturesque, naturally beautiful scenes. They had just finished tying all the lines down and were discussing dinner as the sun sank on the horizon, when the lantern Jimmy had just lit suddenly went out all on its own. There was no wind. It was pitch dark. Only stars in the night-time sky were visible.

Jimmy's eyes were working to adjust fully to the darkness when suddenly someone put a hood over his head. His years of martial arts training were of no use; he'd heard them approach from behind due to his training, but they were too quick for him to react. He thought he heard Bernd struggling with someone to his right. Jimmy's arms were pinned to his sides by someone who was very strong, and his hands were tied in an instant. He heard all their belongings being hurriedly deposited back into the backpacks.

"You okay?" Jimmy forced a muffled shout towards Bernd.

"So far," was all Bernd got out before they were both hoisted up, each slung over a very sturdy shoulder and whisked away. Backpacks, filled with their goods, were taken—so no sign of them remained. Brush was laid down to cover any steps or tracks.

Bernd's mind was ticking. *Who had captured them and why?* It seemed rather odd that two foreigners would be abducted along such a famous pilgrimage route, but that was precisely what was happening.

Where are they taking us and why? Jimmy wondered. It was beyond his imagination to think that someone wanted to harm pilgrims. It didn't make any sense. Everyone had generally encouraged him to go on the pilgrimage since he arrived in Japan. Then he remembered a news item he'd seen while in Japan some years back. Along the pilgrimage route in Shikoku, there were thirteen sites in which were found signs warning against damaging the pilgrimage route. One said, "Please protect our sacred sites from rude Koreans who are posting stickers (giving directions in Korean and Japanese) and spoiling the route." The police noted that a group that posted signs were "claiming to be in charge of protecting Japan's pilgrimage routes." (Japan Today April 11, 2014).

Did that have anything to do with what was happening right now? He sure hoped not. After all, his experiences in Japan were filled with people who were the opposite of that—they were kind, especially to foreigners. It was unlikely that there were people who wanted to kill foreigners…Right? He kept telling himself this, but his beating heart betrayed his fear about what was to happen next.

As far as Jimmy could tell, for some time they went up a slope, and then they walked across a flat area, with Jimmy's feet hitting tree branches from time to time along the way. Each man was shifted from one shoulder to the other and between people, and by Jimmy's count, there were at least four of them. The path wound back and forth. They had gone around the slope of the mountain. Jimmy felt, *It seems that we are heading away from the pilgrimage route.* The breeze picked up as they moved along, and the sun had been down for some time. The abductors apparently knew their way. Jimmy, sensing Bernd's fear, too, began to pray the Vajrasattva prayer, the only one that came to mind in his panic. *Would purification of his being help?* He only hoped so.

Eventually, they were brought into a camp or compound. They were released from the sacks and locked in a wooden shed. Fortunately, it was a warm summer night. Jimmy was thirsty from the sweat of pure fear. As his eyes adjusted to the dark, he searched for Bernd's form. Bernd had crouched down, and his face betrayed his equal fear, but his logical mind must have been hard at work. Eventually, they could see each other. The light of a campfire that peeked through the cracks along the door and through two small windows provided flickering light. Outside, the crackling sounded as though there was a fire in the middle of the compound or whatever the place could be called. Jimmy had only a very brief glance around before the door was slammed and locked.

Are we about to be burned alive? Jimmy's mind tried to make sense of such an unanticipated situation. He listened. *It seemed there was some kind of council convening there, probably not for the first time,* Jimmy imagined. He wondered how many others had been captured, but since he'd not heard of anything in the news or in any of his studies regarding religious conflict in Japan, he feared that their situation was, at least in the modern period, unique. That didn't make him feel any better. The smell of wood smoke and a heated discussion did not bode well.

Then the fire was snuffed out, and the captors retired for the night.

What the hell was happening? Jimmy grew concerned and increasingly agitated at their predicament. After a short discussion carried out as quietly as they could, both men in the little shack grew more and more worried as the night grew closer to the next day. They both knew that most Japanese understand a fair amount of English, so they didn't want to say too much. They finally agreed to rest to save energy for what came next.

After a small breakfast of rice and fish—and it was emphasized, *traditional fare*—they were left to sit and wonder just what they were doing in the custody of this group. Given only a little water to drink, they were told that tea wouldn't be wasted on them. Bernd, like Jimmy, wondered, *what could that mean?* Seemingly if they were fed, they were not going to be killed. At least not right away. This didn't assuage their fear because they were still prisoners.

Luckily, their captors hadn't thought that the foreign gentlemen might hide their phones on their bodies—not giving them the credit for craftiness. Still, they were able to use them for only a limited time, since Bernd was wise enough to have them shut down power, which allowed them two things: the possibility to reboot, and should they be able to escape, find a library to recharge them, and second, not having the screens light up and draw the guard's attention. Jimmy prayed that the charge would hold out.

Later, after meditating, hoping to calm his unease, Jimmy thought he heard the guards posted outside the shack say, "Glad we have someone allied with our group at that temple signing pilgrim's books. So many people leave Japan, and when they come back to Japan, they can no longer be trusted. That guy is solid. His grasp of English is invaluable." Jimmy recognized that he was referring to the calligrapher at the recent temple who'd used English with Jimmy and Bernd. Apparently, that same man had alerted the captors that there were two men on the pilgrimage, and although Jimmy and Bernd had been careful, he'd overheard them talking about trying to solve the case of the monk. This fact made them stand out. No one was supposed to know what really happened to the monk. Jimmy's intuition had him being the closest so far to figuring it out than anyone in the group's 120-year history.

Odd. The group did not seem to be counting on Jimmy's level of understanding of Japanese. He understood much of what they were saying, but he couldn't hear it all, so some pieces remained a mystery. He chided himself for not being more careful at the temple. He, too, had believed incorrectly that the man there wouldn't understand as much English as he obviously did.

"*Honto da*—or *that's for sure,*" the other guard said. She was the 29-year-old who'd followed them. She had a personal interest in making sure that these guys would not unveil the secret. After all, the work of the Samurai Clan, a small group that wished to rid the island and eventually the nation of foreigners had not, at this time, achieved their aims and wishes. The monk was one issue, but keeping the group's existence hidden was even more important, she believed. It only grew harder each year as more and more foreigners trapsed across Shikoku. Again, she bristled. And there was the mandate, the need *to not disgrace her ancestors…*

The Samurai Clan had set up moles at as many of the 88 temple sites and beyond in hideaways such as this one—as they could. It was imperative that no one learn of not only their existence, but that they continue as they had been gradually and carefully taking measures to rid Japan of foreign influence since they had to go underground, as Jimmy had accurately guessed, during the Meiji Period in the late nineteenth century when the samurai had been eliminated and any hold-outs had to go underground. Bernd, of course, had agreed that Jimmy's intuition made sense in his logical mind. Unfortunately, for them, Jimmy's intuition was right. They'd both hoped he was only imagining things.

To Jimmy, the fall off the side of the trail was beginning to look like a pleasure trip compared to what may be in store for them. Bernd had been pretending to meditate to not only let on that he knew a lot about meditation in hopes that the fact would make him more acceptable to his captors but also to allow him to measure up how the shack was constructed. Instead, the action linked them to Buddhism in the Samurai Clan members' minds, unfortunately backfiring in its attempt, even as Bernd noticed the hinges were simple rope, something neither of them could snap with their bare hands. It would take a formidable fulcrum—Bernd's scientific mind was trying to figure out a way.

After the "meditation" session was over, Jimmy checked in. "You sleep at all?"

"No, not really, but I did rest my body by lying down."

"Same here. I heard them saying that the guy at the temple speaks good, er, my language…so he is a trusted member of their society, whatever it is." Bernd knew of another secret society, but he feared that this one was not after wholesome pursuits, unlike the one he was affiliated with. "I thought that is what was said, but I'm unsure." Bernd's Japanese was good but not nearly at Jimmy's level.

"They do use older Japanese, making it hard to tell what they are saying," Jimmy offered. "I studied ancient scripts as a graduate student, which helps." The experience with Saori was becoming invaluable in understanding what they were saying. They'd be shocked to find out Jimmy could follow what they were saying.

"Yah, it's like they are somehow lost or frozen in time. It's comprehensible that this Clan, or whatever it is, doesn't like foreign influence in Japan," Bernd expressed, his disbelief was evident even in his whispered voice. "Are these guys for real? I mean, foreign influence is the norm these days except on the remotest parts of the planet."

Jimmy, too, was certainly amazed at the development. "That's for sure. It's hard to define Europe without thinking of international connections."

Jimmy added, *"Honto da,"* mimicking the guard's earlier statement, but this may not have been the best thing he could have done.

The guards began to take a closer interest in what their prisoners were saying. The two of them couldn't have known that most of the Clan, which treated each other much as a family might, did not speak much English, thinking it was below them to muddy their minds with foreign words. If the world thought it was passing them by, they didn't care. They were on a higher mission—to purify their homeland.

Bernd leaned up against the door while listening to Jimmy, making a show of how dejected he felt at the same time. Jimmy began to breathe in a way that brought on calm. He started to think about the needs of the Clan. *What would satisfy them? Is there any chance of reasoning with them?* He thought about his Buddhist training, which teaches that no one harms others without being in pain first themselves. He wondered if there was any way to address their concerns and show that he and Bernd didn't mean any harm. How could they even think so? He began to call on his polite, formal language form, especially the antiquated Japanese learned from his lessons and discussions with Saori.

In the most innocuous tone of voice Jimmy could muster, "Hey, why have you captured us?"

"*Damare*—Shut up."

"But we have done nothing wrong, broken no laws," Jimmy said as politely as he could.

"There are many kinds of laws. You have gone against the laws of nature by bringing foreign influence into Japan. Now, shut up." Jimmy took the cue; this was enough for now.

By now, Bernd had almost rubbed through the lower rope hinge on the door by using his watch clasp to wear it down. He didn't finish cutting the rope, hoping to not raise any concern, at least not just now. He figured that Jimmy would catch on quickly enough and would forgive him that he had to keep Jimmy in the dark about his plan. The element of surprise would be essential for them to escape. He'd be for-given once he'd broken them out of their prison.

He looked around the wooden hut. He hoped breaking the door off its roped hinges would allow them a chance to run. Either way, his logical mind concluded, they had to get out soon. The longer they were there, the greater their captors' anger would become, the more danger they would be in—and the less energy they would have.

Jimmy secretly scanned the ceiling, while giving an exasperated exhale of air. It was not unlike tea ceremony houses he'd seen. Indeed, it seemed to be just that, a tea ceremony hut complete with a varied wooden ceiling. It didn't make sense. Wouldn't the tea ceremony be a prestigious element of Japanese culture? Something of importance? Why would you put foreigners, especially if you thought of them as impure, in here?

"They have something against foreigners. That's the thing I feared the most. *Kuso*," Jimmy cursed. He'd no idea that this made one of the guards smile, since it was so odd to hear a foreigner cussing in Japa-nese. It had in fact, been a first for this guard who assumed all foreign-ers only learned Japanese for their own economic advantage and not for the beauty of being able to converse with another, to be truly con-nected with another. Foreigners simply weren't that intelligent.

"Is this any way to treat guests?" Bernd asked in a way that sug-gested the feeling of *amaeru*—or creating a connection by suggesting a need another could fulfill.

"Keep quiet" was said this time in no uncertain terms. There was a finality about it. This too, had been part of the woman's training in the Samurai Clan. Both captives understood the need to comply.

After several hours and only water to drink from a nearby pond, Jimmy attempted the conversation again, being sure to address only Bernd—and to avoid the guards, who by now had changed. It centered on the accommodations. Jimmy considered that the pond water was safe but not the "good" water flowing down the mountain to the local, ancient, hidden shrine he'd heard them talking about in rough, purposefully gruff voices. He started this way to find out whether conversing was safe and in hopes that water as a topic wouldn't be perceived as threatening. Jimmy and Bernd agreed that the *pure* mountain water was reserved for the "pure" Japanese people, the members of the Clan.

Chapter 11
AT THE COMPOUND

While pretending to sleep, with the change of the guard, Bernd had noticed the secret exchange of their guard's symbols and signs. Hand signs were made by clasping one's index finger with the other hand. Bernd recalled the secret signs and symbols of the Secret Society, the organization he belonged to but, having been sworn to secrecy, was unable to tell Jimmy about. The guards didn't think these stinking foreigners posed any danger, and so they relaxed the normal protocol, not using the customary look-over-the-shoulder to ensure no one was observing them. The protocol of safety having been neglected, their actions were observed by Bernd.

When Bernd told his observations to Jimmy under his breath, Jimmy perked up and offered the following. "That symbol is from the Zen teaching of the one. Samurai would be familiar with it. It is being used in an insidious way by this group, I imagine."

"It could be some kind of expression of unity," Bernd suggested.

"That's originally what it did mean, but I have no idea with these guys. After all, embracing things foreign would be an unwanted form of unity for this samurai-like group or Clan. Regardless, whatever it means, it's brilliant. Anyone witnessing it would immediately think of Zen and not some secret cult," Jimmy said. Bernd agreed. This cult or society or whatever it was, was both secretive and successfully hidden from the mainland. No one seemed to know they were here.

Bernd relayed to Jimmy that he'd asked his university colleagues about taking the pilgrimage, including what they thought of it. None of them suggested that it was anything other than a very, very long hike, and some told Bernd that he'd probably be better off taking a bus tour of the route than attempting to walk it since it is said to take six to eight weeks to do so.

Since the adventure with Yuri several years earlier, Bernd felt he was up to any challenge. He accepted the challenge of walking the route simply to see if he could do it. He was up for anything he'd thought but not what they were going through right then. He was getting tired, and his mind was racing and racing. He realized that he longed for home. Jimmy silently held the same thought, his breathing rough enough for Bernd and the guards to perceive.

Bernd had dropped off his meditation practice; however, Yuri had continued over the past few years he told Jimmy. He understood that, while he liked the calm that it brought, it came much easier to her. He wished now, because of his growing anxiety, that he'd continued his practice in earnest. After all, he'd gotten a good start, but like so many, after some time of experiencing calm, he thought he was healed of worry. Now the fear he felt told him that was premature. Making himself come back to the task at hand, he dropped that thought. There was no time for self-pity.

Bernd took the opportunity to express how ironic he thought it was to be in the building that they were in. "See that spot over there? It looks like it's a pit where fires are burned to heat water. I think, Jimmy, that this is a tea ceremony hut, isn't it?"

"Yes, I believe so."

"Doesn't that strike you as weird? Seems to me like the tea ceremony would be sacrosanct, unassailable in Japanese cultural history. If these guys are against foreign influence, then why would they allow foreigners in such a significantly *Japanese* place?"

"I have an idea about that," Jimmy started to share his knowledge of Japan. "The tea ceremony, of course, was introduced to Japan by Eisai, the Zen monk, late in the twelfth century, from outside, from China. Gee, I wonder why that would be a problem?" he followed up sarcastically. Bernd understood right away.

"Another meddling foreign influence as far as the Clan was concerned."

"That's gotta be it. These guys are intense," Jimmy mused. "Clan, huh? Seems we have a common term for this collective," Jimmy said hoping to not be understood.

"It is said that love is blind. Perhaps one's love of country or home can also be as blinding." Bernd's logical side was assessing the motives of the Samurai Clan, as well as what they'd both discussed, the enduring strength of the idea of *furusato*, the deeply held belief in Japan of the importance of where one comes from, one's hometown, one's home.

The Clan decided they had waited long enough. Jimmy and Bernd had a meal of fish and only a little rice; the small portions were served on purpose because they were not wasting food on foreigners. Then the Clan members brought the two out into the open to interrogate them. Jimmy started to get nervous; it was simply too much to bear calmly. It wasn't that there were so many of them; it was more that they were so purposeful—and Jimmy worried that their purpose was not good. A quick look revealed that Bernd shared his concerns. Fortunately, it had been over a week since Jimmy's fall. His hip was feeling as normal as could be expected. This new development on their journey seemed unreal, as though a dream.

Then Jimmy wondered if that was it; he had to remember his dream! Wasn't the aggressive man dressed as he imagined a samurai would dress? Could the dreams be related to an earlier member of this group, what they were coming to call the Samurai Clan? What did they want? It all went through Jimmy's mind. *Sakoku*—exclusion, ridding the country of foreigners, the master having taught his disciples about the purity of Shinto, the monk falling off a cliff near Temple Number Thirteen…

"Is Zen something you all practice? I heard it is a favored practice of the samurai along with the Shinto—" Jimmy asked.

"*Damare!*—Silence! How dare you even say the word Shinto! You dirty foreigner." Jimmy wished for the first time that he didn't understand as much Japanese as he did, but Bernd could follow the tone of voice even if some of the antiquated words were unfamiliar to him. He prayed that even if he were harmed in some way, Yuri would be all right.

"But didn't I see one of your brethren when I visited Mount Kōya?" Jimmy recalled his visit to the museum at the temple he stayed at while there and the samurai armor he'd seen.

"*Baka*. Fool. What are you talking about?" The interrogator asked, but the clear undertone was, *how could you know that?* adding more to Jimmy's comment than was there. "Our concern is with Shikoku first. The rest of the country will be ours in due time." His explanation betrayed his confidence that Jimmy and Bernd were completely at their mercy. "It is true that we want to eliminate the impact of Kobodaishi, the crazy monk who polluted so much of Shikoku with his stupid Shingon Buddhism. That was unnecessary. Shinto is far superior. As for Zen—"

"Enough for now," said a man who looked extremely advanced in age. Everyone quickly deferred to him. It was easy to see that he was their leader, the one wise enough to not want to reveal that it was one of their founders who went to Mount Kōya to eliminate the influence of Kobodaishi. It was midday and getting hotter. Still, the interrogator didn't realize that Jimmy had seen the samurai in a dream and that samurai had gone to Kōya in the nineteenth Century. He couldn't fathom that Jimmy would know anything about that venture because it was a strictly guarded secret.

Jimmy and Bernd were made to kneel in the sun. Others walking by them threw side-long looks of disgust. They spit near them. However, the two were not spat upon, which would be too uncivilized, even for an enemy. This was also why they were given food. It was uncivilized to not feed even prisoners, and besides, Japanese food was better than other types of food, so they figured it would be good for allaying some of the dirtiness of the pair of foreigners if they *had* to be around them.

Bernd picked up on the man's comment, telling Jimmy as quietly as he could. "What was unnecessary? Eliminating Kobodaishi or going to Mount Kōya to do it?" This had not been explained, so Jimmy was considering his response when—

"Why are you here?" The interrogation was resumed by the elder man they had encountered moments before. The interrogator sat with his legs open wide and an elbow resting on one leg, a position of cocky authority, Bernd thought, as the man looked at them sideways. Being polite to him, to all of them, is paramount, Jimmy realized.

"On the pilgrimage?" Bernd responded.

"No, fool, in Japan. You are trespassing on hallowed ground." The older man named Umura, a name Jimmy thought was uncommon, continued the conversation. "Too many are trespassing. It hurts my soul," the elder said, then looked away from them.

Hurts his soul, Jimmy thought. *That's pretty sensitive if not just plain crazy*. He had an idea. He decided to sit in Zen-styled meditation form. As he got into posture, the others only laughed, some muttering, audibly, "There's no way he could comprehend Zen, one needed the gods for that." *The gods?* Both Jimmy and Bernd, who also understood the word *kami* in Japanese, were perplexed. Zen practice was, as far as they both experienced or read about, a god-less endeavor.

"Jimmy, I can't do Zazen," Bernd was playing along. They were looked on, at least for the time being, with a kind of detached amusement and told to "shut up" again. Still, the atmosphere in the compound, a series of barracks and buildings likely constructed for living and training, felt oppressive in its intensity. Neither man thought that this would last much longer, and both were concerned that this interview would end suddenly, perhaps by sword, since all Clan members wore them.

There was more muttering about how or why they knew the terminology they did, but that meant absolutely nothing to their leader. "Stinking foreigners might know the words but could never understand," Umura said. The explanation came from their angry responses—that the only reason the samurai were able to utilize Zen in the first place was because in the land of the gods, the *Kami*, Zen had a leg up on other pursuits in helping the samurai to be like gods themselves. This had been, of course, up until the time when they started to allow into the country foreign influence in various forms of innovation and technology. Each hung his head at this last comment, referring to the revolting weapons called *guns*. The elder viewed with some interest Jimmy sitting comfortably in *zazen*, the Zen form for sitting meditation, but he only grunted something harshly and then looked away when he noticed Bernd looking back at him. Bernd averted his eyes.

"What was unnecessary about going to Fukuchiin?" Jimmy realized that even if this drew an angry response, taking action was the only thing that just might keep them alive.

"What'd he say? Fukuchiin? What would he know about that?" They talked about Jimmy in front of him as if he wasn't there, obviously unconcerned that he was. The truth was that Jimmy had not been sure that his interpretation of the dream, that someone from Shikoku went to Mount Kōya in Wakayama Prefecture was even correct. *What was it on Mount Kōya that he had yet to understand?* he wondered since he and Bernd both had walking sticks from Mount Kōya, and his recurring dreams led him to guess that Fukuchiin was in some way connected to all of this. If not, then what was happening in his dreams?

"I have been there. That's all. I saw the Samurai Armor, was extremely impressed—"

"Stop. You mean to say you saw the armor of that foolish samurai there?" Others exchanged looks, stunned that Jimmy had understood them.

"Well, yes, but I don't know what you mean by foolish. Seemed pretty norma—"

"*Damare!*" They were both getting used to the word for shut up, although this time it came with a slap across the back of their heads, very effective for getting them both to stop talking. Jimmy noticed that the two who slapped them did so in unison without having to talk about it. These people were highly trained.

The aged interrogator continued. "He was foolish in that he adopted Christian beliefs. How could anyone not see through the phoniness of that religion? It is beyond belief. Stinking foreign religion."

"That was one of your...Clan?" Jimmy asked. There was no holding back now. The elder had stopped the man next to Jimmy from hitting him with a slight raise of his hand. At this point, the conversation began to shift. Umura let on to his group that he wanted to know what Jimmy was talking about in more detail. All this was done surreptitiously. Bernd was totally at a loss, and Jimmy followed only in a general way as much of the communication was done through Samurai Clan secret code and protocol.

"Noooo. Certainly not," came Umura's response. "Our guy went to eliminate a different fool but met this Christian fool—and lost his sword. Some kind of cheap, Christian, foreign trick. The Christian was working in service of the local *daimyo* or regional lord." Much to their disbelief, Jimmy nodded his understanding. Umura continued. "A

Christian samurai protecting a monk of a foreign religion. Now that's laughable. Or at least it would be if he hadn't relieved our esteemed leader of his sword."

Jimmy searched the memories of his dreams for an answer, anything to move this conversation forward. When he'd visited the temple on Mount Kōya, a sword had been in another case nearby the armor of the Christian samurai. He hadn't bothered to read the inscription. He had been shown it by the staff who wanted him, as an historian, to encounter, connect with something from the Edo Period. Jimmy had held the sword, but with his quest being to understand the Heian Period at the time, he didn't think much of it aside from what seemed masterly workmanship; however, sword making was far from his expertise. And he had no idea who that Christian Samurai was—he was certainly an anomaly working for someone who controlled the area and wanted the monk protected as he was now told. The Christian samurai had come through but had no idea what can of worms he'd opened by besting Suzuki. *Who was Suzuki?* Jimmy wondered.

Thinking back to holding the sword, Jimmy realized that it didn't match the Christian samurai's armor. Was it someone else's? The sword was a real object, something that tied that man's spirit to this world, and Jimmy was surprisingly able to once more access that essence even over time. That is exactly what had happened with Saori. Now it was happening once again, and Jimmy began to move in and out of consciousness as though dreaming. This connection across time was what prompted him to make these distinctions while talking to the Clan and Umura; it was also true that he did not yet understand what it all meant.

Somehow, the contact with the sword allowed Jimmy to connect with the intruding samurai's thoughts across time during the interrogation:

The hall was dark. The shoji—paper doors hid the occupant in the next room from the samurai's view as he looked down the temple hallway. Muttering, "I'll kill the baka"—fool. It was clear to Jimmy that this man didn't think anything of his wish to kill within the temple grounds. That it was a temple was to him insignificant. *The samurai began to walk and closed in on the room where the monk resided. He became quiet, almost silent in his approach as he neared the room in which the man was studying and praying.*

"It is only a temple, not a Shinto shrine," the samurai thought, then moved along the hallway. This place is not a holy place such as that of the gods.

Of the gods? Jimmy wondered, coming out of the dream-like state.

Buddhism was a religion devoid of gods other than to express ways of being, including varying types of consciousness. *What could he have meant?* The connection to the vision resumed.

Behind the shoji paper doors, a lamp betrayed the studious monk. This student of Shingon—the Buddhist sect began by Kobodaishi in ninth century Japan—was, like Kobodaishi the sect's founder, known for his skill in Chinese calligraphy, and he was practicing that now, brush-writing classical Chinese, prior to meditating. This was still another reason for this samurai to want him dead. He was muddying Japan with foreign words. The Shikoku samurai went to strike the monk but was surprised and intercepted by the Christian-warrior who'd been trained to hear the quietest of steps. He emerged through the shoji paper doors that had kept him hidden from view in the adjacent room.

Based on his studies, Jimmy assumed that the Christian samurai, on site to provide protection, was there because of the precarious nature of the times in the later part of the Tokugawa period.

The alert was sounded, and the chase ensued. The "Shikoku Samurai," being unsworded in their encounter, cursed the Christian, who'd been revealed by the cross insignia on his arm, then fled, barely making it out of the temple compound safely before descending the mountain. It took him several days to get back to Shikoku in one piece. That the man who unsworded him was a Christian especially irked the Shikoku Samurai, adding insult to injury.

Jimmy came out of the trance and through the conversation began to understand that his vision revealed the beginnings of the Samurai Clan that now held him and Bernd captive. Jimmy wondered, *is the proximity to Umura? — the Clan responsible for the detail revealed in his connection to the past? Is that why things are coming to me now?* It became apparent that upon returning to Shikoku, the man had been so angry at being blocked from his mission to kill the Leader of the Shingon Sect of Buddhism on Mount Kōya that he and the grandfather of Umura, the elderly man who currently sat in front of the two pilgrims under scrutiny, started the Samurai Clan. Jimmy had already let on that he understood a lot about history and Japanese culture. While Jimmy had hoped that it would make amends, to Bernd's eyes, the opposite seemed to be happening.

Certainly we are to be killed, Bernd's logical mind proposed — since the two men had come to know so much.

Umura's grandfather was related to the lineage of Shinto priests dating back two full centuries. In his dream, Jimmy had heard the cursing and then the discussion as the two men in the past — the samurai and Shinto priest — made a pact to start the Samurai Clan, swearing their lives and their progeny to the effort. It was, they said, a pact made between them and the gods: Shinto and the samurai. The messages came in fits and starts to Jimmy, some inaudible as it had been with the ghost in the recent years. This was informed by his dream of the Master, who Jimmy now believed was a Shinto priest, in some untold earlier time in the Tokugawa Period.

That was a first for Jimmy, who wondered, *Never have I experienced a dream while awake during the day, a feeling of non-awareness of the present and the vision of another scene.* He was not only concerned at the development but realized this meant that he may be prone to having these kinds of "attacks" or whatever they could be called, for the rest of his life. Jimmy had kind of hoped that after Saori was integrated, he'd be able to go back to a "normal" life. That obviously wasn't happening. But perhaps that was for the best as he and Bernd weren't out of the woods at this time, and this knowledge may come in handy. He was worried, but his heart warmed a little, making him just a little calmer. *Breathe, Jimmy, Breathe. The old man is the grandson of the priest in the Shinto lineage from my dreams...*something was coming together. *Stay focused, Jimmy*, he told himself.

"How are we going to get out of here?" Bernd whispered, growing more worried by the second. For several minutes, Jimmy seemed to be lost in meditation: he wasn't responding at all, and those around were losing patience with his unresponsiveness. Bernd was beginning to panic. He'd not been this anxious since meeting members of the Secret Society several years earlier.

"Jimmy, snap out of it," he implored.

"I'm back. I just saw the samurai in my dream again. He said something very interesting in the vision. Give me a minute. I have to think of how to say this."

"We may not have a minute," Bernd said.

Jimmy said, "Your grandfather would be proud of you," looking in the direction of the elderly man. The man had had enough. "*Damare,*" he ordered.

"Put them back in the foreign tea ceremony room. The only place suitable for them." They were rushed back to the tea ceremony hut and given a little water. Jimmy thought he heard of a plan to get them to some kind of ship. *Are we being shipped off the island? Sold into slavery?* he wondered. *And what is up with considering tea rooms foreign?* Jimmy prepared to fill Bernd in about his insights once back in the hut.

"Any other ideas? That didn't work," Bernd said, continuing to be both worried and anxious. He went back to wearing down the rope hinges on the door in another place and pretended to be angry at Jimmy to take attention away from what he was doing.

"The old man is the grandson of a Shinto priest who connected with the samurai in my dreams. Of the two in my dream, the samurai went to Mount Kōya to kill the leader of the Shingon Sect of Buddhism, the sect began by Kobodaishi—and was somehow stopped by a Christian warrior. Did you see the Christian symbol on the armor in the museum at Fukuchiin?"

"Yes, but what are you saying is the connection to our current dilemma?"

"That warrior, the one who had been wearing that armor, stopped the Shikoku Samurai, making him leave without his sword. The Christian samurai had been hired to protect the calligraphy-writing monk in an uncertain time."

"And you just thought you'd bring it up here and praise them for hating foreigners? Brilliant, Jimmy. How dumb can you be? These guys want to eat us for breakfast, and you're trying to get chummy with them."

"Excuse me. I thought that you'd like to know more about this place. Next time I'll think twice before sharing." Bernd was happy that Jimmy had gone silent after this exchange because it drew attention away from him. He figured the second rope hinge was about ready to break when they needed it to. He reached over and steadied his hand on Jimmy's leg when the guards looked away for a moment. Then, he pulled his hand back. "Try again tomorrow, Jimmy. It may be of help. Who knows?"

Jimmy nodded, gathering that Bernd had some kind of plan, and that his anger was intentional. Jimmy wondered: *Can we find a Clan member who would actually trust us? Will we have to break out and run?* Neither seemed like a good idea nor even remotely possible. It was true, too, that they weren't terribly far from the pilgrimage route but certainly far enough. If they called out, it was more likely no one was in earshot, and besides, when caught, they'd really be under strict supervision or perhaps killed outright. Maybe they could swim away from the ship.

How can we get out of here? was foremost on Jimmy's mind. After their small dinner meal, there was time to think. They had been made to wait, seemingly to make them nervous. He considered being compassionate, a major teaching of Jimmy's own lineage, and what that could mean in this instance. *Is there a way I can help them?* It didn't seem likely. He eventually came around to the idea that Bernd was right. They'd have to break out and make a run for it. *That might be the only compassionate thing to do, survive and somehow prove that at least they, as two foreigners, weren't evil.* Even as he thought this, he realized how hard it would be to change their minds. Understandably, they were set in their extreme views. The chirping crickets announced the onset of night, although it didn't afford their usual comfort on this, the second moonlit evening of their unwanted stay. The humidity, common in July, let up only a little as the night wore on.

Bernd said, "Surely there is no way we could outrun them. They must know the area like the back of their hand. Each could catch us before we made it to the trail."

"Even if we broke out, they'd round us up long before we could get back to the pilgrimage route however near or far that is," Jimmy said.

"I'm sure you're right, Jimmy, but it's our only chance. Right now, I think they are only playing with us for fun."

"No, we are not." In the hot summer evening air, the woman guard had understood or at least intuited the gist of their comments related to having fun with them, since "fun" was the farthest thing from the minds of the Samurai Clan, a very serious group. So their conversation was stopped dead by the guard, the woman who'd followed them on the trail, as she returned to her post. "It's that we simply want to get rid of you." This Japanese was understandable to both men, stopping them short. Jimmy gasped.

Unfortunately, she left it at that. This allowed the minds of both men to wander, concerned whether that meant death, being sold into slavery, or something else. It was agonizing not knowing what would happen nor how soon. On top of this, she'd obviously heard some of what they were saying. How much could she have understood? They had no idea. Bernd's logical brain calculated her chances of knowing passable English as anathema to her, so likely she had picked up only some things from her compulsory studies in junior and senior high school.

"She probably understood the word 'area,'" Jimmy suggested, "since it is a term pronounced almost the same in Japanese and English. If she understood much more of our conversation, they would have increased our guards by now." Bernd showed Jimmy how he'd been able to scratch through nearly all of the rope hinges on the door. It was lucky that the group had such little regard for foreigners, resulting in the belief that the animosity between them was real, and that there was no risk of them trying to or even being capable of escape. Fortunately, she had looked away long enough for them to have a brief exchange. She began talking to a guard about how revolting foreigners are.

"Jimmy, we have to do something or we're done," Over by the other side of the hut, Bernd began even more quietly pretending to be fearful and worried while rocking back and forth. The guards looked on but then seemed to grow disinterested in this *stupid, foreign display of weakness.* He expressed an interest in breaking out of there sooner rather than later, and Jimmy nodded, following the idea of breaking down the weakened door.

"To be sure," Jimmy said. "We need to confuse them. If we run off without doing so, they will be organized and capture us as soon as we're out the door," he said while formulating an impromptu plan.

"You think so? What's your plan?"

"You're right. We must try. I say we bust out of here, after they think we're so angry at each other that we'd part. You go to the right of those buildings, and I'll go the opposite direction, to the left of those trees. Do you think you can find the pilgrimage trail?" Jimmy asked.

"Yes, we have no choice."

"Good. I am pretty sure I can, too. It's risky since we will need to go back via a leg of the pilgrimage route different than the way we came along Temples Twenty-Two and Twenty-Three. If I can get to another area along the route, we can meet up back at a previous site, but don't go in, just meet there," Jimmy finished explaining his plan.

Bernd followed up with, "Looks like we'll be camping for a while, with or without the tent, if we can even get out of here alive."

"Camping beats being sold into slavery, Bernd."

"Yes?"

"They're not going to stop looking for us."

"I know, but I have an idea. Let's see what you think. Did you have any papers in your backpack that would reveal who you are?"

"No. I have everything right here. I'm sure they're about to take anything we have," Jimmy responded.

"Same for me. Well, that means that they know only what we look like. They don't know where we work, live and so on."

"Besides, their influence seems only to be in Shikoku," Jimmy chimed in. "Once we get back to Honshu," the main and largest island, we'll be okay, I think." Jimmy hoped that this wish would be a good omen for them.

"Nobody's going to believe that this happened to us," a worried Bernd said.

"Right. I suppose that is why they've remained undetected for so long." Jimmy realized that this tale was as unbelievable as having a ghost from an earlier generation appear before oneself. He couldn't help but smile, which Bernd did not detect in the darkness.

"You two, that's enough. Get some sleep." It was the male guard telling them that it was *lights out*.

"Okay."

"There you go again. These guys want to cook us and eat us for breakfast, and you're Mister Nice Guy. You're stupid. You give foreigners a bad name in Japan by being so dumb."

"That's a bit much, don't you think? What's wrong with being agreeable? After all, it's their *furusato* or hometown."

Shut up came once again. *"Damare."*

"I don't care what it is. I'm sick of hooking up with you. I hope they kill you first."

"Settle down in there...."

They began to wrestle, which caused a commotion. They were about to make break for it when Jimmy said, "Wait!" loud enough for only Bernd to hear. After three rounds of battling, the guards began to take less interest and only threw water on them the last time, telling them that if they argued again, they'd be separated. As the guard turned away, both men hit the door with their full weight, causing the weakened ropes to snap and the door to knock down one of the guards with Jimmy landing on the other, pushing him aside.

Jimmy went left and Bernd to the right as planned. This caused anyone following to split up—and left the nearest guard, the woman, with the idea that they wanted nothing to do with each other. She informed the others. The searching parties set out in both directions. The men had only a brief head start. Branches hit Jimmy most of the way until he was out into the opening where they'd been questioned by the interrogation committee. He went for the most open path, and soon it narrowed. He hoped that this direction was right.

Bernd had to use his scientific mind. If he went down the way he'd come, he figured they would know he'd done so based on his knowledge of how people solve being lost.

They had no time to lose. Finding their backpacks strewn down the hillside, where Jimmy thought he'd heard them fall after being thrown, he grabbed his with the tent, minus some of the stakes, and went down, not further up. Bernd came around to the backpacks a moment later, hoisted his and was off in another direction.

Jimmy followed the ravine for a distance until he came to where he thought the previous pilgrimage site was. He hid the belongings and came up the slope part way, trying to stay hidden from sight but also looking like a pilgrim in case he was discovered. He hoped that Bernd would show up too and the clue of the stacked rocks he left would point Bernd in the right direction.

Chapter 12

OUT OF THE FRYING PAN
AND INTO THE FIRE

"Yes, it worked," Bernd, coming up the ravine behind Jimmy, reassured him.

"Now to get off Shikoku in one piece. It looks like you won't be going to Temple Number Seventy-Five any time soon."

"Bernd. It won't be that easy," Jimmy said. Neither man thought that getting off Shikoku without the Samurai Clan seeing them would be easy. In the back of his mind and with a warming heart, the indicator that some kind of insight was arising, Jimmy thought *leaving would have to wait.* "Bernd. We have to discover what happened to the monk who fell off the slope. His story seems even more important now. It's what brought us together here. It must have some importance for us."

"You're crazy. These guys will kill us," Bernd said, but his expression made it evident that he wanted in, regardless of thinking that this wasn't a good idea. "What do we have to do?"

"I don't think we have to go all the way to Mount Kōya to find clues. They must be here, but where, and if at a temple, which one?"

The next day, after sleeping several miles farther ahead on the route, they got out of the tent, packed up and went toward the town they'd seen on their way the night before. Jimmy caught a glimpse of the woman, one of the guards from the compound, searching the road, but ducked under cover, hoping that she hadn't seen him.

"They're nearby somehow, Bernd. Stay down," Jimmy said, motioning for Bernd to get down. "I don't think she saw me, but the guard woman is over that way about a hundred yards. She must be onto our trail."

"I guess you're right. Hard to know what to do next. How'd she stay so near?"

"It doesn't matter. She's nearby. Let's keep moving."

"Agreed." Bernd followed up with, "And let's stay quiet, using our phones to text anything we need to say."

Jimmy nodded approval. After a while, when they figured they were far away enough to be safe, Jimmy got an idea. "We need to go back."

"What? Are you crazy?" It was Bernd's turn to worry. After a brief explanation, he understood Jimmy to mean that they were not only looking for details about the monk's death but also those of a member of the Samurai Clan. Neither seemed like a very good idea. Jimmy continued with, "I think we should keep them in sight instead of having them trail us."

"I see what you mean," Bernd concurred.

As evening came on, in his heart Jimmy thought he heard familiar murmurings that said, *"You can help her."* He wondered to himself. *What was that about? Why is this familiar experience happening to me? Oh dear*, he thought, but the present predicament demanded attention to stay alive.

The next day, Jimmy and Bernd caught up with the person they began calling Samurai Clan member number 1 or SC1, the first Clan member that they'd encountered, their guard, the woman. Now that they had doubled back and were able to find her, they discovered that another guard, the one who'd been with her at the compound, was with her once more. The two men dubbed him, SC2. After trailing them for a while, the men believed that the two were acting as a team. They were dressed in simple garb, not wearing anything that might draw attention. After trailing for a distance, Jimmy saw them split up.

Bernd suggested that SC1 and SC2 might circle around if they noticed the two guys following them. Therefore, they split up too, in hopes that they'd be able to circle faster and keep their plan. For now, cell phone coverage would allow for coordination via text message on silent mode, called *manner mode* in Japanese. Jimmy was grateful that Bernd had told them to turn off the phones as they entered the hut at the compound, allowing them to reboot and find somewhere to charge. Jimmy went in the direction the woman had gone and Bernd the other. Soon it became apparent that they were hopelessly outmatched. Both Samurai Clan members had vanished. The two men decided they'd be better together. They met on the middle of a slope along the pilgrimage route. Cover was provided by young pine trees.

They progressed on the journey, even being able to blend in with a group for a short time. Eventually, they came upon the next Temple site, but they weren't sure which it was until they conducted a search on their phones. It was a temple back where they'd already been. *Have we been led here by the universe for some kind of purpose? We must have taken a route over the mountains and backtracked farther than we thought.* Without knowing for sure the reason for them all to be going this way, they pushed nearer Kumadaniji, Temple Number Eight on the pilgrimage route. Beside the temple was Benten Shrine with a beautiful red orange *torii*, an entrance "gate" to a Shinto shrine.

They may have gone right past SC1 but for her audible expression of obvious disgust at the small size of the Shinto Benten Shrine as compared to the Buddhist structure of Kumadaniji. As incensed as she was, she didn't see them. It seemed odd, her stopping in a random town like this. She'd obviously stopped at the shrine to pay her respects, bowing twice, clapping twice, and bowing once more with apparent, sincere respect for the *kami*, the god of the shrine. The *kami* was Benten or Benzaiten, the goddess of music and eloquence, but this woman knew that, before being conjoined with the Buddhist tradition, Benten was a Shinto Goddess of reasoning capacity, something far superior to the foreign idea representing mere eloquence. She knew this because after all, she'd grown up in the area only a stone's throw away, as Jimmy and Bernd were about to learn.

The two Samurai Clan members had split up for the day so the woman could visit her aging mother. Having already lost her father, she knew it was important to spend any time with her mother she could. It was the Japanese way, the respect for one's elders, especially parents, notwithstanding that this, too, was influenced as well by Confucianism, a foreign influence strongly impacting culture throughout Japan.

After a visit to a local market to buy flowers that she placed at her father's grave, a purchase of some fish and some pickled plums, she went to a house at the end of the street. Everything was conveniently nearby. Jimmy and Bernd couldn't imagine what was going on. If Jimmy hadn't been so shaken by their earlier encounter, he'd have thought that he'd like to live in that place; the quaint town was serene. But at this point, anywhere but Shikoku was all he'd consider. Solving why that monk died seemed imperative now. He'd explain his thinking to Bernd the first chance he got.

That night, after seeing SC1 enter the small wooden house at the end of the street, they went back up the hill, found what seemed to be a secluded place to put up their tent and get some rest. They knew that even if they lost her trail, they needed even more time to plan and to solve this riddle before getting off the island, hopefully for good.

"Jimmy did you see that? She must know someone who lives there. She walked right in like she owned the place."

"Yeah, I noticed. Could be a relative. Could be her own home. Has to be a relative in parts like this. Why are we back where we've already been? Obviously if they knew we were following them and brought us here on purpose… No, ah, wait a minute. I must go to the temple as soon as it opens."

"Why is that?" Bernd asked.

"There were a series of temples marked with a plaque explaining the connection of the important monk to the route. If only this temple were one of them…we have to find out."

"And?" Bernd asked.

"If we can find out which temples he is associated with, maybe we can find out what happened, some clue." Jimmy was certain that he was supposed to figure this thing out. He just had a feeling. The summer air was still warm, even though it was late. The evening crickets began to chirp, only slightly easier to listen to than when held captive in the secluded tea hut.

"Well, we should be planning our escape from this island at the same time. I'm getting nervous. I look over my shoulder even if I just looked over my shoulder, ya know," Bernd explained.

"I think that makes absolute sense. I say we continue in this area, at the temples around here. I expect that the Samurai Clan will be looking for us, thinking that we continued the journey. While we were in their custody, I mentioned Temple Seventy-Five because I really would like to see the birthplace of Kobodaishi. I figure that they must have alerted anyone they know around there about this fact. I guess that journey will have to wait till another time. If there *can* be another time. Man, this is crazy."

"You got that right. Now let's get some sleep. We're going to need it," Bernd said amidst a yawn. Jimmy lay back in his sleeping bag, considering once more what was the reason for him being on earth. *How am I to help others*? His thoughts went out to the universe.

The next day, they found one of the plaques Jimmy mentioned, in the temple complex. The monk was affiliated with all the temples by way of his association with Shingon Buddhism; however, it seemed that his residence was in Temple Number Nine Horinji which, by a stroke of luck, was only two and a half kilometers away. They'd travel off the trail using an internet map. As they turned to leave, Bernd pushed Jimmy up against the gate of the temple, one of the most elaborate they'd seen. About a hundred meters along the path was SC1. She was hurrying along, perhaps to catch up with SC2 again. They followed.

About one kilometer further, Jimmy witnessed something totally unexpected but fully familiar to him. In her wooden clogs, and because of being in a hurry, she slipped and went sailing over the side of a steep slope. She didn't stop rolling until her leg got caught between two rocks. She'd just missed a pine tree by inches. She had rolled over a few protruding rocks on the way down. The underbrush was present, but sparse, providing little cushion for her rolling fall. By a strange coincidence or perhaps because of a feeling, she looked up and right at them. They looked back. This was their chance to get away. *She'd be okay,* Jimmy thought.

Bernd looked like they should go, but both breathed deeply and then without talking about it, following Jimmy's lead, the two men went down the slope after her, both wanting, needing, to be of help. They slid down the slope, catching their footing on rocks and tree roots along the way. She noticed their choice, but her attitude belied that she was unaware of what they thought was their obvious willingness to help. *Anger can make one overlook a lot,* Jimmy thought. *It can be so poisonous.* Worse, what if she thought this demonstrated foreign weakness, assuming they had the urge to kill her in her current predicament?

"*Daijōbu*? You okay?" Jimmy asked when they reached her, concerned because of the way her leg seemed to be pinned between two rocks that had rolled down the slope with her.

"Oh, it's you two. What are you doing here? You should be far ahead on the trail. We thought it would take days to catch up with you." Ignoring her question, they started to see if they could get her leg out.

"What? Are you going to take advantage of me in a weakened position? Just like foreigners to do such a treacherous thing."

"Let me think." Bernd's scientific mind flew into action. He found some pieces of wood, created a lever and began to count. "One, two, and three." Jimmy pulled her leg out from between the separated rock.

"Now are you going to kill me?"

"No. We have to, ah, go home," Jimmy lied, hoping she'd soften.

"What are you going to do with me?"

"With you? Nothing. Is it broken? Can you move it?" Seeing that she could move her toes, and observing no visible bleeding, the two were amazed that she'd come out seemingly unscathed, just some soreness and muscular bruises.

They helped her, but mostly she wanted to walk on her own, and it was obvious that she didn't appreciate them touching her, however kindly. It was also obvious that she couldn't have gotten up the hill on her own; however, she did all right once they were on flat ground, on the trail once more.

They went on to the next site, leaving her for the time being, as she obviously didn't want anything to do with *foreigners*. They split up, hoping to throw her off. As soon as they were out of sight, she called SC2.

Some things never change, Jimmy thought sardonically. *Her attitude seemed in sharp contrast to his understanding from his teacher that all things change. Always things are continually changing.*

Chapter 13

CLUES AND MUTUAL UNDERSTANDING

After entering Temple Number Nine and walking around the building to the back, Jimmy nearly fell over. It was the scene of his dream. He grabbed Bernd's arm and said, "This is it."

"What do you mean?" Bernd helped him get steady and then extracted his arm from Jimmy's tight grip.

"In the dream, this step is where the one man was shot with an arrow. The other, the monk who fell down the slope, ran along the building this way, and it was the same building, however, it has obviously been restored since the events of the dream." Bernd looked down at the step on a building that seemed at least several hundred years old. Since Jimmy was moving while speaking, Bernd realized that he had to keep up.

"Jimmy, this is a long way away from where he fell. That's miles away."

"I realize that, but this is the place. I *saw* it," an excited Jimmy said.

"Okay. Now what?" Bernd's mind was ticking again. He looked around the complex. There were various buildings: the *hondo* or main temple hall, guest houses, a cafeteria for pilgrims, and other buildings that likely held memorabilia and artifacts from the long history of the pilgrimage.

"I say we check in. We have to risk it and see if we can find any clues." *How could I have seen this place?* Jimmy stood more firmly now on the belief that the samurai sword that he held in his hands at Fuku-chiin must have made a difference. That might explain why his dreams recurred; they must be tied to the owner of the sword in some way. It made sense, too, based on his experiences with Saori and being able to connect with her and relive her experiences after encountering something associated with her.

Bernd agreed with his explanation of the phenomena despite it betraying scientific logic. He was no stranger to unusual happenings of the universe, and Jimmy was coming more and more to understand this. Jimmy once again grew concerned about his ability to pick up on traces left on ancient items. It wasn't always welcome. He'd considered now and again that it was very special but also acknowledged the discomfort that came with the ability, an example being their current predicament. He wondered if there was a way to control it so that it didn't seem so random, which was the main reason for it being uncomfortable.

They checked in. Realizing it had been several days since either had bathed, they took turns, each on lookout for the other. No sign at this time of the Samurai Clan. They had no idea that their luck was lasting, mostly because as foreigners, they were underestimated. Their earlier breakout was considered a fluke. The Samurai Clan didn't send additional resources, allowing SC1 and SC2 to do their job as quietly as they could. This level of caution, too, was why no one had heard of them up until now. This temple wasn't one they had an insider stationed at. It was *too close to home.* Jimmy remembered the previous time he was there; he had his temple book signed, and moved on, eventually to his fateful fall. He hadn't looked around at the buildings as he did this time with such careful interest.

Later that night, Bernd stirred when Jimmy suddenly bolted upright, saying, "Too close to home?" Waking from his dream, Jimmy wondered what this meant.

"Bernd, there is no way to confirm it, but this temple is safe. This place would be considered *too close to home* to plant a spy for the Samurai Clan. And, if it is safe, then it makes sense to fully search this place. Hopefully, they *can't* come in here to take us."

"I hope you're right, but let's not take any chances. Let's look around tomorrow and then get the heck out of here."

"That's fine with me, even if I am not a scientist," Jimmy said as both formed uneasy smiles that were a combination of relief and a much-needed pause in their anxiety.

They laid back down to get some sleep before the explorations of the coming day. Jimmy had a dream related to his encounter with the sword at Fukuchiin. *It was Mr. Suzuki witnessing the blessing given by the Shinto priest responsible for Mr. Suzuki's harsh training. The blessing of the sword with an ancient, secret Shinto rite was supposed to uphold the beauty of Japan and its people.* Jimmy woke briefly wondering, *Who is Suzuki?* but exhausted, quickly fell back to sleep.

In the morning, they ate a traditional breakfast of rice, locally grown vegetables made into pickles and other dishes, roasted fish, and a choice of green tea or coffee. The Samurai Clan members as a principle were appalled that *coffee* was included in the *traditional* Japanese breakfast. Feeling fortified for the day, Jimmy and Bernd went down to the museum and found several unique paintings of swords among the pictures of Kobodaishi and other Buddhist imagery, such as three-pronged vajras, associated with Shingon Buddhism. As they discussed this, the vajra in his recovered backpack burned at his side, making him pause for a moment. Jimmy didn't tell Bernd but was delighted that he was able to continue his contact with the treasured item. As they continued their talk about the paintings, Bernd concluded, "I haven't seen any pictures of vajras in Japan aside from those in the Shingon images we're looking at. Same for you, Jimmy?" Jimmy simply nodded his agreement, deep in thought about all they were experiencing.

The painting with a sword leaning against a bamboo tree was striking. They both thought that the images had been inspired by Benten, for her part as the Shinto Goddess of Art.

Next, they walked through the hall and found plaques of people who'd donated a significant amount of money to the temple. Among them was a Mr. Suzuki who donated in the Tokugawa Period and was listed as a samurai. The curator mentioned how the head monk had kept elaborate books, but this wooden plaque, associated with Suzuki was without record. When they asked the curator, they found that there was no record of a receipt being provided to Mr. Suzuki. In addition, Suzuki was credited with the donation of funds to build a dojo for martial arts in a time when martial prowess was in great need. Suzuki's philanthropy for the temple was apparently legendary in the area. Jimmy and Bernd could imagine the gratitude the regionally important head monk, they confirmed was a Mr. Tsuruya, must have felt to have received so much from this Mr. Suzuki.

They took the day to strategize, and especially to rest up before walking on, and later that night, as they planned their next steps in Temple Number Ten, one stop further along the route, Bernd stopped short. Obviously, his brain had been ticking again.

"You okay?" Jimmy asked.

"Yes, but listen, Jimmy."

Jimmy waited for him to continue. "I think no receipt for the donations given by Suzuki is significant."

"How so?"

"Well, if Mr. Tsuruya was meticulous about keeping records, and then a large donation comes in, wouldn't he have kept a record of it? Is there something he was trying to tell others by doing this? Perhaps some kind of clue?"

"You mean like this samurai guy—hey, wait a minute. That could be it. Samurai as in Samurai Clan. And there was the painting of the samurai sword by the bamboo, right?" Jimmy's dream of the samurai warrior came up in the conversation.

"Yah, so what?" Bernd replied.

Jimmy was figuring it out…although he still didn't understand some things. Did the reclining Buddha, only at this site along the entire 88 temple route, mean anything? There was a man named Suzuki in his dream. It seemed likely that the Suzuki connected to this temple and the Suzuki of his dreams are connected, but Jimmy considered that Suzuki is such a common name, among the most common surnames in Japan, that there was no way to be sure.

She needs your help, Jimmy, the familiar voice sounded in his mind. *There it is again* he thought to himself. *Saori? What help?* "Who needs my help?" he wondered out loud.

"Jimmy, you're not making any sense." Bernd wondered further, "Do you mean the monk's case we are trying to solve?"

"Bernd, this is going to be hard for you to believe."

"Well, maybe. Let's have it. Remember, I've encountered some pretty strange things in Japan myself."

"Not like this I'll bet." Jimmy was already starting to backtrack, unsure about sharing his ghost story of the previous few years with Bernd. "I mean, it's utterly fantastic. Unbelievable, I think."

Bernd wanted to solve the problem at hand, so he urged Jimmy to get on with it. He figured it couldn't be any stranger than meeting a Secret Society in an old, apparently abandoned building. He wished he could tell Jimmy about it.

Jimmy looked concerned. Bernd, too, realized that it was about time to decide—was he going to inform Jimmy as much as he could of his strange adventure of several years ago? Seeing Jimmy's hesitation, Bernd first sought to put him at ease. "Jimmy. It seems that we both have some unusual stories to divulge. If I promise to tell you mine, and that is what I am proposing, will you please tell me yours? I'd like to figure out what we're in the middle of, and I don't wish to be in that same cell again. I don't think we have much time to figure these things out. We must act." Bernd finished with both a sense of urgency and a sense of seriousness that Jimmy hadn't encountered outside of his relationships at Open Breeze, the meditation center in Canada.

Jimmy made his mind up to tell Bernd. He prepared himself for not being believed once again and began. "Bernd, it started several years back. Appearing a little at a time."

"Oh, I can see from the look on your face that this is difficult for you. Please go on. If it is some kind of secret, I promise not to tell anyone, except I don't keep secrets from my wife, Yuri. She is completely trustworthy; I can assure you."

With no way around the weirdness, Jimmy decided to take the direct approach as he, too, believed they didn't have a lot of time to discuss this—that action mattered. "Bernd, a ghost from the Heian Period visited me. She needed me to go with her to Japan and heal her karma or something like that. It was all very strange. If you even believe me, I can tell you about it sometime."

"That is quite shocking, but considering my experience was really strange, I don't want to suggest that you're lying. My story, too, is fantastic. Why are you telling me now?"

Jimmy's jaw almost dropped. This was the second person, aside from his meditation teacher, McDougal, who talked with him about the ghost as if it were nothing out of the ordinary.

"Bernd. I am glad that you, well, *believe* me. I have a hard time believing that you do because those I have tried to tell, haven't." He remembered the skeptical and then dismissive math teacher from their trip to the Rocky Mountains several winters ago. "I tried to tell my teacher friends, and they brushed it off as tiredness, thought I was crazy," he said, getting back to his normal sense of humor, if only for a moment. Bernd smiled along with him, and then waited for the rest. "The reason for bringing it up now, is that it worked. We got her healed, and she went back to Heian Japan. Or at least that is what I thought until just now."

"Excuse me. What do you mean?"

"Well, I think she just told me telepathically that there is someone who *needs my help*. Of course, that would mean *our* help."

"Oh, now I see why you're having two conversations. That makes more logical sense. But who needs our help, and how would a ghost know?"

"She is connected to me somehow, and therefore, connected to this story. Her otherworldliness allows her to see or sense things from the past, and recently that has meant across time. I don't pretend to understand it, but here she is suddenly appearing in my thoughts. As for who needs our help…"

SC1.

"Oh dear. She just said, 'SC1.' She's been able to track my thoughts somehow."

"You mean she's back now?" Bernd asked, his voice sounding shocked.

"Yeah, but again, I only hear her. Believe me, I am just as surprised as you this time. I thought she was completely healed, integrated, and gone from this earth. I have no idea why she is able to connect with me now. In Minnesota in the United States, she used to show up as a guest at my house. I never knew what to expect. It was very unnerving, even after I got used to her appearances."

"I can only imagine. This is strange of course, but the logical side of me says, we need to look for clues and be ready to leave at a moment's notice. I'm sorry Jimmy, but my story will have to wait until another time, although I can tell you that it includes, like yours, a secret. If we survive, I shall be *filled with joy* to tell it to someone that I trust."

Grateful for their shared trust, "I understand," Jimmy said, while starting to pack, and he couldn't help but be a little disappointed. "I want to hear your story, too," Jimmy said. He noticed the slight bow as Bernd put the computer they'd been using to search the internet in his bag.

They went through the temple to all places that weren't off limits. The other buildings, too, had various paintings on display. In paintings that hung on the wall were bamboo forests with samurai swords. Bamboo trees were cut by swords, even if the sword didn't exist in the painting. *This has to mean something*, Jimmy thought. *Were all bequeathed by Suzuki?*

"Who painted these? They are such nice representations of Buddhist art," Jimmy asked the caretaker at the temple. It seemed to Jimmy that whoever painted them understood well the idea of one-corner, the Zen style of painting developed in China and adopted in Japan, by representing images with as few strokes as possible, called "Thrifty Brush" in Japanese.

"Why, the monk who fell over the side of the cliff while on duty," the caretaker responded. "He'd been traveling for work, we think, when it happened. You saw the plaque near the entrance, I guess?"

"Yes, we did." They both nodded. Things were coming together, including the monk from the pilgrimage route, the previous temple, and their shared dream of him falling over the side of the slope. His name was prominently displayed nearby the paintings. Jimmy said it out loud, "a Mr. Tsuruya." The caretaker told them that Tsuruya had been given that name upon his ordination. It was because the name Tsuru means cranes, symbols of celebration in Japan—and joining the order to benefit all was cause for celebration. He'd been given it because he studied so much that it was believed he'd always had something to celebrate, being so knowledgeable of things domestic and foreign. Ironically, Jimmy realized he died quite young before any final celebration could happen. When Jimmy told him what he'd learned, Bernd nodded in agreement. It was apparent that these images were not from Suzuki.

"Perhaps inspired by his generosity?" Jimmy wondered aloud.

"So, what do we know?" Bernd began to take stock of what they'd discovered. "The monk Tsuruya died falling off the side of the mountain, a samurai named Suzuki donated a lot of money, but there is no receipt, and SC1 needs our help, but we don't know in what way."

"Right. And I am beginning to wonder how these all relate. SC1 is of the Samurai Clan, Suzuki is a samurai, and Tsuruya was the manager for temples along the route as the caretaker confirmed when he told them about Tsuruya. Let's ask the caretaker of this temple whether Tsuruya was responsible for all, only a few, or many of the temples."

"Okay. Anything is worth a try at this point," Bernd said. They went back to the front desk to ask. "Pardon me. Was Tsuruya responsible for all 88 temples along the route?" Jimmy asked the caretaker in as polite Japanese as he could.

"Yes, but ah, well yes, yes, but of course he had help."

"Help?" Bernd inquired.

"Yes. He asked Suzuki, who seemed to know the route so well. You know his great granddaughter lives back near Temple Number Eight with her mother, Suzuki's only remaining relatives. Mr. Tsuruya asked Suzuki to check in on some of the temples. He figured with the outlawing of samurai families in the Meiji Period that it would be a good way to keep the man busy and use his array of skills to protect parts of the pilgrimage route. It was likely that Tsuruya wanted to take Suzuki's mind off disbanding the samurai in 1876. It seemed to work well, at least until Tsuruya fell over the cliff. Suzuki was so put out by the fact of the monk's death that he didn't show up for work for several days afterward.

"Oh, I see. Thank you," was all they both said, one after another.

"Bernd, we have to talk," Jimmy pulled him aside. "I just thought of something." Jimmy was getting somewhat excited. He realized the connection he was trying to make. It was about a samurai, Suzuki the samurai. They went back to their room.

"Bernd, Suzuki may have done more than work for Tsuruya. And if his great granddaughter lives near the previous temple, then we better hope *she is not SC1*. That would be just too weird."

They could overhear something out the window, some kind of commotion at the entrance gate. The curator was talking to a young woman asking about two foreigners.

"SC1 is here, and she's not alone," Jimmy said. The small tatami room became almost claustrophobic in an instant. Bolting to their feet, each grabbed his backpack and sprang into action.

"Go to our planned spot. Go now," Bernd blurted out as both men dove out the door and the window, as previously planned, in opposite directions. Their exit was across from where the voice had come from, where the two Samurai Clan members were standing talking to the person by the gate, and perceptively they both noted the movement of the brush behind one of the men.

While Bernd had set this plan up before they'd settled into the room—the plan was to exit as quickly as possible, not giving the Samurai Clan members a chance to think—it would work only if they were confused. Bernd had realized that while the temple was considered by them to be safe, other temples along the route could not be considered so; therefore, they put this protocol in place already, which was lucky as Temple Nine was no longer "safe." Jimmy was glad to have Bernd's scientific mind along on this journey. *Did it work?* was Jimmy's thought.

They met halfway up the hill behind the temple at a gnarled tree, *one that would have been perfect for a Zen painting,* Jimmy imagined. When making plans to meet at this spot, Jimmy informed Bernd of this "Zen" look. Bernd laughed nervously upon seeing the tree again. He wasn't feeling very *Zen* at the moment.

They pressed on, moving up the hill. Breathing heavily, both stayed low, trying to stay out of sight. Fearing SC1 and SC2 would be right behind them, they looked over their shoulders but continued until they crested the hill to find a view that displayed an open valley below somewhere along the route in Shikoku. *Will we ever get out of here alive?* Jimmy wondered. Exchanging glances, Bernd seemed to have the same concern.

"Jimmy, whether we solve the riddle or not, we have to start thinking about how to get off this island."

"Of course, you're right. I hope we can get a chance to talk soon; however, I think I am piecing this together a little at a time. Suzuki was the name I said, right?"

"Yah, it was. Now come on." Bernd was forming another plan while they were on the move. They descended the hill in the opposite direction from Temple Number Eight, going around small trees, some sparse tall pines, only to find, to Bernd's joy, a complicated maze. Jimmy chimed in with his thoughts.

"Bernd. This must be used for training monks about being mindful; however, I don't want to go in there. It seems like a bad idea." From behind them SC1 appeared, running toward them, this time with her sword unsheathed. She looked determined and crazed. The two men had no choice; they ran into the maze.

Realizing that there wasn't time to peruse detailed instructions, and prior to going in, pausing only briefly at the entrance, and in a voice low enough for her to not hear, Bernd said, "Jimmy put your right hand on the wall here and walk to the right. Keep your hand on the wall! You will find your way out." Without time to spare, breaking away immediately, Bernd went left with his left hand on the wall. This was a good idea, because it meant that SC1 had to follow only one of them and not both. Unfortunately, as she and Jimmy disappeared to the right, SC2 entered the maze and saw Bernd go to the left about one hundred feet ahead. Bernd began to run. He hoped that Jimmy understood his directions. He'd learned to solve mazes while in college as part of an experiment. He was glad that he'd chosen science as a profession.

They saw wooden boards and hedges. Every one hundred feet or so, the maze turned, causing this hundreds-of-meters-wide maze to be filled with many twists and turns. The variation of the hedges and boarding, along with signs that urged one to "Be Mindful" and "Don't let yourself get in the way," made it a confusing and intense training ground, especially while running at full speed. No one had envisioned anyone having to be mindful while being chased by two crazed sword-wielding samurai in the 21st century.

Bernd had gotten significantly ahead of SC2 since he was following the wall with his left hand and didn't need to think about where he was going. He thought he heard someone a few sections back yell "*kuso*," the Japanese term for cussing, as if the man following him ran into a dead end. Bernd thought, *That must be at least two sections back, judging by how far along he was into the maze.*

Bernd formed a quick plan. Since the maze was a mixture of boards and hedges, he climbed up the hedge wall he was standing next to and got a look at the man following him about three turns behind, and now closing in. He grabbed a board off one of the wooden sections of the wall and hoped that the universe would forgive him for damaging the work of Buddhist monks.

Jimmy moved as fast as he could. His thoughts became a jumble because he had no idea how to solve a maze, let alone do so while being chased by someone carrying a samurai sword. He wiped his forehead with his right hand, wiped his hand on his shirt, and then realized that he'd done the one thing Bernd had told him not to do…take his hand off the wall. He stopped running and listened. He could hear steps; it must be SC1, and she was not far behind. Then he heard *"dame,"* a term that signified something was wrong. He imagined she was in front of a section of the maze that was a dead end.

Suddenly, a sword came thrusting through the hedge, missing Jimmy by inches—and then disappeared. *Can she hear me breathing*? He began moving again and did his best to calm down. He tried not to step on anything that would make noise. He began sliding his hand along the wall again. He hoped that this was still the right wall to have his right hand against.

Desperation caused his nervousness to leave him. He became energized, thinking that Saori was somehow connecting with him but was realistic enough to realize he'd have to get out of the maze first for that to matter. He kept moving at an increasing pace, hoping to put more and more space between him and the woman. This went on for a few minutes. He must have been halfway through the maze; at least that was his best guess.

Bernd kneeled on the man's lower back to hold him down. The man had literally fallen for Bernd's plan. Bernd had torn one of the boards off the wall, placed it across the path and let the man hear where he was. He'd coughed to let SC2 know his whereabouts and cursed *kuso,* pretending he'd run into another dead end. When the man came running around the corner, he tripped over the board Bernd had wedged into the hedge, so it was across the path. As SC2 fell, Bernd had leapt out of the hedge to kneel on his back while tying his hands with rope from his backpack that he'd already looped to catch one hand quickly and then wrap up the other. The man screamed, but Bernd gagged him with a handkerchief. *Now to find Jimmy and get out of here.*

Jimmy wasn't faring so well along the right side of the maze. SC1 leapt down from above, just missing Jimmy with the samurai sword.

"Suzuki, stop it." Her face went white and she, momentarily, lowered the sword.

"Eh? How could you know my name? You've been calling someone SC1, I heard several times, but wait a minute? How could you know?" she said again in disbelief.

"Suzuki was your great grandfather, wasn't he?" She looked at him in disbelief because what he said was true. She grew worried and raised the sword again.

"So, you've killed many foreigners?" he boldly asked.

"You will be my first. It will be for the honor of Japan." Her face wrinkled up, smoothed out and scrunched up again, revealing an emotional battle inside.

"What are you battling inside, young lady? What is it that concerns you so much?" he asked as kindly as he could while fearing she'd strike at any second. He heard Saori's imploring voice, *She needs your help. She, too, is tied to your karma.*

"Ahhhh!!!" she let out a war-like scream. Woosh, the butt end of the handle connected with his cranium, knocking him unconscious in the process. She turned, but because of her distress, which made her unable to see clearly through the tears welling up in her eyes, didn't notice she was too close to the wall. The sword bounced off the wall and cut a nasty gash in her arm. She couldn't feel it completely, adrenaline rushing through her body, but the training told her to keep her attention on the battle in front of her.

Bernd came around the corner. Because of the commotion, he was able to find them based on the sound, but it hadn't been easy because he had to take his hand off the wall and work toward the sound. He bent down to get a cloth out of his backpack to dress her wound, but when he did so, she ran past him pushing him over in the process. She was holding her arm as she had been taught to do. Bernd thought, *She could have killed me but didn't.*

Jimmy came around. "My head sure hurts."

"Lucky that's all, Jimmy. She's gone. She may come back with SC2. Since she has her weapon, let's get out of here. Can you walk?"

"I think so," Jimmy said getting to his feet. "She may be hurt bad…and she's hurting pretty bad inside." They didn't know how tough she was and that it wasn't that deep of a cut.

It had been enough to cause her to leave the scene, but she'd be ready for action after having it stitched up. Both she and SC2 would have to answer for their blunders in failing to capture the two stupid runaway foreigners—of this SC1 was sure.

As she looked for SC2, her imagination went wild. *This was the first time I've botched anything related to battle.* She was ashamed. She sat down to cry. *I can't believe I allowed my emotions to cloud my thinking*, not considering how this was what separated humans from animals, making her normal. *My first time messing up anything. I've been perfect so far.* After sobbing for a while, she got up to look for SC2. She was relieved that no one else was there. It was her error for which she alone felt responsible. Recovering composure, she secured and tidied up the makeshift bandage, torn from her shirt, around the wound. She continued to look for Jimmy when from the opposite direction there came a noise. *It's coming from near where I'd entered the maze.*

Officers entered the maze, having been called by the head of the temple because of the commotion. The sound was coming from the direction of where SC2, a Mr. Kinoshita they later learned, her team partner would have been. Happening on a nearby exit, she silently slipped out hoping that Kinoshita, too, was safe, and she left the maze to reconnoiter the area. Since it was crawling with cops, she left the area. SC2 got out unscathed, claiming he was all right, and he'd been jumped by some mangy foreigners he'd followed into the maze to see why they were wandering around there after hours. After giving a fake name and seeing paramedics at the site, he left, having received the gratitude of the officers on the scene.

Jimmy sensed SC1 was gone. He was amazed that he could feel that in the present and not across time. *This woman needs help*, he thought. Saori was right. His Bodhisattva vow, to be compassionate to others, caused warmth in his heart center.

<h1 style="text-align:center">Chapter 14
RIDDLE SOLVED</h1>

After the two exited the maze by applying Bernd's strategy along the righthand route, Bernd surmised that enough was enough, and he should tell someone that they were being followed by some crazy local gang. He'd finally had a chance to breathe and think logically about it, something he was unable to do while being so anxious the past several days. Fortunately, they were able to charge their phones at places set up to accommodate pilgrims along the way. Via text, he contacted some people he knew in the Secret Society, an organization he was connected to but couldn't talk about—and found that one of his "organization's" associates, the organization he now was forced to tell Jimmy about, worked in the local precinct. He'd start there. He'd wished he'd done this earlier, but the past was the past.

"You mean to tell me, Bernd, that there is a local gang acting right under the noses of the Shikoku Prefectural Police Department?" said Hata, head of the "Gangs Unit" for the local precinct in Shikoku, who usually kept tabs on organized crime.

"Yes, Mr. Hata. I am afraid so. One of them was tied up in the middle of the maze just a few minutes ago. I hope he is still there." Hata sent someone to find out—and then made arrangements for the two young men to stay in a safe house overnight with an armed guard. The next morning, they both woke early, understandably a little on edge.

"Bernd and Jimmy, Good Morning."

"Ohayō gozaimasu—Good morning" Jimmy gave the normal morning greeting in Japanese. "And thank you for having us put up here. Even though I woke up early, I haven't slept that soundly in a while."

"You're welcome. Come, let's have breakfast. I have some news." After sitting, he continued, "The man was not still there in the maze when my people arrived. The officers on duty had processed him and let him go, as he seemed the victim of some kind of attack. I went along to be sure of what we'd find. Took us a while to get to where he'd been lying. I'm not much good at mazes myself," he chuckled. "And I can't believe that I had no idea the Samurai Clan existed; apparently, it's been a well-kept secret. It will remain our secret, too, at least for now. Understood?"

"Yes, sir," they both replied.

The two pilgrims exchanged a knowing look but said nothing as Jimmy rubbed his right hand. His head was feeling better after sleeping. The bump from where she'd hit him with the hilt of the sword was still tender, but the swelling had gone down by morning and was only a little sore. Hata continued, "Since we weren't able to question him, we're starting from scratch, so to speak."

"That makes sense," the two men said almost at the same time. After they gave a statement to the police, which took just over an hour, they went into town to get answers. Jimmy was wondering about how well-known Mr. Suzuki had been in the local area, and for that matter, he also needed to find out about his great granddaughter. What they found out at the local indigo dye company was that the older Suzuki had been quite well-known in the area, a local daimyo or regional ruler prior to the law of 1876, demoting the samurai as the Meiji reforms were in full swing.

At a nearby temple, not part of the pilgrimage route, supposedly the one that the Suzuki family had belonged to, the monks looked at them in disbelief when they asked if he had also given them, too, a large donation. They made it evident that they doubted he would have given any kind of donation at all. He seemed angry about life, according to the collective memory that ran deep in the local area, at least according to those men.

Jimmy and Bernd checked in at a nearby hotel and relaxed on either side of a table to begin to reformulate their plan based on the new information.

"Bernd, it makes sense that he wouldn't have given a donation to a local temple. Now that we have a chance to talk in private, I must tell you what I suspect." Bernd was all ears. "The woman's name is Suzuki. She is the great granddaughter of the man in my dreams. My intuition, based on the dreams I have been having, is that he probably started the Samurai Clan. I could see that she held a position of status within that group while we were there, based on the elder's reaction. Couldn't you?"

"Yah, I guess so, but I didn't really notice it until you pointed it out now. I was too busy trying to wear down those rope hinges on the door and formulating a plan to get out of there."

"Of course. Thanks to you, we're not still there."

"I think we make a good team. Glad I met you," Bernd said knocking Jimmy on the shoulder and smiling.

"Likewise. Uh, so, what is that secret you were going to share? This seems as good a time as any."

"Jimmy, I can't tell you everything, as it is a requirement of being a member of our group that I don't, but what I can say is that I've met a group of sincere people who really care about the planet. I almost never see them, but several years ago, Yuri and I came across some good information which tells me that someday humans can truly work together despite the perceived differences we often let get in the way."

"You mean like the Samurai Clan do?"

"Exactly! As a race, we humans will get past this, I just know it. But really, I can't say more than that. I hope you can trust me with that."

"Well, I'll try," Jimmy said teasingly. In some ways he felt that he owed Bernd his life. They could take it slow for now. With that realization, Jimmy's heart warmed, but he realized telling Bernd more about Saori wouldn't be any easier.

"So, Jimmy, what did you figure out about the riddle? You know, why the monk fell over the cliff. Was it an accident as it originally seemed?"

"Not entirely sure yet, but here are my thoughts. I think that Suzuki, the samurai from my dream who made an attempt to kill the serious Shingon monk on Mount Kōya was thwarted by a Christian samurai and as a result sulked all the way back to Shikoku."

"Okay. That seems understandable. Anything else?"

"Well, if he was angry enough, it might have pushed him over the edge, so to speak."

"Making him do what?"

"Oh, I don't know, form the Samurai Clan," Jimmy said, hoping that Bernd wouldn't counter with something logical that contradicted Jimmy's thoughts. This time, it sunk in for Bernd.

"I could see that. It's hard to get all the pieces since so much of it is from your dreams. I had only the one dream. Let's go over them again. Perhaps that can help me better understand."

"Right. First, I had a dream about someone who'd learned from a master that things foreign were detrimental to this place, the place called Japan."

"Check."

"After that, I have been having these recurring dreams about someone, who I now believe was the monk, Tsuruya, from Temple

Number Nine, who became responsible for the care and maintenance of the temple route in the latter part of the nineteenth century."

"Wait a minute. How do you know that?" Bernd asked, noting how this was not previously divulged.

"Bernd, that is what makes it hard for me to explain my mystery, my secret. I just know these things sometimes. I am not always sure why. It could have to do with…oh, of course," Jimmy smacked the fist of one hand into the palm of the other, something he'd picked up in his first stint of living in Japan. "Bernd, did you see the samurai sword at Fukuchiin? I haven't told you about its impact on me to this point, have I?"

"No, you haven't told me, and yes, I saw the sword. It's a prized possession prominently displayed in the temple's museum."

"But did you do more than *see* the sword?"

"What are you getting at, Jimmy?"

"You know, I held it in my hands," was Jimmy's response. Bernd nodded but seemed to wonder about the significance of the point. "You see, the person who was acting as the docent must have sensed that I was in earnest about my research on things Japanese and Japanese history. He took it out of the case and let me handle it but for only a moment. Said something about not wanting to cause trouble, so we put it back. Not sure what he meant by that. Perhaps other monks at the temple would be jealous. Who knows?"

"No, I didn't hold it like you did. What's the big deal?" Bernd leaned toward Jimmy, an elbow on the table.

"Well, in my recent experience, coming into contact with something from another time brings back memories for me—of that time."

"You mentioned something like that, but I'm not sure what you mean. You weren't around then. What memories?"

"I didn't say *my* memories."

"You're sounding a little weird…You mean you see someone else's memories?"

"Not so sure about what is happening now, but it has happened in the past. It would explain why I saw Temple Number Nine in my dream. Remember my saying there were two monks? One was shot by an arrow; the other ran out of the temple grounds to escape. I'm not saying I know exactly what these images mean, but it's clear-cut that they are not my own."

"Yah, I remember, but…fill me in. Do you mean that you came in contact with the sword on Mount Kōya, and it was something from the time when the Samurai Clan was formed?"

"That could be the case, but, of course, I have no way of being sure."

"Jimmy if what you say is correct, it would explain the dreams, at least the strength or intensity of the dreams. Especially if you're right, and it's not your own experience, but you have been surreptitiously experiencing someone else's view of something that happened. Up until now, I thought the dream I saw, that paralleled yours, was my own." Bernd's logic was working through the situation, proving once again that they made a great team.

"It must be true that these dreams come from someone's experience and not ours. Bernd, you must have been impacted even a little by staying at the site with the sword on Mount Kōya, causing you to have the dream. As for me, I couldn't have been around when the monk fell. In fact, up until now, I kind of thought I was the monk or the one falling off the cliff because of my fall along the route. I wasn't there in the dream at all; someone else was experiencing the dream, but who?"

"Jimmy, whose sword was it again?"

"Suzu-ki's sword. Of course…Oh, my god; that's what I heard in my most recent dream several days ago. It must have been Suzuki who was there. He *must* be the connection. He may have started the Samurai Clan. He was at the temple as the two monks fled—one being killed, and at the slope when the monk fell over the side."

"And it seems that your connection with the sword, while you were visiting Mount Kōya, somehow connects you to Suzuki's experiences."

"Right, as strange as it may sound."

While Jimmy's assessment of the details, including the final piece that perhaps the monk was shot, pushed, or at least chased by Suzuki prior to falling made sense to Bernd. He added, "You're being too polite, Jimmy. Suzuki must have been responsible for the monk's death. It's the only thing that makes sense. After all, what would cause a monk, trained in awareness, to fall over the side of a cliff?"

Jimmy understood the point, but when he felt that Bernd was picking on him, it also hit a sore spot. He had done just that—as someone undergoing daily awareness practice, he'd fallen off a cliff.

"Well, I can attest that it can happen," Jimmy said smiling.

"No worries, Jimmy." Bernd returned the smile, realizing how it came across. "On second thought, I guess it could happen to anyone."

"Still, as you say, it is unlikely," Jimmy said. "I'm convinced. Suzuki must have done something to make it happen. Bernd, let's go over all the details. And we need to go back to meet with Hata if we can."

"Right. That sounds good." There was a noise outside the window, but when the men looked out, no one could be seen, and though there was no wind, the branch of a bush alongside the corner of a nearby building was moving.

"Someone is still watching us," Jimmy grew concerned all over again. "Wonder if it is young Ms. Suzuki or some other member of the Samurai Clan?"

"Damn, these guys are persistent. I thought with the connection to the local police, they'd leave us alone," Bernd suggested.

"Bernd. This is very upsetting. They won't likely leave us alone. We are the one thing that betrays their existence outside of their organization. And we don't even know how extensive that is. It could have infiltrated much of Shikoku, even the police. That would be a good way to keep themselves secret. In fact, they would benefit by—"

"Us no longer being around," Bernd finished Jimmy's ominous thought.

Chapter 15
IN THE MOONLIGHT

It had been no use. After all they'd been through, they were exhausted both mentally and physically. Whoever looked in on them would have to be sought after another time. They gave up the hotel and went back to the place arranged by Hata. They both thought their contact with the police would have kept them safe and now knew this was premature.

"Mr. Hata?" Bernd asked.

"Yes. Is this Bernd? How are you guys getting on? I hope the safe house is comfortable. Is there anything you need?"

"There is nothing we need, but something I'd like to tell you, and I want to do it in person."

"Okay." They arranged to meet with Hata in a secluded area of the safehouse compound moments later. Aside from the remote possibility that any ninjas were hanging about, Bernd figured they were relatively safe. He'd heard that the ninja had died out long ago, so wasn't truly worried about ninjas dropping in on them. Later, to his surprise, Jimmy was to find in his coursework that one scholar believed that the ninja never really were a thing. The men and Hata had no idea that SC2 was able to observe them from the rafters.

SC2, who was as much ninja like as samurai, thought, *I'll stay up here in my hiding place where I can hear and see things in the "safehouse."*

Jimmy and Bernd took Officer Hata into their confidence more fully about what they knew about the Samurai Clan, not realizing how much they were implicating him in their dangerous adventure since SC2 was eavesdropping on them. After a brief discussion about what to do, they parted, having agreed to meet early the next day as Mr. Hata had somewhere he had to be. By the time they finished their meeting, it was already evening. Jimmy and Bernd risked a moonlight walk, feeling the need to stretch. And they'd gained confidence, protected by an increased police presence on all sides of the building they were staying in.

"I love the moon but sense that tonight's moon gives a feeling of coldness rather than warmth," Jimmy said, revealing his mood.

"I'm worried, too, Jimmy. I had arranged to text Yuri every day but haven't, so understandably, she's been worried. Our time at the Samurai Clan's prison without communication, and now being forced to have cell phone silence once more, must be driving her half mad."

"Yeah, I know what it is like to really want to communicate with someone, somewhere in the depths of your soul, and not be able to do so. It's excruciating, isn't it?" Jimmy missed Saori right then in a way he hadn't in days.

"It sure is. Can't be put into words, can it?"

"No, not at all," Jimmy said, his thoughts trailing off to Saori's integration. Jimmy looked around. There wouldn't be a better opportunity. Even if someone were to be lurking in the shadows, they'd be too far away to hear what he was about to tell Bernd.

"Bernd. Listen carefully. You are one of the only humans I know who hasn't flinched at the story of my intimate connection with a ghost. I'd like to tell you more about that. In fact, there may be something, after I have told you what I know, that your logical brain can help me with, but I need you to promise something first."

"Go ahead Jimmy. What is it?"

"Promise that you won't tell anyone, and even if you tell Yuri, it won't be right away. It could make a difference to us getting off this island alive or not. First, I will tell you about Saori," Jimmy continued. "After that, I'd like to consult. Do we have an agreement?"

Bernd took this seriously and thought it over for a moment. He'd need to exact the same kind of promise from Jimmy if he were to tell him about the Secret Society, so he thought it was only fair. "Yes, Jimmy. I'm in. I promise. What is the nature of your experience? I hope it can help us. Her name is Saori, huh?"

"That's right" he started—and then hesitated because of being burned before with Thomas, the math teacher. Jimmy started slowly, but then began to gain steam. "Bernd, she was not only in need, she was beautiful, as odd as this may sound, in a human sort of way, even as a ghost."

After explaining for a while, Bernd asked, "So, you're saying she showed up while the moon was out. On nights like this one?" Bernd said this while looking around. Jimmy thought he could see worry on his face in the pale moonlight.

"Bernd. It isn't likely she is able to appear to us. I think her integration took care of that. However, I must admit that I spent many nights—despite knowing she wouldn't return anymore—somewhere in my mind, wishing she would reappear. This was despite my sincere wish that she is completely whole and safe wherever she is. My feelings for her are quite complicated."

Thank you, Jimmy. It was her voice again in his heart and his head. He'd never forget it, he hoped. Jimmy froze. *It'll be all right.*

"What's wrong, Jimmy? You look pale even in the light of the moon."

She still needs help. Perhaps more desperately than before.

"It's nothing," he said snapping out of it. "I mean. Let's come back to what just happened—later. I'd like to consult, but it can wait. I need to finish the story first, so you have the information you need to help me think this through."

"How can you say that it will be all right?" Jimmy said.

"I didn't say that." Bernd was now worried for Jimmy more than himself and was increasingly confused.

"Of course you didn't." Jimmy pressed on with the story of the last few years. "Bernd, the ghost and I had to go to Japan together. We found her family of origin, and by a strange and lucky twist of fate, I was able to not only see a diary that hinted at what had happed in 1180 CE, the year she died in life, but also receive a bell that, when matched with a *vajra* I'd received, also under unusual circumstances, was able to help her integrate, heal I guess. Saori, or her energy at least, was integrated about a year ago."

Don't forget that your good karma helped me, she continued communicating telepathically. Jimmy had a cold flash this time as part of her sudden communication with him. *This is her voice in my head. She is with me now. How can this be?* He pulled himself together.

"And Bernd…Saori and I made a good team—our karma being somehow connected across time.

Yes, a good team. She chimed in.

"So, you two were able to help her energy heal, and now you think she is out of your life for good?"

"Well, I want to talk to you about that, Bernd. I think she is communicating with me right now but had not been until the pilgrimage. Saori wanted you to know that our shared karma worked together to help her heal. This experience of her communicating this way is new. I thought I was dreaming or imagining her voice earlier when I told you about her—it is as though she is here with me, us, *now*."

"Is she speaking to you? I can't hear anything."

"Well. I don't think it is audible. It's in my mind and my heart, as strange as that sounds. Like I said, I think it worked, and her energy was integrated. As such, I can't imagine why she can communicate now. For example, I don't see her, either."

"But you did before?" Bernd confirmed.

"That's right."

You're standing in the moonlight, Jimmy. He shook his head. It made sense out of the senseless situation.

Saori, can you see me? He sent his thoughts back to her.

Not clearly. It's more that I can feel the connection to you and the moon. It's night here, too, in whatever time and place I am in Japan, she replied. Jimmy nearly fell over. She was in Japan.

"Bernd. We are communicating. We can communicate through our thoughts." He didn't say it was because of the moon. It was all so unexpected that he became unsure what to explain next.

"Jimmy. Is she telling you anything useful for our journey here? This crazy adventure that we're on?"

"Yes. It's something about SC1, I mean, Ms. Suzuki. Saori thinks that Ms. Suzuki somehow needs my help, our help."

"That's right. You mentioned that before. Has she said what kind of help? Wait a minute, Ms. Suzuki…Did she tell you her name?"

"Well, not exactly. I called her Suzuki to rule out that she is the relative living near Temple Number Eight, and she was stunned and confused and confirmed that she is indeed a Suzuki, wondering how I could know that. I'll ask Saori if she can be more specific about the help Ms. Suzuki would need from us."

Jimmy asked through his thoughts, but Saori's response was inconclusive.

Jimmy, it is nothing specific. I just have a feeling that you must help her. Your connection to her has connected me to this need, whatever it is. The only way to save yourselves, the only way to save all of you, is to help her. I'm sorry Jimmy, I have nothing more to offer, which is what the universe has been telling me for several of your days. It tells me now that I am here because of your karma pulling me to you, to help you. Jimmy had gotten used to things being inconclusive with Saori. In fact, like other times when he asked more of her, for that night, she didn't respond. He told Bernd about how common this being cut off suddenly had been in the past few years.

Wonder what has become of her? Is she safe in her Heian homeland? He couldn't know she was no longer in Heian Kyō. Her body had died that night of the Gion Festival, and now her soul was intact, sort of, thanks to their joint efforts. She had been healed and died a "normal" death. However, after her death, she was still attached to him, only this time through Jimmy's karma, not hers. That is why she had been able to speak to him this night from the later part of the nineteenth century — no one, including her, knew the time or place she was in. His karma had again pulled her into his life.

Where is she? Jimmy couldn't imagine.

Chapter 16

ON THE RUN AGAIN

After meeting with Hata the next morning, Jimmy had a sense that something was wrong, an intuition that literally something was up. He did just that—he looked up. In the rafters he saw the back of a person who ran along a wooden beam, jumped to the ground, and ran out of the building.

Someone had been listening in on their conversation. If this was someone connected with the Samurai Clan, the gig was up. They'd have to flee once more.

Hata took no chances. He drove them in his car a few kilometers farther along the trail. He knew some backroads, so he believed they hadn't been followed. While Hata drove, Both Bernd and Jimmy were on the lookout. All agreed…likely they were safe, for now. Hata told them that he'd get to the bottom of what was going on. He knew some good sleuths who specialized in infiltrating groups. He'd try to cause as much trouble as he could to keep the Samurai Clan busy. He hoped this would slow down their desire to rid the island permanently of Jimmy and Bernd.

Upon return to the police compound, Hata went to confirm the investigation with his staff. They had seen the man who fled the compound. One officer recognized him as the man from the maze several days earlier—they told Hata that they'd lost him in the woods. All they knew was that he had overheard them. There was no time to waste.

Certainly, he would let the Samurai Clan know that Jimmy and Bernd were talking with the police. This assumption was right since it was the thing to do according to *the Clan's training—clean up after any mistakes.*

So that is exactly what SC2 did when he returned to the group. This helped regain standing for him after being "overcome by the weak foreigner." The "training," in the present day, was reminiscent of the training that Suzuki's great grandfather had received from the eminent samurai Shinto priest years ago, one who'd passed down the tradition from the early Tokugawa period. The training had continued uninterrupted, all this time, only more intense and more anti-foreign after Mr. Suzuki instituted the Samurai Clan.

Suzuki, the young woman who was after Jimmy in the maze, had been the best student to come along in a while, thought the aged Umura, the Clan's current leader in the samurai complex where Jimmy and Bernd had been taken. This is why she'd been allowed to trail them ever since. SC2's ninja-like efforts were a help to her, although his being overcome by one of them, Umura believed, was unforgiveable.

Umura thought, *The two foreigners had to be eliminated somehow. The continued existence of the Samurai Clan, its purpose and the strength of Japan depended on it. Ms. Suzuki's "missed opportunity" would be dealt with in time; she is too valuable to the Clan right now for other measures.*

The previous evening, Suzuki had sat on the ground, alone in between some shrubs, once more sobbing. She didn't know why. *Am I as weak as these damn foreigners?* "Kuso," she cursed. Her sobbing continued unabated for some time until she fell asleep. In her dreams, she was strong again. She knew she could catch the two meddling foreigners. They'd be dealt with soon enough. She awakened with renewed vigor and resolve for the task.

Jimmy and Bernd for their part walked right past Temple Number Ten Kirihata Temple, called *Kirihataji* in Japanese and around to the back of the complex. In a secluded area, they set up a simple campsite and started planning their next steps. How could they get off the island? It would mean, Jimmy believed firmly now, that they would have to forgo visiting Temple Number Seventy-Five, Zentsuji, the place of Kobodaishi's birth. Jimmy figured the members of the Samurai Clan would be waiting for them there, and Bernd agreed.

While in the area, Jimmy read up on the history of Kirihata Temple. According to his guidebook, Kobodaishi, the founder of the Shingon School of Buddhism as well as many of the temples along the pilgrimage route, was meditating or undergoing austerities at the temple when a young woman cared for him and gave him a *kirihata*, a piece of cloth that she had woven. After that, he carved for her a statue of Kannon, the deity of compassion in the Japanese Buddhist Pantheon. The story states that the woman became a Buddhist nun.

Feeling queasy—and with no idea why—Jimmy sat down on a rock in their simple campsite. He wondered whether in some way this meeting of a man and a woman, and a story that included a piece of cloth, was related in any way to him and Saori. After all, the cloth from her kimono was also something that bound him to her and helped with her redemption and the integration of her karma back in Minnesota. Again, he was amazed at the coincidence, if that is what it was. Every year, it seemed to Jimmy that the universe was more and more mysterious. Of course, this led him to want to check out the temple. Fortunately, there was still time. Most temples close around four or five in the afternoon, and it was only two o'clock. Bernd promised to keep watch.

Jimmy entered the gate, and since he had his temple book stamped the first time he was there, he went directly to the statue of Kannon and prayed for compassion to be spread throughout the world but especially at this time in Shikoku. He was saddened that people tend to have a hard time looking past differences to see how very much we are alike. He prayed fervently along these lines and lost himself in the mantra of compassion for about thirty minutes. Then, when he discussed the legend of Kobodaishi with the local attendants and monks, they told him the usual thing: Kirihata was like so many temples on the route, a Shingon temple, started by or related to Kobodaishi.

As he was about to leave, he found out another interesting fact about the temple: In the late 1800s, the pagoda had been moved from the shrine and temple complex of a Shinto shrine in Osaka that shared the grounds with a Buddhist temple—to Kirihata Temple. Jimmy wondered what impact that where the pagoda was moved from would have had on Mr. Suzuki, as he now tied his own backpack, hoisted it onto his back, and looked around to make sure that he wasn't leaving anything behind. *Would Mr. Suzuki have been disgusted at the shared grounds for the temple and shrine since he favored Shinto as the indigenous religious tradition?* he wondered. Then, satisfied that he wasn't being watched, Jimmy began walking once more.

Just as he left the temple grounds, he was seamlessly forced into an arm lock, then dragged around the side of the temple. When his head hit the wall, he blacked out. Having been worried about how long Jimmy was taking, Bernd had come around to meet him at the gate when he saw Ms. Suzuki carrying Jimmy off into the woods. Somehow, she covered her trail, another piece of her training, and Bernd lost them almost as he'd begun to follow. Suzuki leaned Jimmy up against a rock and tied his hands so he wouldn't cause any trouble, should he awaken before the others arrived.

Suzuki went over her own training again, wanting to find where to perfect it. She didn't want others to slip up as she had done. *Always train harder* had been her motto for as long as she could remember. Stupid, weak mistakes couldn't happen if they were to sanctify the homeland.

During training, each day for a month, they got up and took a cold shower. All summer long, they were trained to ignore the heat. In this way, they became inured to the heat and cold. She took it on herself to train holding her breath underwater or just to be able to breathe slowly, imperceptibly slowly. The Shinto of old, not Buddhism of the pagoda moved to the temple below the hill, was among the things that she wanted to *save*.

I'll go to Ise the first chance I get, Suzuki thought. *It has been too long, and now with this blunder…*

Ise is a trip she took once a year to purify herself with help of the main goddess of Japan, Amaterasu, who is venerated there. *This is necessary since so many things foreign are now in Japan. It seems like it is the only place where I can be at peace. As the national Shinto shrine of Japan, it is truly the home of the Yamato damashi, the soul of Japan*, Suzuki thought.

Ise, the place not far from where the Kingdom of Yamato was located, appealed to the Samurai Clan since they believed in things Japanese as being supreme. Yamato was the first somewhat centralized and unified area of Japan right in the middle of Honshu, the largest island, even earlier than the Heian Period of Saori's time.

"Yamato damashi," Suzuki said proudly. Jimmy heard her as if in a dream since he was floating between conscious and unconscious. It was the same term he recalled from the dream about Suzuki's sword, *the soul of Japan*. Jimmy realized that someone nicknamed Suzuki's sword *Yamato damashi*, meaning something like, *Long live the soul of Japan*. Now his great granddaughter was following in his footsteps, Jimmy believed, as he began to slowly regain consciousness.

Bernd calculated the most likely route from a topographical map — and logical considerations, such as she was carrying a man who probably weighed more than she did. He admired her strength but figured that she could have managed only two hundred yards farther. One route was an incline and the other sloped downward, so Bernd started with that one. Unfortunately, it was the wrong one.

Jimmy came around. "What the heck?" his head hurting something awful. Fortunately, she had bandaged it. *Seems kind of strange to bandage someone's head if you're about to kill them or have them killed,* Jimmy thought.

Shizuka ni! "Stay quiet!" she insisted. He complied, hoping that it would give him time to think and to relax into the pain that eased when he didn't speak. With her, seemingly a trained samurai sitting across from him, his lessons on samurai came to mind.

Samurai were instrumental in controlling Japan, and Japan's native Shinto Gods looked favorably on Japan during the two Mongol invasions of 1274 CE and 1281 CE, sending *kamikaze* or divine winds each time.[3] Suzuki came from a proud heritage, a good lineage.

He couldn't stay quiet. "Why are you doing this?" He figured that if she was going to kill him, he might as well try something, anything to find out why.

"Quiet, I have to think," she said in Japanese.

"About what? I am sorry you have such anger for foreigners. I mean…ow." She'd smacked him in the face to shut him up.

"You talk too much. Another weakness of foreigners." Her face betrayed disgust.

"Have you ever even been abroad?" At this her face scrunched up, displaying a pained expression mixed with surprise. She looked away.

"I have no interest in going to other lands. Why should I? Japan is far superior to them all." Jimmy was unconvinced by this comment that came across as something she'd been fed by someone else. In line with Jimmy's intuition, truly, it had been part of her training.

"That seems to be a little strange to say, if you have never been to any place outside of Japan. I mean, how could you know? Ow." Having stood up, she kicked him in the leg this time to get him to be quiet and sit down.

"I hate you; I hate all of you."

"You don't know me."

"I don't have to. All foreigners are dumb and want to cause trouble for Japan, to dilute our ways."

"I am on a pilgrimage route to explore the beautiful things about Japan. You, Ms. Suzuki, make no sense."

"And, how do you know I am Suzuki?"

"You are your great grandfather's great granddaughter." Her mouth fell open at this.

"What do you know of my great grandfather? How dare you."

"No. How dare *you*. At least I have traveled abroad. I have seen other places. I have seen kind people in Thailand. I have learned to love Japan as my second home. Japan, damn it, IS my home."

"Japan can never be your home. It is ours. Don't dishonor my family's name by saying such a thing. My great grandfather went through the most important Shinto training and concomitant samurai training that existed during his time. His austerities were legendary. He spent time in the mountainous region of Nagano Prefecture simply so he could demonstrate and fine-tune his innate skills of self-survival. Oh, what am I telling you this for? Stupid foreigners could never understand the greatness of Japan. I not only hate you all; I also feel sorry that you can never understand my Japan."

"*Your* Japan. Japan is bigger than you, than your group. *The world* is big enough for all of us." Jimmy couldn't believe that this was coming out of him, but it was what he believed, and it was inspired by his practice, his attempts at connection with the universe.

Suzuki pulled him to his feet, but she left him tied up and made him walk to the top of the hill. She'd taken him about one hundred yards up the hill. The others were told to meet her and her captive in the valley after she'd doubled back. When Bernd saw them crest the hill, he heard footsteps behind him and hid.

Chapter 17
SUZUKI'S TRANSFORMATION

Jimmy and Ms. Suzuki made it about a half a mile down the other side of the mountain-like hill. The cedar trees shot straight up out of the slopes among red pines, bushes, and some low underbrush. They really were in the wilds of Shikoku, having left Temple Number Ten and town behind. Jimmy wondered if she even knew precisely where they were. She'd filled a water bottle in a nearby stream and shared it with him by pouring water into his cupped hands. Between the two of them, they had a couple of simple snacks they'd have as their evening meal. It was obvious she'd shared what food she had to keep the prisoner alive and that it was begrudgingly. She seemed as conflicted as ever. She'd had her orders to keep him alive for questioning, but they didn't expect much from him since he was a foreigner. She would have preferred to kill him and get it over with.

Suzuki took on a concerned look, but it wasn't because of him. It was that she'd broken protocol for the first time in memory. She had always been the best. She'd always done everything perfectly. *What was different this time*? She needed to talk this through internally to figure this out for herself, not realizing that was a major part of the problem—relying only on herself to the exclusion of others and their input. She kept going back and forth since the confrontation in the maze. Was it his karma that was impacting her now? She wished she could have simply killed him and moved on. She turned away from him.

Something inside of her couldn't carry the weight of the family tradition, her training, and her natural compassion that had been stifled by growing up in this lineage. It seemed her karma, too, was ripening.

"Don't speak. Let me think," she urged him into silence as his expression gave away that he was about to ask more about her—and what they were doing there. After a long pause, to both of their surprise, she began to apologize.

"Jimmy, right?"

"Yes, that's right Suzuki *San*." He'd recognized her change in tone, and that she was reaching out. "Jimmy, I too, wanted to travel, but in my family, that of the honorable Mr. Suzuki, my great grandfather, there was only one option, which was to become a member of the Samurai Clan. At first it was all fun, running and jumping, training in martial arts. I don't even remember when it became a passion. I have been totally blinded by *the training*." Her sincerity caused compassion to well up in Jimmy.

"Can I ask, what do you mean by *the training*?" He was grateful for her sharing and wished to know her, truly know another person perhaps more fully than at any time in his life.

"We are indoctrinated with the information I have been telling you: foreigners are stupid and the cause of all trouble; Japan is special, and so on. Oh, I have been so foolish. My schoolbooks contradicted this way of thinking, but I just ignored them, blinded by hate." She began to sob lightly; this had been coming on for some time. She was perhaps most amazed by the improbable transition unfolding for them both. Jimmy had seen transformation at Open Breeze many times.

"You are an amazing human, you know." It was Jimmy's attempt to be of help.

"Don't patronize me."

"I'm not," he said in a calm, low, undertone; continuing, he asked her, "How did you get so good at fighting?" Jimmy was intrigued by this fine specimen of humanity in front of him.

"Well, the samurai, the mainstay of my training, were supported by Zen in two ways, both morally and philosophically. We take to a course of action, and we don't look back, as well as we do not uphold life over death. We gladly die for a cause." She broke down, unable to speak momentarily since she was already mentally distancing herself from this sense of "we." "The Samurai Clan has taken it upon themselves to train more broadly to preserve the various traditions of Japan and, as you can imagine, help us be really tough fighters."

"Zen doesn't condone killing?" Jimmy countered.

"No, far from it. This was the invention of the samurai as they utilized Zen—we utilized Zen—for our own purposes."

"In what ways has the training in Zen worked for you?" Jimmy wanted her to keep going, accept what she'd done as Zen would suggest she do and move on. "One's karma can be healed even if it takes a long time." He knew what he was talking about based on his experiences with both Saori and his distinguished teachers at Open Breeze. At the term *karma*, Suzuki winced but regained composure quickly and then…

Bernd came out of the bushes. She lurched forward ready to fight, her instincts always prepared for battle, it seemed.

"Bernd, hold on." Jimmy stopped them both with a look and a wave of his hands. One of her arms had gone up to block any attack, and she had drawn her sword with her other hand. Bernd was shocked into silence at first, but eventually, he did move over next to Jimmy. He started to untie Jimmy's hands. Scowling, she lowered her sword. She knew what had to happen next.

"New guy, stop what you're doing and get over here. There isn't much time. My guys will be here any second." Jimmy helped with any translation of what Bernd didn't understand.

"What is going on here, Jimmy? This is a strange turn of events."

"We were just figuring that out when you came out of the woods."

Suzuki blurted, "There is no time to lose. Hit me with this rock. If we get caught, it needs to look like you ambushed me. However, if we are caught, that will be the least of our worries. In that case, you'd better be prepared to run. This is only a measure aimed at giving us some time, precious little time. When I was given the mission to recover you both, there was quite a furor over who gets to kill you to save the homeland. You're a real pain in the neck." Jimmy finished translating.

Bernd accepted the rock but logically chose to wait until someone did show up to use it.

"What's going on?" she said.

"I can hit you with this rock when and if anyone does show up. Do you mean that someone is definitely coming this way, and why are you worried about that?" Bernd asked.

"Yes, I contacted them already. They should be here soon. I am not one hundred percent sure what to do. This isn't part of my training."

"But it is exactly what my training has been. You have to be at peace yourself. Then you can make better, ah, I mean *balanced* decisions," Jimmy offered. "Trust yourself."

"Now is not the time to talk. We have to move. My group is pretty intense," she finished, pointing them in the direction she wanted them to head.

"You've got that right," Jimmy said, while rubbing the bump on his head that still ached as they began to move.

Chapter 18
NOW THERE WERE
THREE AND A HALF

*Jimmy, I can sense that her heart is good…*Saori reached out to Jimmy while they crested a mountain, which was terrifying under the circumstances. The moon being out again this evening made them visible for miles around, exposed by their silhouettes from the top of the mountain. They hurried over the top and began to descend to the other side. If it hadn't been for Ms. Suzuki's intelligent sense of strategy and directions, even though it meant taking the long way around, they would have headed directly into a trap set up by the Clan along the temple route on either side of the road where passing the temple became too narrow to slip by. It was a place where it would have been impossible to go around someone waiting in the dark. Rest being necessary, they eventually stopped several kilometers from where Bernd had caught up with the two.

"Bernd, thank you for coming after me. I am in your debt," Jimmy said.

"Not really. Wouldn't you do that for me?"

"Yes, I would."

"Oh, my," was all Ms. Suzuki said, and then looked down.

"Suzuki *San*, what is it?"

"Well, it is obvious that you both have a lot of respect for each other, and you are not even from the same country, are you?"

"No, we aren't," Jimmy replied. "We've built our trust up a little at a time."

"It's just that we've been told the opposite. For so long we've been told that you have no honor, no redeeming qualities. After a while, you believe it without really thinking about whether it makes sense or not. And it really *doesn't* make any sense. I feel very ashamed."

"Why? How could you have known better? You were only a young girl when you first heard these things, not the grown woman standing before us," Jimmy said as compassionately as he could. Bernd nodded gravely in agreement.

"But I was the strongest advocate of hate. The one who went to the utmost for our, our *cause*," she finished and buried her face in her hands. She realized that being a member of the Clan wasn't her final destiny. She was both distraught and relieved. Everything would be just fine, but she'd need time to heal—if the Clan would allow it. They'd have to understand, or she'd be dead before she had a chance to integrate her understanding.

She didn't really believe that the Clan's forgiveness was possible. No, it was *impossible*. She was too good to have been done in by these men. The Clan would judge her as having grown weak and, surprisingly—become a lost cause. She'd also be killed with Jimmy and Bernd. The Samurai Clan wouldn't understand, she believed, so escaping with the two men was the only option available.

"*Yes, her heart is good*," Jimmy said, replying to Saori in his thoughts. Then he relayed the message from Saori to Bernd quietly and briefly. Suzuki didn't seem to be listening, lost in her own thoughts.

"You two, they'll never believe that I have been 'duped' by you. I was too good at the training, excelling in every way, especially strategy—which is why they haven't found us up to now—but mark my words, they will, and then, we will all have to pay. We must keep moving. I will never be allowed to go back, and I will be lucky to be alive in three days."

"I see," both said in unison and somewhat subdued. After moving on for another hour and then pausing for a rest, Jimmy's fascination with the samurai could not be stifled.

"Ms. Suzuki, what about the samurai? How did you use Zen?" Jimmy asked for Bernd's sake and for clarification. He wondered if it really was like what he'd read in his studies, that Zen augmented the practices and was instrumental in the training of the samurai.

"We used the practice of *zazen*—sitting meditation—to calm our minds. It helped in two ways. We were psychologically prepared to fight and go through with whatever it was, the needs of a battle, because we didn't value staying alive over an honorable death."

"And the other way?" Bernd astutely asked.

"Morally grounded in the meditation, we were, and are, strong enough to not back down in a fight, like the soldiers who followed chivalry in the Middle Ages in Europe I learned about in junior high school, only we did it even better." She paused, seemingly deep in thought, then continued. "My great grandfather taught that the Shinto master had prepared him in all ways, better than any foreign religion could. This belittles the efforts of those in other lands, without *really* having any way to be sure, to confirm that it is even correct." She'd been pondering what Jimmy said earlier.

"Go on" Bernd urged, showing that both men were intrigued.

"Shinto, the native tradition of Japan is not a religion," Bernd continued, having learned about it while visiting Kasuga Grand Shrine. "The statement was rather that "Shinto *is* in the Japanese, and the Japanese *are* Shinto."

"Interesting," was all Jimmy could say. He'd imagined the close connection between the samurai and their native tradition. "However,

I thought the samurai were more closely aligned with Zen than Shinto."

Suzuki said, "That is what the books say, but while it may have been a calming practice for us, it would not have half of its power elsewhere. Amaterasu, the Goddess of the Sun in Japanese mythology, gave to us the powerful spirit, the *Yamato damashi*," Jimmy said it with her, causing her to pause.

Suzuki continued, "Yes, the Japanese spirit, given by the gods, was of the utmost importance as I had learned in studies of the Kojiki, the ancient creation story of Japan. It explains about the beauty of Japan, the sincerity of the Japanese. Without our soul, Zen is only a toy for fools to imagine they are superior to others who cannot sit cross-legged for long periods of time. For the Samurai Clan, in *the training*, we proved that action was what was most important. Our training was rigorous. We were planning how to spread our group onto the mainland, Honshu, when you two jerks arrived at our doorstep."

She truly is going back and forth, and as such, could turn on us at any second, Bernd believed.

"I see," Jimmy said warmly. Saori's voice rang in his head again on this moonlit night. *She needs your help, perhaps more than ever.* He pressed on with what he thought was most important. Rather than harping on how crazy the Samurai Clan sounded, he decided to see about getting her to take responsibility for her own actions.

"And about the healing process…"

"It will have to wait. We must move. Staying still is very dangerous in the mountains and hills of Shikoku." Suzuki urged them to leave, got up to leave, then turned back around and stopped.

"You guys ruined everything, at least temporarily. Since I was a major part of preparing your demise, I cannot help but feel anger about the plan being ruined. However, my heart tells me that your karma and my karma have made a connection today. Healing will come later. We need to move on now, but this'll get sorted out soon." All stood and prepared to move on.

Suzuki continued. "You have no reason to trust me, but—"

"Wait right there. Yes, we do. Your life is on the line now, too," Bernd stated logically.

"Well, it may not be that easy," Jimmy said under his breath to Bernd, recognizing that she might still be a covertly hidden plant, but continued louder with, "What should we do next?" He'd evaluate her plan to see if she was with them for real or not. Bernd seemed to understand or at least was willing to wait to find out more. Jimmy and Bernd didn't realize that the Samurai Clan training included not leading someone on. That was considered beneath them. They'd simply kill offensive people outright and not play games with them.

Based on her explanation of avoiding famous areas along the route, they all continued to transverse the slopes. Skipping temples along the route served two purposes. It would make the Samurai Clan have to work harder or at least split up to chase them and would also avoid high traffic areas whose docent might remember two foreigners walking by on pilgrimage with a Japanese woman dressed in traditional clothing.

Suzuki's next suggestion sat well with both men. She said they'd have to go back. They agreed because it was what Bernd thought was their only way to throw the Samurai Clan off their trail, and Jimmy knew that compassion dictated that they must at least try to let the Samurai Clan know that their goals were in error in so many ways. They must go back even at the risk of their lives. This was part of Jimmy's training. He hoped that he was up to the task. He was grateful that Bernd was willing to go along. His way of talking about being raised in Germany, his schooling about Hitler and the Nazis, may have been responsible for Bernd's compassionate side in the face of bias.

Recognizing they understood that she'd overheard them speaking of going back to talk to the Clan, and to allay their concerns, she said, "At the point when I heard your plan, I was the only one following you. I hadn't had an opportunity to tell anyone else, so *only* I know of your plan to do so."

Great, Jimmy thought. This didn't make it any easier to trust her. *Should we take her at her word*? The men exchanged looks, shrugged their shoulders and followed Suzuki as she turned toward Temple Number One. As the dawn approached, they holed up in a small ravine with limited access, it seemed, even to animals. After a short nap, they all began to talk once more in low voices.

"Are you ever going to be able to return?" Jimmy asked as the breeze picked up and morning neared, foreshadowed by the sky getting lighter. Sunrise was not far off.

"I don't know at this time. I am more concerned with us not being killed in the next few days. Sunrise will be in about three minutes. I know this from the many sleepless nights when I trained into the next day."

"Killed in the next few days. That sounds pretty scary," Bernd expressed his obvious concern.

"Suzuki *san*, is there anything we can do to make it right?" Jimmy continued to reach out.

"I know that this must all sound crazy, but no. In my area, we all have planned, trained, and striven to *purify* Japan somehow through our training in earnest; however, none of us has had an opportunity to kill anyone up to now. We were steeling ourselves, assuming that is what is coming next. Momentum has been building. Everyone has been wound up. There's no telling what they will do. We were just about to take action on our beliefs—and then you two showed up."

"Us?" Jimmy wanted clarification.

"Yes, with you two being captured because you were getting too close to figuring out what happened to that stupid Buddhist monk, and as a result of finding out about us, and then escaping, it is no longer viable to only talk tough. We felt over the past few days that we'd have to do something about it. Despite the many hours of training, in my area at least, no one has gone to the extreme of killing someone up until now."

"You mean no one has killed anyone; is that right?"

"Well, yes, but unfortunately for us now, my group is about ready to go crazy since you guys slipped out of our compound. Things have changed incredibly fast."

"No one has killed anyone," Jimmy repeated out loud. "But I think that is mistaken. I think that—"

"That can wait." Bernd cut off Jimmy. "It's important to keep moving. You heard what she just said." All agreed. Jimmy pretended to understand her to mean that no one had been killed *recently*. So far, it was just a stroke of luck that they weren't lying in pieces on the side of a mountain somewhere. Jimmy figured that she had been prepared to kill if necessary.

The next stop they made was several kilometers away from the beginning of the pilgrimage route. Suzuki told them they were between Temples Nine and Seven, but not really near any temple. She also told them the positioning was on purpose. She was taking them along a route that was parallel to the routes used by the Samurai Clan. It was risky but perhaps their only hope. After a rest, they pushed on.

The day moved on fortunately, with little change other than their hunger. Pine tree after pine tree lined the mountains, hills, and fields. The mountains still sloped, causing a beautiful straight line of trees to be juxtaposed to the diagonal of the slope.

The rows of trees trailing off into the distance are the epitome of beauty, Jimmy thought. The sun, climbing from the horizon, warmed the day.

Soon, the movement of animals would be slowed by the summer heat. Suzuki filled all their water bottles in another of the many mountain creeks that lapped, burbled and flowed along, not caring who was foreign or from Japan, oblivious to such concerns.

They made a detour into town, a little village of small shops that fed pilgrims, provided supplies, and were open to visitors from all over the world. While the men stayed on lookout from a designated place where she knew they could not be seen, she went into town and bought some food, hoping to draw as little attention as possible, being Japanese. Still, both men acknowledged that her strikingly fit, muscular form would draw attention almost anywhere she went.

Suzuki was brilliant. She played up being clumsy, which seemed to work wonders, drawing attention away from her looks to her obnoxious actions. People would talk about the clumsy girl who came into the convenience store that evening; however, she hoped that not too many would. If many mentioned it, some of her group may be able to figure out it was her. They'd realize that this rang true of her kind of behavior. Many, however, would not remember her description as much as her clumsiness.

After eating, they pressed on. By sunset, they had to rest, and the sound of the cicadas had stopped as the air cooled somewhat, and the evening breeze flowed. They took a moment to rest and visit before moving on.

Jimmy could wait no longer. "I think this is a good time to talk about the monk dying along the route in the nineteenth century."

Suzuki let on that she knew the story he was talking about. "He fell over the side of a steep slope. Everyone knows that. The story is very popular; it's folklore around here."

"But that isn't what happened, I don't believe. I am sorry to give you bad news, but I think your great grandfather killed him, if only because he chased him over the cliff."

Suzuki blanched. "Jimmy, how could you know that? I thought it was a family secret."

"Sorry. Hold on a moment." The moon was just coming up again. It was Saori again. *Jimmy, there's more to it than that.*

What do you mean? He sent a thought back to Saori. The other two could sense his growing distant but waited to see if he was alright. Bernd thought he was on to something. Suzuki was worried that he was exhausted and delirious, which would be a problem since they had so much farther to go that night if they hoped to be safe. Little did any of them know their journey was about to take a turn.

Jimmy said that they should relax as he was having a vision related to a recurring dream. Bernd understood and took Suzuki aside to explain while Jimmy connected with Saori.

Saori continued in Jimmy's thoughts. *Suzuki's great grandfather's dying words were that of regret that he'd ever started the Samurai Clan.*

That's stunning, Saori, Jimmy sent a message back.

Saori continued…*Yes, and additionally, he regretted that it was too late to change the group in his advanced near-death state. You see, it had taken on a life of its own by then. Jimmy, go slowly and carefully with this topic. Ms. Suzuki doesn't know this. No one alive does. I only know because of this place I am currently in. A Fukuchiin. Oh, why am I here?*

Jimmy thought: *Oh my God. Because I was there, I wonder. As for Ms. Suzuki, I'll be careful, Saori.* He realized that compassion was becoming his calling—and was perhaps the only thing that would save them in life or even in death.

Saori's message continued: *Jimmy, Great Grandfather Suzuki was too weak to talk at the point of realization. The Shinto priest present, a Mr. Matsuya, was also a disciple of Great Grandfather Suzuki's own Shinto master.*

Is that so? Jimmy was following.

Saori continued. *Great Grandfather Suzuki's master descended from a lineage of Shinto priests that began sometime in the Tokugawa period.*

Matsuya, the Shinto priest who was with Suzuki when he died, was Umura's father's teacher and grandfather. Matsuya was privy to Great Grandfather's last thoughts. As such he made sure that everyone knew of Suzuki's final words by revealing what he'd understood was Suzuki's final wishes silently communicated because of pre-death frailty. In the end, he revealed nothing out of the ordinary to others. As a result, Suzuki died a hero to the Clan he had formed.

Wait, it may be that Matsuya had no clear idea of Suzuki's wishes. In his weakened condition he may have been unable to share his new understandings, his feelings…. I'm not sure. It is something coming through about notes… His connection to Saori trailed off as it had other times.

Jimmy came out of it and was back with the two in the present time. *What were Mr. Suzuki's wishes?* That would have to wait. The two in front of him needed an explanation.

While Ms. Suzuki went into the woods alone, Jimmy sat down and related to Bernd what Saori told him; then he went into a trance-like state listening to Saori once more: *Jimmy, as I am now on Mount Kōya and no longer in the Heian capital, I am not sure what time period this is. And there is something missing. It has something to do with Great Grandfather Suzuki's sword.*

What is it, Saori? Jimmy asked her and the universe once more.

Something to do with his sword, if it still exists, she repeated.

"Does your Great Grandfather's sword still exist?" Jimmy asked tentatively as Suzuki returned.

"No, ah—what do you mean?" Suzuki acted nervous.

"I know that he lost his sword on Mount Kōya."

"Wait; you know that?"

"It's a long story," Jimmy said.

Suzuki obviously did not want to talk about it, but after thinking for a while and allowing everything to sink in, she resigned herself to following through. "You know, we have his scabbard, and it is considered prominently in the Samurai Clan heritage, a symbol of why we are fighting. That damned, sorry, that Christian disarmed him on Mount Kōya...." She filled Jimmy in, confirming what she knew of what he'd been told by Saori, and continued.

"Christians, we have been told, never had any business even being in Japan, let alone being of the samurai class. The scabbard is all we have left. It is displayed at my mother's home. Since my father died while being away from Shikoku...oh, this brings back memories I trained extra hard simply thinking of a Christian samurai..." Her voice trailed off.

Jimmy urged them to go with him to get it, as dangerous as that would be. "Then we must go get it. It holds some clue to all of this."

"How could you know that?"

"Suzuki *san*, I just do. No time to go into that now; it is related to dreams I have been having, and a kind of intuition I have had for several years leading me to well, ah, have a deep connection with the Japanese past. A deep awareness of a lot about the past." Jimmy finished with what under any other circumstances would have been a gross understatement.

They'd found a place that they hoped would be secure to rest for some time that night. Taking turns as the lookout, they slept.

Chapter 19

RETRIEVING THE SCABBARD

The next morning, the three of them set out. It was more dangerous to travel during the day, but both exhaustion and the urgency of the need to act before being found out, created their current karma of needing to continue. Still, if they hadn't slept, they wouldn't be able to travel farther, and now that it was morning, they couldn't wait until dark to travel. That would take too long, be too risky. They had to keep putting distance between themselves and the members of the Samurai Clan. *This is much more precarious than it sounded*, Bernd thought. *Members of the Clan could be anywhere.* After letting them know his thoughts, Ms. Suzuki confirmed his concerns.

"Watch your head, Jimmy," Bernd warned him. It seemed as if the tree branch had come swinging at Jimmy out of nowhere. Bernd realized, *These pine trees and branches provides the kind of flexibility that could be harnessed for dangerous traps.*

"Get down," Suzuki said quietly but convincingly. "That is a very bad sign. You've sprung a trap. They're either nearby or have guessed the route I'd take you along. Extra care is warranted." It was already getting hot and humid, the norm for summer in Japan.

Finally, this quick and sincere reaction by her convinced them, probably along with her reaction to the revelation of her Great

Grandfather's note and dying wishes, that she was in earnest—and was not leading them like lambs to the slaughter. Still, Jimmy signaled to Bernd to keep an eye out for trouble.

"Oh, wow. You mean that was a booby-trap?" Jimmy expressed his concern in a barely audible whisper.

"Yes, it is meant to either startle someone into making noise, or if it hit them, well, you can imagine."

"Yah," was all Bernd said, continuing with, "Lucky that Jimmy is so calm and composed—and didn't call out in his surprise."

"Be careful to make as little noise as possible!" Suzuki commanded. Silence ensued for a time.

"Anything we should be looking for?" Bernd's logical mind was rubbing off on Jimmy, aiding his inquisitive mind in making sense of the situation.

"Hard to say. Just *be careful*, hyper aware of your surroundings." They were now all on hyper alert. They had several kilometers to travel cross country to get back to her town, the town with Temple Number Eight Kumadaniji, and of course, her beloved Benten Shrine with its brilliant red orange *torii* or shrine gate.

After a while, Jimmy burst out with, "This is all too fantastic. Along the most famous Buddhist pilgrimage route in Japan lies in wait a group of Japanese nationalists with a strong interest in Shinto, the indigenous religion of Japan." Jimmy let fly both his exasperation and frustration at their predicament. Initially, he assumed he was just going on a little adventure—but it had turned out to be a harrowing journey. He was temporarily at his wits end. He began to breathe, remembering that everything wasn't about him; what matters is what is best for all. Immediately, he began to calm down. *Remember your Bodhisattva Vow,* to awaken speedily for the sake of all sentient beings, he told himself. His calm state retuned in part because of the encouragement of the other two. *So helpful to be together,* he thought.

"Keep moving. I will tell you more about our interest, ah, as you say, the Clan's interest in Shinto when we stop to rest—if they haven't caught us. Be quiet." Suzuki tapped Jimmy on the shoulder and walked ahead to lead them. They started taking special care not to trip on twigs or brush against low-lying branches.

"Keep an eye out above," Suzuki stated, as if it was the next, logical thing to do, which it was. Jimmy felt better now. He'd thought of that, too. His awareness training was beginning to help. Just thinking about the need to breathe to stay calm made him *feel* calmer. He was alert and focused but also understandably tired. Bernd, too, had admitted as much.

Suzuki pushed ahead, her eyes peeled for anything out of place; she seemed unstoppable. "Stop," she whispered fiercely not long after they'd began moving. She pointed to a pine tree ahead and to the left of the trail that they were forging along the mountainous slope. "See that?"

"Yes, but what does it mean?" Bernd asked while Jimmy nodded.

"It's a sort of challenge. Cut that way to demonstrate they think they can find us. A "See who can catch the foreigners the fastest" challenge. I guess I *am* one of you, now."

"It feels very different being the one who is followed, doesn't it?" Jimmy asked quietly in the way his teacher often did to increase insight, rather than place blame. Suzuki couldn't bring herself to answer but nodded, putting her head down for a brief pause, and then she advanced once more.

Then, she let them in on an insight that had come right from her training. "This part is most important. Don't let them in our heads. If we can do that, we have a chance."

Both men nodded agreement as they climbed over some rocks and made their way along a trail that had little in the way of brush but lots of trees to cover them from a distance. This made them all feel a little safer. No one could jump out of the bushes and ambush them. Bernd continued to look around. Jimmy was a powerful observer as well and was thinking of a plan in case anyone attacked. Suzuki continued to pray to the gods for confidence. This time, her shrine was nature itself. Jimmy just had a feeling that her training would prove useful.

Later, when Jimmy told Bernd his plan, his response was, "I hope you're right."

Suzuki thought it was worth a try, but only to gain some time, not at all something that would fool the Clan.

Jimmy's plan was that if anyone attacked, the one in the lead would take the rear; anyone in the middle would move to the front, and then the person in the rear at the time of attack would move to the middle position. Then they would all lock arms and spin twice, pushing anyone away from them—and then separate, but meet at Temple Number Eight as soon as possible.

While Suzuki had never heard of such a plan before, being used to having to primarily fend for herself—she thought it was a good one. If anyone was caught, all would not be caught. She liked it and agreed. Bernd gave assent to the plan as well, enjoying the idea of using confusion to overcome. Jimmy tried to keep himself as loose as he could, both in terms of muscle and mental energy, a combination of techniques gleaned from meditation and martial arts training. They neared the area in which Temple Number Eight was located. Jimmy grew nervous, as he had an ill feeling about the place. It was about an hour before sundown, but he anticipated the dark, hoping that Saori would be of some help.

Suzuki took them along the back way, a way she'd never shown anyone before, not even members of the Clan, so that it would be her own way of getting *home*. The men had traveled only part of the route and were amazed by the small-town sights, mountain views, bridges, and quiet trails that allowed one to sense the spiritual, even if they weren't religious, as they advanced but off the pilgrimage route.

Her mother was still up, sitting at a low table in the living room watching TV. It looked as if she'd finished dinner not long before, as the dishes, small plates, and a bowl for serving rice sat on the table, her chopsticks neatly aligned on top of it.

Suzuki entered and silently sat by her mother, being careful to stay out of sight of anyone looking in from the outside. Jimmy was impressed by what seemed like her innate ability to do that. She told them to stay hidden since the Samurai Clan members would be watching her ancestral home for sure. Her mother was startled, then moved to do something, but her daughter blocked her movement.

"Mother, I realize this looks bad, but before you reveal us, as is protocol for the Samurai Clan, think about my many efforts for the society. Doesn't that give me the option to make my case before I am tried and sentenced without the opportunity to defend myself?"

"They said you might say that."

"Yes, I know. And, even I wouldn't have listened to myself earlier, but I was a naïve little girl only days ago," she said with such gravity that her mother, who'd been leaning forward attentively up until then as a proud samurai family member, suspended her attempt to contact the Clan; the compassionate mother began to yield but only slightly.

"Child, I hope there is a good explanation. If not, you are dead to me. Are you with those unclean foreigners?" Her mother was firm; however, she had a mother's human sense of imploring in her response. The woven *tatami* reed mat ran cold beneath Suzuki as she looked past her mother at the wall hanging in the *tokonoma*, the alcove where the scabbard lay in honor. It read in a mocking way, "Monks will die for Buddhism," sounding like religious ecstasy, yet rather sinister now, the young Suzuki thought.

"Mother, I will tell you what has caused this. A change was bound to come over me. It was not their fault nor their responsibility." Her voice wavered, but unlike what her mother thought, it was not because of fear. *So much time has been squandered,* Suzuki thought. *It is because of my sincere regret about how I've lived the years of my life.*

Jimmy and Bernd could hardly hold it all in. Both were tired, hungry, and scared. Jimmy wanted to move on, and Bernd wanted to develop a contingency plan. They both prayed that Suzuki would get the scabbard and get out of there—in one piece. The house could easily be surveilled according to how many members they'd been led to believe that the Samurai Society had. The sun went down. Jimmy attempted contact with Saori as the mother gave a sign that would prompt the watching Clan members to come into the house. The mother would come to regret having done so.

Saori, is there any help you can offer? Jimmy reached out.

Jimmy, be careful. They are near. Usually, they guard the house as a group, though all but one went to get something to eat. You are not safe there for very long. Jimmy figured that he'd have to get that message to Suzuki inside the home.

In a text, Jimmy wrote, "Bernd, we have to tell Suzuki that the time is very short. We have to get the scabbard and get out of here. There is no time to look at it here. Saori indicated those watching this house could be back any moment." He used every strategy he knew to keep himself from breaking the protocol of absolute silence.

"Oh dear." Bernd moved toward the house, trying to stay in the shadows and form a rational plan. Jimmy followed while concocting his own strategy.

"We don't have any choice." Bernd was about to urge them to action when Jimmy grabbed a uniform shirt off the neighbor's clothesline, wrapped a towel around his head and began to knock on the door of the family home. Bernd stood in the shadows amazed at the transformation. As the door was opened, he invited himself in and looked to see if Suzuki was there. She'd hidden herself only until she heard his voice. She closed the door while remaining behind it. Jimmy relayed Saori's message. *"We have to leave right away."*

A moment later, her mother looked furious and sounded determined. "You will only take the scabbard from our home—over my dead body. It is the last souvenir of your great grandfather's courageous voyage to Mount Kōya."

"Mother, we have proof that we are not crazy."

"Then show it to me." She was standing firm.

Outside the house, Bernd was getting increasingly on edge. The watchers could return any second now, so he moved deeper into the shadows.

"It *is* the clue. The scabbard itself!" The daughter was imploring her mother to listen to her.

"What do you mean? We have seconds. The Clan, of course has been notified of your presence here."

Jimmy watched, having the sense to keep his *foreign* mouth closed. Suddenly when it was time to speak, Suzuki spoke before he could. "Let's take a look at it without taking it out of the home, and I will show you," she implored her mother.

"It's right in the alcove. Be careful. It's old. And if you try to run with it, I will scream," her mother reaffirmed.

"Mother. It will all be okay. You'll see. I seem crazy to you, but I have never felt better about myself than right now." Jimmy felt proud of his willingness to get into danger out of compassion for her. His heart warmed, but it was different this time, a warmth of loving kindness, not self-aggrandizement. Suzuki continued, "Jimmy, I will need your help. Hold it so I can look at it while the light goes down the tube."

"Not a chance. No foreigner can touch it. I'll do it." As her mother manipulated the scabbard, and everyone grew more and more nervous, Suzuki directed, "Stop!"

Suzuki had observed the artifact so carefully that she knew of nothing that was inscribed on the outer part of the scabbard. She assumed any clue must be *inside* the family's prized heirloom.

"You see anything?" Jimmy asked.

"Not sure. Move a little to the left, Mother." They hadn't realized that when she did so, it made her elbow just barely visible from the road as the watchmen returned to their posts, rice balls in hand, made with *umeboshi* salted, marinated plumb and *shiso*, a fragrant leafy plant. One member began to eat and looked at the home. The men had been called back by the member who'd seen the mother's signal. None of them had seen him as he had hidden himself in the shadows so well. He'd seen Jimmy and Bernd approach the home.

Bernd observed Samurai Clan members observing those in the home and threw a small stone, a pebble at the side of the home; all inside froze at the sound. In that instant, Suzuki said, "I see it." Outside, Bernd had the sense to move on to the agreed upon meeting place, should they be separated.

Everyone dropped to the floor, and Suzuki crawled to the kitchen for some chopsticks. She poked around, and after several tries, succeeded in drawing a small scrap of cloth out of the ancient scabbard. "Here it is, she exclaimed." The markings were old and hard to see but had been unmolested. Lucky for them, the scabbard had been persevered in a place of honor, a treasured remnant, evidence of the great grandfather's heroic effort. Unbeknownst to anyone, this note had been stuck to the side of his scabbard all this time, scrawled on a piece of ancient cloth.

Chapter 20

CALLING ON THE
SECRET SOCIETY

Suzuki's mother was unhappy about the visit, not wanting to turn in her own daughter, but assisted their escape based on what the note read. Seeing it was in familiar handwriting, both convinced her—and vindicated her daughter and these strangers. How could a foreigner be of help in this private Japanese matter? She had much to think about. But things began to move too quickly to take anything back.

The Samurai Clan members circled the house while Ms. Suzuki slipped out of the passage only the family knew about. As the Clan members approached the front door, Jimmy barged out, chased by Suzuki's mother. His uniform said that he was a gas company employee. He was able to hide his face temporarily as she yelled, "Get out of here. I didn't call for gas repairs. That is the other Suzuki down the block." Jimmy quickly sulked away, apologizing in Japanese the way he'd heard so many times, "*sumimasen. sumimasen. I'm sorry. I'm sorry.*" After he rounded the corner, he began to run.

Suzuki's mother made a scene while two more men approached. As was protocol, she pretended that she didn't know they were Samurai Clan members. "How awful young people are these days; we need to get back to the way Japan was when I was young."

"That's totally right," the Clan members smiled, pleased at her energy being used in this way. "Our honor is achieved through such efforts," one of them said when they were certain no one else was in earshot.

Continuing in a low tone, Mrs. Suzuki apologized profusely. "I'm ashamed for the false alarm of calling you because of a phony salesman. Let me get you something to drink." She provided chilled *mugicha* or barley tea to help them stave off the heat of summer, still hot even as evening turned into night.

After putting some distance between herself and the Clan members, Suzuki reunited with Jimmy a few blocks away, both sliding between homes with barely enough room for their rib cages. Bumping into each other, Jimmy noticed that, this time, she didn't bristle with the accidental contact.

Once the three were reunited, Bernd called on the Secret Society.

"Hata here." It was the chief of the Gangs Unit once more.

"It's Bernd. We need the help you and I planned when together earlier."

"Understood. I will personally call for additional help," Hata said.

Bernd, Jimmy, and Suzuki stopped running only after getting back to Temple Number Eight. They finally got a chance to look at the note together. It read:

> *"It has been years since I returned. I have worked to restore Japan to its rightful place in the world, to purify it of foreign influence. Of that endeavor, much remains to be seen, but of Japan's beauty, I have no doubt. Indeed, it was never lost. I regret my misguided efforts have led so many astray as well as killing the monk, done without my sword. I am glad now that I have no sword with which to commit more crimes. I must make amends, but how...?"*

From her place in between worlds, Saori began to fill Jimmy in from she'd witnessed on Mount Kōya where the note left off. Saori was revealing Suzuki's thoughts that she was able to connect with due to her nature as a ghost and proximity to Fukuchiin. "Great Grandfather," Suzuki began out loud and quickly went silent. Saori continued expressing great grandfather Suzuki's thoughts, *"Someone approaches. Where can I hide the note? I only have my scabbard. I'll use my short sword to slide the note into the small scabbard. I still have this beloved sword all these years after the mishap on Mount Koya. Ah, it cut the note in half instead of pushing the note farther into the scabbard."*

Jimmy, Saori went on, *half of the note fell onto his chest while half was in the scabbard.*

Saori continued, *Great Grandfather Suzuki's thoughts were of a sharp pain as he lay dying. With his last breath, he saw the Shinto priest enter the room and take the note, not realizing that it was only half of the note and that Great Grandfather Suzuki had put the other half in the scabbard. The Shinto priest treasured what he believed was the dying man's last words and said, "I will keep this note and give it special significance all my life." Then, the Shinto priest gave Suzuki some water. As Suzuki started to drink, he began to cough and, after that, was unable to speak, having grown so weak. Perhaps he even died right then.*

Saori continued in her own voice: *This must be where the Shinto priest took half of the note from Suzuki and kept it, ostensibly, on Great Grandfather Suzuki's behalf. Jimmy, I heard Great Grandfather Suzuki read the whole message before it got cut in the scabbard, a kind of dying prayer. I heard the full note while on Mount Kōya oh, the other day, but like before, I am unsure how many days have passed since arriving here.*

That's right. You're on Mount Kōya, Jimmy thought.

Yes, Jimmy. I'll tell you what I remember of the other half, the part the Shinto priest obtained.

Saori divulged to Jimmy what Great Grandfather Suzuki said in the note, what he read in his thoughts that she could gather as part of her ghostly ability. *"It was a close call. I was stopped by the Christian, losing my sword in an instant. I vowed to make him pay if I was able to meet with him again. Alas, I did not. I wanted to go back to Mount Kōya, but after returning to Shikoku in one piece, I believed that it was a miracle and never had the opportunity to go again. The gods had favored my life, so I lived for the glory of Japan ever after that."*

Saori finished explaining, *This, Jimmy, was the note received by the priest at the time of Suzuki's death. It had always been attributed to Suzuki. It convinced others, wrongly, that he was against anything non-Japanese, which, of course, isn't the same as glorifying Japan—nor true to his dying wish and understanding. Instead, it was what the Shinto priest believed that Great Grandfather Suzuki wanted all to think. The other half is what was in the scabbard all these years. The note in the scabbard reveals that before death, Great Grandfather Suzuki had a change of heart.*

Ms. Suzuki confirmed, "Jimmy, 'Living for the Glory of Japan' is the motto that the Samurai Clan used to spread its influence in Shikoku. It was the rallying call for the group after Suzuki's death at the time of the Clan's rapid growth late in the nineteenth century. This was the legacy of the Shinto priest's message of Suzuki's last dying breath. 'Purification at all cost' we were told were his last words."

Saori chimed in. *What the priest didn't know was that his interpretation of Great Grandfather Suzuki's dying message was wrong since he did not have the rest of the note.*

Jimmy replied with his thoughts. *Perhaps he simply didn't care, being the nationalist that he was. Either way, the Shinto priest's legacy ensured the continuation of the Samurai Clan.*

Jimmy shared with the others what he learned from Saori, what she was able to know by being on Mount Kōya and in part through her connection to Jimmy who had held Suzuki's sword, if only briefly.

They all sat stunned and in disbelief at the story—and the contents of the ragged note from the scabbard. Saori had been able to fill them in about the events on Mount Kōya and Great Grandfather Suzuki because of the sword on Mount Kōya. Jimmy's karma had pulled her closer to the present day—the nineteenth century, and she accessed the history of the notes through his encountering the sword and her close proximity to it. These things allowed her as a ghost to connect to Great Grandfather Suzuki's mind stream from long ago. Saori herself swooned in and out of her ghostly consciousness but recovered. Swooning was a new experience for her. In the past, it had only been a kind of unworldly mental discomfort. This time it was a fuller feeling, something she'd not experienced since being alive, she imagined, but couldn't remember.

The current Suzuki was the most put out by the messages. She'd been living a lie. She was raised in a family that praised Japan and disdained the rest of the world. Her love for her country was not misplaced; she really did love the things that came with being from Japan. Up to now, she realized there was much about the world that she did not understand. To judge something without knowing didn't make any sense to her anymore...and now she was visibly shaken.

"But wait. Jimmy, how am I to believe you about the first half of the note?"

"Well, you lived that experience, the story of the angry Great Grandfather Suzuki experience thanks to the Shinto priest, right?" She nodded. "What you didn't know was in the second half of the note, hidden until now, about how he'd come around prior to dying."

"Yes, but there's no way to prove that the two notes or halves of one note are real. There's only proof of *this* one."

"True, but..."

"You guys. Remember, our lives are on the line. Let's be ready to go. Details will have to be ironed out later." Bernd was right. They all steeled themselves for what was still to come.

Jimmy thought, *I wonder if Umura can confirm the first message. Hmmm. But first, there is a person in front of me who may need support to continue her transformation.* "I can also see you are proud of your great grandfather's awareness; it seems that he was a truly amazing human."

"That's true, but my feelings are very mixed right now. In the Clan, we are not even supposed to *have* feelings. Ah, you see it's all very complicated. It was legendary that Great Grandfather had been so angry for so many years prior to writing this note."

"I'm sure it is challenging; however, from what I've witnessed, if anyone can get through this, it's you," Jimmy said reassuringly.

Bernd brought them back once more. "What do we do next?"

Jimmy answered first. "Of course, we must tell the Samurai Clan they are living a mistaken path, that the original Suzuki had a change of heart, and he never meant for all of this to continue." His compassion meter was buzzing.

"That won't be easy, Jimmy. Many of our group firmly believe in the cause—and like me, have done so for very long—so a change won't be readily forthcoming. For me, there had already been lingering doubt, things that were somewhat unclear, as well as karma perhaps from a previous life. I feel, well, sort of lucky to have met you—still, I'm not sure how the others would take the news, especially the part about you just knowing something. They'll want more proof, I think. We will need proof of both halves of the note, Great Grandfather's dying message."

"Of course," was all Jimmy could say as he sat down to contemplate what to do next.

Chapter 21

THE SECRET SOCIETY SHOWS UP

After waiting for an hour, both Bernd and Suzuki were noticeably anxious and wanting to be on the move. Jimmy, too, was nervous but was meditating and waiting patiently when members of the Secret Society emerged out of the mist. One was stocky and carried himself confidently. The other, who was taller and lanky, wore a patch over his left eye and spoke for them. "Here we are, specially chosen to help you all."

"Hi there. Who are you guys?" Jimmy had the sense to ask, not taking any chances. They exuded confidence, and having seen them put their fingers through their hair, Bernd's eyes showed that he believed they were using greetings that members of the group he'd contacted use—putting the others at ease.

"Why, we're members of the elite group, of course, two of Hata's men." Bernd figured the "elite group" referred to the Secret Society. He believed this to be a ploy to make sure Suzuki and Jimmy weren't privy to more information than was necessary. Suzuki had an air of caution around her the entire time, something Jimmy attributed to "the training." All this tension made even the trees, already nearby, seem to push in on them.

"Why are you guys wearing swords?" Bernd asked the logical question. The Secret Society members pushed to get moving, telling Bernd they would forgo the usual secret greetings and such to keep their cover. With the others looking on, Bernd understood and agreed that the work of the Society was too important to take any risks, to give anything away. They seemed on edge, as if they believed all of them should hustle.

While walking, the taller man began to explain, "As for the swords, how else are we to look like the people we are trying to impersonate? Let's keep moving and avoid us all getting captured and killed while we bring you off the island." Bernd smiled. Once again, simplicity was chosen over elaborate displays.

Jimmy nodded approval and understanding, and then said, "Bernd and I can't leave just now; our time on the island will have to be extended a little." This caused the group to stop.

Perturbed, the man with the patch over his eye said, "Oh, really. What do you have to do? You know, we are risking our lives just being here."

"It's just that we have something to reveal to the Samurai Clan. It's of the utmost importance. We have a message for them."

"What kind of message?" the other member mentioned, looking keenly interested, but Bernd pulled Jimmy aside.

"Jimmy, I think it is better to tell them more once we've started moving." His intuition told him that they'd been in one spot long enough. "We have to move on," Bernd said to the group, and all seemed to agree. They picked up their backpacks and gear and began to file once more along the narrow mountain path. A wave of exhaustion flowed across Jimmy, but he pressed on since there was nothing that could be done about it. Suzuki and Bernd also showed signs of fatigue. Night grew deeper as they continued to run from who knows what.

Saori reached out while Jimmy wasn't talking to anyone. *Jimmy, don't let on that I am communicating with you.*

Okay, he said to himself and her. Next, she clarified her concern.

Jimmy, I am not sure what it is, but you must be careful. It could be that you will walk into trouble, a trap with the Samurai Clan, and I have an ill feeling. It started as soon as these two men arrived at the place where you were waiting for them. If you can, keep moving.

Thank you, Saori. I will keep us moving and be on alert. I won't let any-one other than Bernd know that you are communicating with me, he said, while trying to make it seem like he was looking around for others who might jump out of nowhere—for Samurai Clan members. They moved on for a while.

"We take a break here," one of Hata's men said.

Suzuki asked, "Which direction are we going? We need to be heading back to the start of the route, but this feels wrong."

Jimmy thought he saw one of the men wince slightly. He was used to looking for clues on people's faces in the moonlight after his many experiences with Saori in the past few years. Bernd continued to size up the men but figured that since they were Secret Society members, they were completely safe.

"Well, I did want to ask that we go to the Samurai Clan's compound, even though it will be risky," Jimmy urged once more.

"Risky? Risky and far," the man wearing the patch broke in, seeming to want to settle everyone down. Bernd listened, feigning disinterest. Jimmy wanted to consult with him, but they couldn't split up right then. The two newcomers were right in the middle of everyone.

"It's risky, but we could be saving a lot of people a lot of trouble if we can talk with them about something we found out about Mr. Suzuki, the founder of the Samurai Clan." The men seemed to stand taller at this point, realizing how important Mr. Suzuki was to the Samurai

Clan members. "It's very important, I think," Jimmy said, as convincingly as he could.

"Wait here, I think I see something," the man with the eye patch said as he left with the other man to go ahead a little. Jimmy took the time to tell Bernd in a voice only Bernd could hear that he was communicating with Saori. He'd only just expressed the concern she'd told him about when the two men returned. Suzuki had, unbeknownst to all others, clandestinely followed them. She shot a warning look to Bernd and Jimmy, but they were all urged forward before any words could be exchanged.

The two men mentioned that the Samurai Clan was known to work in this area, which Suzuki confirmed with a nod that only Jimmy and Bernd could see. Having been told to be silent, they complied.

About a half an hour later, while coming out into a clearing, they heard a twig snap—and Suzuki, trusting her years of training, was gone. Bernd turned to head back into the woods while Jimmy began praying, but both were taken by surprise as the Samurai Clan members surrounded them, bound and gagged them, and then walked them about a quarter mile—seemingly deeper if that were possible—into the mountain. The breeze had disappeared, and the sweat running down Jimmy's back caused a chill to run along his spine, sending another reminder of Saori, since so often that had happened when she was around.

Jimmy grew increasingly scared this time but prayed that the universe would give them the opportunity to reveal what they'd found out, namely that Mr. Suzuki had had a change of heart not long before he died, and that his dying note had been misinterpreted since the nineteenth century—in no small part due to the spreading of the incorrect message by the Shinto priest who'd been with Suzuki at the time of his death.

Unfortunately, Suzuki, the great granddaughter they had come to trust, was now a mystery once again. Why did she abandon them? She seemed capable of taking out the two who grabbed them. Bernd, for his part, worried about the fate of the Secret Society Members. Would they be killed?

"Jimmy, they got all of us, even the two members of my organization."

"Yeah. That was shocking to see."

"Makes me scared to think that the whole organization might be at risk. Besides, I didn't think it was possible since the organization has been around for so long. If only I'd observed more carefully."

"Don't blame yourself. It won't help anything. Keep alert now. If I had to be in trouble with anyone, I'd wish it were you," Jimmy said as warmly as he could in the low undertones they were using.

"You two knock it off. Silence now," said one of the Samurai Clan's members, and then there was laughter throughout the group.

While the two men were mulling over mistakes made and the predicament they were in, the caravan arrived at the Samurai Clan's compound. Still tied up, they were placed in the familiar tea ceremony hut, but this time the armed guards were inside the hut with them, and they were placed together in the middle of the hut. Jimmy was not inclined to observe the pattern of the ceiling and check its austerity against his learning in his Japanese culture course for *wabi-sabi* or beauty in imperfection. Instead, Jimmy and Bernd were bound together, and the other two members of the Secret Society were tied together.

Suzuki is long gone, Jimmy imagined. *I wonder if she has anyone she can go to for help, if she even would want to help?* He began to imagine Kobodaishi walking along the route between temples in ancient Japan. In this situation, what might he do? Jimmy hadn't studied him enough to know the answer to that question. Then he allowed his thoughts to go quiet. *There was another who might be able to help, another from Heian Japan.* He hoped that it was dark enough as night was falling.

Saori, are you there? We're back in the Samurai Clan's compound. Lucky for him, she was only in a parallel time. She was also just experiencing nightfall in the nineteenth century.

Yes, but now I don't know what to do, Jimmy.

Anything you can do will help. I know it. He was encouraged being in communication with her.

Bernd wanted to talk to Jimmy, but Jimmy's nudge and glance told Bernd that now was not the time. Bernd seemed to understand. He looked with increasing interest at the Secret Society members. They looked totally unconcerned. There seemed to be only three possibilities in Bernd's mind: they were crazy, they were beyond concern because of their Secret Society training, or they were…oh no.

"Jimmy, don't say anything out loud," Bernd whispered while the moon shone in through the small windows, and the evening summer breeze blew through the hut. "This place is not safe with Clan members being so near." As he waved his head toward the Samurai Clan guards, he pushed Jimmy's hand toward where the "Secret Society" members were sitting. Jimmy tapped Bernd once. While staying together earlier, they'd decided that two taps meant "No" and that one tap meant "Yes." The one tap meant yes, that he'd be quiet, and Bernd took this to mean that Jimmy understood.

The Secret Society members seemed to be compromised, as unlikely as this was. Both men knew what that meant—likely the Secret Society members had been killed by the Samurai Clan when they were intercepted coming to the help of the young men. The Clan couldn't risk more people being aware of where they were and what they were up to, and the two men tied together in the hut were Samurai Clan members posing to be Secret Society members. Fortunately, the imposters hadn't noticed or at least didn't let on that they understood

Jimmy and Bernd's interaction. Jimmy returned the focus of his attention to what Saori was saying in her thoughts.

Today, I saw Mr. Suzuki's sword. It had some writing etched into the metal near the scabbard, "Eien to Yamato Damashi"—Eternally the Soul of Japan.

Okay, so what does that tell us? He sent his thoughts back to her.

I don't know Jimmy. You'll figure it out, find a way. You always do.

Jimmy thought for a moment, then communicated. *It's a long shot, but when the timing seems right, I have to say, "Eternally the Soul of Japan" and pledge myself to it like I mean it.*

What? It won't be easy. They won't think you are one of them. Even Jimmy himself wasn't sure this was the thing to do.

Maybe not, but they will see my spirit, Jimmy was increasingly confident.

Saori continued. *And my senses tell me in a tingling sort of way that you will be telling them what they need to hear, even if they don't like it.* Jimmy and Saori agreed that even if there was a better way, they must trust in the universe.

One thing is for sure. They'll either like it or they'll be totally offended and kill me right then and there!

One Samurai Society member cut a bamboo tree diagonally—and as Jimmy had heard once, it was often used for testing one's skills. In this case, it had the secondary purpose, which both men guessed correctly, of instilling fear in them—and it was working.

Bernd found that he wouldn't be able to confirm his concerns about the two men who claimed to be Hata's men. After a short time, the two who Bernd supposed were "imposter" Secret Society members were taken away, ostensibly for questioning and were not seen again.

Chapter 22

IN NEED OF HELP

Bernd had no plan this time. Even if they could free themselves from the bonds joining them, they'd then have to confront two sword-wielding Samurai Clan members before even reaching the door.

Eventually from exhaustion, they both slept leaning against each other. The Samurai Clan guards seemed to think, the next day when they woke, that the fact they had slept was a sign of weakness inherent in them because they were foreigners. A samurai, they believed, would have stayed awake and alert, even if exhausted.

"To your feet." As they got up to that command, Bernd saw out of the corner of his eye first one of the other men, then the second. They were talking to Umura, the elder. Bernd's misgivings that they were imposters were confirmed. The Secret Society had been compromised. He wondered how far the Samurai Clan had infiltrated the Secret Society. His assumptions were made, not knowing the Secret Society members had been killed in their attempt to come to the rescue. He was worried that the Society's cover worldwide had been blown. The two saw Bernd, and looking his way, nodded and bowed toward him. Understanding their intent, *Very rude*, Bernd thought and looked away.

Jimmy finished blinking the sleep out of his eyes and conferred with Bernd briefly before being told to shut up. Bernd confirmed what

Jimmy came to understand—that the Secret Society wasn't coming to help any time soon, and it probably didn't even know where they were.

"Now what?" Both seemed to be asking with their eyes. Jimmy knew he must try what he and Saori discussed, but he also was pleading with himself to trust in the universe, hoping it would help. His gut told him the dying message of the founder would have an impact, especially with the elder, Umura, if he had a chance to talk to him.

Jimmy and Bernd were taken out as before and made to sit in the open. They were given a little water, but verbal jabs were spoken purposefully loud enough to hear, "That's enough; don't *waste* water." No explanation needed.

Bernd was rested, so his mind began to work again, but however he figured it, an escape as before didn't seem likely since they were being watched so carefully.

"So, you didn't expect dumb foreigners to escape last time." Bernd was trying to draw them in, hoping to learn something that could help. Jimmy looked at him like he was crazy. Bernd thought, *then go ahead, have a go at getting us out of here,* before staying quiet.

Jimmy did try. "Eternally the soul of Japan" he said as seriously as he could: "I support this sentiment aligned to what your group seems to value. The soul of Japan is eternal, isn't it?"

"Of course," said the interrogator sitting in front of them. "But what would a stinking foreigner know about the soul of Japan?"

"That since the time of Heian Kyō, it has been tried sorely in many battles and is still here."

"What? *Nama iki,*" "What? You're so green," implying that he believed there was no way Jimmy could understand what he was saying.

"And proudly so," Jimmy continued in the same vein. "I have benefitted so much from my time in Japan. That is why I am back—why I am here. This pilgrimage is another journey in the life of my soul. It has been supported by the soul of Japan. Can't you see how beautiful that is to me?" he finished as solemnly as he'd ever been.

"But you will go back to your own country because it is better? No?"

On purpose, carefully and with determination, Jimmy paused. It wasn't like him. He didn't often wait, pausing before speaking, but this time was different. This was perhaps the most important thing he'd ever discussed. Not only because lives mattered, but because so many lives mattered. After some time, the interrogator seemed to grow impatient.

I *must tell Umura*, Jimmy thought. *I feel that his knowledgeable self will be able to help me now. He will understand; I must tell of why…I love Japan.*" Addressing the elder directly, Jimmy said, "It is because of the understanding that Mr. Suzuki and I share." There had been constant murmuring until now. No one had been taking this trial seriously — because of its foregone conclusion — the imminent verdict of guilty and what that would mean. Now murmurs transitioned to silence as bits and pieces of the conversation spread throughout those assembled. The old man, Umura the elder, leaned forward in his chair.

"No, that is not why I would return. It is not about…"

Damare. Shut up, was heard once again.

The elder spoke about Jimmy. "Bring that guy closer. No doubt he doesn't have anything of substance to say, but because of the samurai sense of justice, I will hear him out." The tone of disgust was apparent, and a wavering of his voice, too, could be heard. The man seemed to be shaken, but certainly not swayed, by Jimmy's words. The elder hadn't forgotten Jimmy's earlier comment about the ancestors being pleased with them, but this time he was less dismissive. *Was this guy for real?* He wondered. *No*, he quickly said to himself. *Foreigners cannot be taken seriously.*

Bernd sat with his fingers crossed. While they were far from being out of trouble, he trusted Jimmy more than ever. His performance just then, spoken with heart, had been amazing. As Jimmy pleaded to Umura, the man in charge, one of the group approached Bernd.

"A little water for the dirty foreigner," was said loud enough for Jimmy to hear. "Do not imagine that guy's fake sentiment, his theatrics, will make any difference."

"And you, little one?" The guy with the patch smiled cynically while offering water, which Jimmy turned down in order to signify the feeling of urgency that he sincerely felt. Then, he was offered *sake*, the Japanese traditional brew made from rice, which all thought he wouldn't accept—but he did—to the surprise of everyone.

Jimmy said, "I am told that on *Omisoka*, New Year's Eve, *sake* is considered a drink that can connect one to the gods. I admire the tradition but do not think myself worthy of the gods. The acceptance of the drink is for all humankind." His point was made, if unkindly received.

"I'll…" Tanaka, the nearest guard, moved to knock the drink out of Jimmy's hand; however, Umura stopped him with an upraised hand, perhaps considering the sacredness of the *sake* above the value of insulting a foreigner.

"Raise your sword, Tanaka." Jimmy acknowledged with his eyes the sword raised above him, that Tanaka was ready to strike when the elder gave the command. Jimmy was unaffected perhaps for the first time in his life. He'd never been so calm in such a fearful position. Was he becoming "comfortable with being uncomfortable," as Sensei had said from time to time? True, he certainly felt no choice in the matter— but to ride the sense of calm.

Jimmy breathed in and out, accessing the meditative ideal of equipoise, not from his efforts only. The energy of awakening, extant in the universe, was aiding him. His calm was not tied to his staying alive; it came from and was only possible because of his sincere, compassionate concern for the others in that very circle in the compound—all of them, something related to the teachings of Open Breeze. It was not different from the understanding that his redemption, he now realized, was tied to his being compassionate and helping the younger Suzuki. He fully understood his life's purpose in that moment.

The pilgrimage was only partially achieved, but it had come through in ways he could never have imagined. He could feel this deeply within. *Don't mention her*, Jimmy told himself, intuiting the importance of leaving Ms. Suzuki out of this conversation.

As for the Samurai Clan, it mattered to Jimmy and ultimately to the world, that they did not continue as they had been. Not for him, nor any foreigners, but because any harm they might do would mutually harm them as well; all those caught up in negative actions would be harmed—doer and receiver. Jimmy knew this belief came from the Buddhist teaching that hatred is harmful. Acting on hatred is likened to picking up a burning coal. It burns the person that the coal is thrown at, as well as the hand of the thrower. That was, he believed, how the universe worked—cause and effect. He needed to stay calm for everyone's sake.

"Tanaka, now!" The sword fell in one swift, precisely aimed, skillful stroke.

Jimmy felt the wind from it as it breezed past his head, as was prearranged. He'd not moved, although he had closed his eyes momentarily.

The old man could give him that. He'd passed this test. It was obvious that he wasn't putting on being calm but was demonstrating a calm state from his years of some kind of practice, just as the elder had when tested so many years ago. The elder was begrudgingly impressed. He had enough years under his belt to understand that this was not "beginners' luck."

Tanaka was told to put away his sword. The elder leaned in again. He had definitely not accepted that Jimmy was in love with Japan, but he was for the time being, willing to at least listen, visibly impressed by Jimmy's demonstration of calm in a test that most had failed. *Could foreigners understand anything about Japan?* He didn't think so, *but if they could*, he thought *it would be important to know*. Part of the training was to know your enemy. For the Samurai Clan's sake, he'd listen to this young man but not just right now. There was one more test.

"Back in the hut." Bernd and Jimmy were ushered back to the hut by their personal guards. After they ate slight provisions given to them, they were tied together very securely once more. Bernd mentioned that Umura was playing with them to get to know his enemy so when other foreigners were captured, he'd know what to do.

"Our efforts matter more than ever, I suppose," Jimmy whispered.

"Right," Bernd replied, and then the day passed slowly but surely, and soon it was, "Lights out. *Damare.*"

Later that night, Saori told Jimmy, through their mental link, that she could sense the men's predicament across time. She told him after that night's dinner, the elder had said, "Even if I like what he says, they are both too dangerous to us. Don't forget that."

Great. There is no hope for us, then. Jimmy sent his thought to Saori who was, as so many times before, already gone.

A new possibility dawned just before Jimmy succumbed to sleep. He believed that Suzuki had been playing them so she could get to know them, which she had done at quite a risk. He realized the Clan was currently, though mistakenly—after her, too. She'd even fooled her mother. *Shame that she hadn't been changed by our interactions,* Jimmy thought as he fell asleep.

Chapter 23
NOTEWORTHY HELP

Suzuki was thinking this through. *The last day may or may not prove useful, but is, I believe, the best chance I have of escaping the Samurai Society and getting off the island of Shikoku. I've discreetly contacted members of the Clan who I hope trust me unconditionally and will at least hear me out before condemning me. It, of course, is a huge risk. Worst case, they will follow the protocol. Of course, even that makes sense since we've all been trained not to trust anyone who is no longer in the group's favor.*

Suzuki was waiting to hear back from one of the two she'd contacted, members who were in her class, who had started the training at the same time as she did. Now she stood on one member's rear doorstep hoping that she would get past the door and not be made to do the Society's version of "walk the plank," which meant to be made to—figuratively and literally—fall on her sword. She'd be forced to kill herself, at worst, or be killed if she refused. It was, after all, the only honorable way for any of them to die, the time-tested tradition that had come down to the present of *seppuku*, a slice across the abdomen. The modern version was a definitive way to end it all.

Having seen her coming, this Clan member, Ms. Fujita gave Suzuki the regular treatment for abduction. Suzuki was covered from behind with a gunny sack and brought into the home. It wasn't the kind of welcome she'd hoped for. Twenty minutes later, after some abuse and being left on the floor of the home immobilized, tied up within the bag and in a panicked sweat, she was released from the bag and kept out of sight with her hands still bound. The twenty minutes were spent undergoing the regular protocol of securing the premises and ensuring no others were hanging around with Suzuki.

"What was that for?" Suzuki cried out to her comrade who unexpectedly had treated *her* like a criminal for the first time ever. In fact, not only were her hands tied, the chair she sat on was also secured between two other cabinets and could not be moved. Suzuki stole a look around. It was a typical Japanese home with tatami woven reed mats, a small kitchen with a rice cooker, and there was a tokonoma, an alcove with a hanging scroll not far from the entryway door. The scroll read, "Never Surrender Your Japanese Spirit." There it was again, *Yamato damashi.*

"Really? You have no idea? Consider our training for a moment. You can imagine what would happen to me if you'd been followed, and I was seen inviting you in. Both of us would be fed to the rats. I'll give you the benefit of the doubt to explain yourself, but after that, dear, if you do not convince me that you are for real, you're toast." Suzuki recognized the reality of the moment. She'd gone rogue, and there was no way for anyone to know for sure what her intentions were. It all made perfect sense. Suzuki was grateful this colleague was giving her the benefit of the doubt. It could go sideways at any moment.

"Ah, of course. I am so sorry for putting you in this position, but there is, as I said in my text message using our private numbers, something you need to know about the lie we've been living. You see, I have met some people recently, now go easy for a moment, they're foreigners." Suzuki closed her eyes, expecting to be hit in the face with the comment, but the other woman just stood there with rapt attention and waiting for the explanation to continue.

"Ugh. Go on." Fujita had obviously received this with disgust.

"We have helped each other, and well, they helped me in spite of my trying to kill them."

"There are more than one?"

"They're the ones currently being held in the compound. Stop right there. You said you'd hear me out before taking action. I know the protocol. *Remember*, I helped, based on what I knew of my great grandfather, to write some of our protocol."

"You have minutes, dear, to make yourself understood. So much could go wrong. You've really mucked things up."

"I know. I think for good reason, too. May I go on? Are you able to hear me?" *I can't believe I said that so, ah, compassionately. What a strange change*, Suzuki said to herself.

"I'm all ears. Spill your guts. It may be the only thing that saves you. And don't take me for a fool. I've got you covered in ways you do not know." A chill ran down Suzuki's spine. This woman she loved for her independence and innovative ways of making things work now gave an ultimatum that didn't bode well for Suzuki. Suzuki trusted that this wasn't only a bluff. Following the woman's hint, Suzuki stole a look upward and was temporarily both wowed and awed into silence.

Above her was a plastic sack of something that looked like kerosene. Fujita stood confidently and defiantly in front of Suzuki. With hair cropped short, she was the epitome of the model modern samurai woman. Her clever reputation was on display; she had hoisted the sack to the shelf. This too, had been part of her actions during the past twenty minutes.

"You discovered it, eh?" Fujita said. Suzuki nodded slowly, thinking it best to not move around too much.

"You see, you are below a ticking kerosene bag. It will melt the bag it is in, begin dripping, and once you are covered, well, you get the picture," Fujita said, taking the lighter out of her pocket, then returning it to its secure place. "You have ten, maybe fifteen minutes to convince me that you haven't come as a ruse, and then I may be able to let you go. If I am not convinced by your story, I will use this lighter, and I have thought of other things in case you try anything smart. Suzuki, don't do that. I'd rather not go to further extremes with you if not necessary. Think of it as the benefit of our training together. Still, my patience is wearing very thin," Fujita finished with a tone of finality.

Suzuki could sense the concern as well as the opportunity in the offer. If whatever they needed to do went wrong, both would be "toast," even if Suzuki made it through the interrogation. The Samurai Clan would make sure of that. Suzuki began in a familiar way to put Fujita at ease before moving to the fact of her inner nature being changed.

"Fujita, our mandate, of course, is to cleanse Japan of foreigners. And this is the best way I can think of doing it. You see, two men were discovered and brought to the compound. They are very dangerous to us. While they are weak, they are resourceful, and they know where the compound is. I figured out how to gain their trust and only narrowly escaped while they were captured and being brought to the compound. But I am in between two worlds. I also think that…"

Suzuki decided to be more direct. "As for trying something foolish with you, I won't. Of course, I remember you will do what you said, and you do not make idle threats. Explain the traps later; what you need to know, I will tell you now."

Suzuki explained pertinent points of the whole time of being with the foreigners, even their weakness in wanting to help her after she had fallen. Fujita was incredulous, and then seemed to go deeper into thought as the explanation continued with the revelations of Suzuki's mother, who realized her daughter's ploy to gain their confidence, but was nonetheless genuinely surprised, as was Suzuki with the finding of Great Grandfather's note on the cloth from inside the scabbard; the note was the second part of his dying wishes that had been hidden for so long.

Fujita considered it good that the mother signaled the Clan, but also noted how her mother didn't turn Suzuki in herself, just as Fujita had done, taking precautions to be in alignment with protocol but found something human within herself that told her to go with her instincts to trust Suzuki. This was certainly true for Fujita as with her mother.

"*Ne,*" Fujita began with the Japanese term that signified softening, and that she'd thought of something and wanted to thoughtfully reveal it to Suzuki. "You know, your mother and I both broke protocol and you are under suspicion yourself for having done so, and the reason is that there is something human above and beyond our protocol that seems to—"

"... have prompted us all to break protocol," Suzuki said finishing the thought. "And what's more, these stupid foreigners don't seem very stupid. They seem rather sincere, something we value to the utmost."

"You know, they could be dead by now," Fujita said. Suzuki sighed only slightly, but Fujita noticed.

"What is this about the cloth you said you recovered from the scabbard? What you said in your text was a bit risky." Fortunately, Suzuki had thought to keep the original when she wrote a copy to give to Jimmy if that even became possible. She figured there would be a need for the original as proof if there was an opportunity to present it to the group for verification. Any doubt could be fatal with the Samurai Clan. *Be careful,* she told herself, as she looked up again. Of course, caution made sense in her current predicament. She realized that Fujita's patience would be limited; Suzuki had to talk fast.

"Jimmy, one of the foreigners, seems to think and act like he somehow knows that my great grandfather was not always the violent Japan purist we have learned about. And Bernd, the other foreigner, is both very, very logical and kind."

"Go on." It was a test, Suzuki knew, but Fujita was playing it by the book. Even having broken protocol, she was still following it completely in other ways.

"I cannot say for sure, but the message on the cloth makes me pause," Suzuki said.

Fujita asked, "What do you mean? As he progressed in years, didn't he grow to hate foreigners and want to purge Japan of foolish outside influence? That makes sense. I get more lucid on this each year," Fujita said, with an air of questioning even while finishing with conviction. Her expression belied a sense of confusion coming over her. Her confidence up until then was an indication of her steadfast training excelled only by Suzuki's level of effort.

"Well, not exactly. I'm starting to think the opposite," Suzuki added.

"Then, what the heck could have changed him? Did he meet compassionate foreigners like Jimmy and Bernd?" Even though she caught the sarcasm in the comment, Suzuki admired Fujita's attention to detail, amazed by her remembering both men's names.

"Experience," Suzuki replied.

"How's that?"

"Well, he began to grow out of his anger as he aged. True, jealous of the invading religion, Buddhism, he did kill the monk." Suzuki was building an old story once more.

"So, what are you saying?"

"There's more!" Suzuki realized she had little time to make her case, and that they had to spring into action if they were to save Jimmy and Bernd. As Fujita mentioned, they could be dead already.

"As you know, when he was found dead, there was a message from the Shinto priest with a note that signified and stated in no uncertain manner how my great grandfather wanted to purify Japan—and that his conviction to renew Japan was definite."

"It was, wasn't it?" Fujita asked.

"I'm not so sure anymore. Your response and recent events have led me to new conclusions. Let me take out the evidence I found."

"What do you mean?" Fujita grew interested but also concerned, as one does who finds the grounding of their beliefs crumbling from underneath them. She was also wary of Suzuki leading her astray simply to escape. Fujita remained vigilant.

"Well, it could be that if the two pieces of cloth were brought together, the tear in them would match half and half."

"There's no way you could know that Suzuki," Fujita said in obvious disbelief. Suzuki, having gone rogue, changed the tenor of their meeting. Usually, Fujita would have referred to her as *sempai* or my senior, one with greater experience and hence status, but that was thrown aside because of Suzuki breaking protocol and her conflict with the Clan. She was conflicted now, as at the same time the crack that had started grew, letting in new light on her world.

"Fujita, it is amazing news, I know." Suzuki realized that this revelation went against their formerly common beliefs.

"Yes, I find that our collective pause is making the ground shift beneath me," Fujita said as she grew quiet.

Suzuki let Fujita know that this was hard for her, too. She was still reeling from the revelation, which had not so far fully settled in her being. She'd come ready to gather Fujita for personal protection and now found herself trying to figure out who was being convinced of what. She was gradually coming to believe that Jimmy and Bernd needed their—*her*—protection, not disdain.

"Let's go over this again. What are we saying?" Both were stunned into silence for a short pause. Suzuki began again as if in a daze.

"Fujita, this is horrible. I think the reality is that my great grandfather changed, and the note written even as he knew he was about to die, perhaps because he was about to die, was supposed to let us know that. If what seems to be revealed in the other part of the note, the other half, proves that, then, that damned Shinto priest has really been the one responsible for the continuation of our beloved Clan. And whether he knew it or not—it was against my great grandfather's intentions. It seems that the truth may have died with Great Grandfather if it weren't for the note found in the scabbard recently."

Fujita softened a little more. "Wait, Sempai. Perhaps the Shinto priest didn't see both halves."

"Well, what is apparent is that he must have taken only half of the note, the one used to further the Samurai Clan development on Shikoku. And call me Suzuki. I want to make changes in my life, but I am still figuring out how. Besides, I like my name." Fujita nodded in agreement.

"He may have wrongly thought that it was the entire note written quickly by a dying man," Fujita said.

"Yes, I think so, too. Perhaps Great Grandfather tried to hide it in the scabbard, and it was cut by the short sword. I'm only guessing, but the Shinto priest obviously was able to obtain the other half of the note from Great Grandfather. Based on what I saw, even inspecting the inside of the scabbard, the priest could have overlooked the part of the note that remained in there all those years." Suzuki continued, "According to this note, recovered from my ancestral home, my great grandfather was even glad that he'd lost his regular sword, so he wouldn't use it on anyone else, a realization coming about as he was lying on his deathbed. I still can't believe it, but to tell you the truth, I always had a background concern over him killing a religious man. And then there's the thread that was hanging from the scabbard. I got into so much trouble when I pulled that off the scabbard as a junior high student, let alone picking it up as a child. No one was allowed to *touch* the sacred item. It sat unmolested all those years."

"Suzuki, remember that Buddhism is a phony, foreign religion. What difference does it make if the man he killed pretended that it somehow could have been a real religion? It's still all fake, unlike Shinto, the way of the gods."

"That's exactly the point. My great grandfather wanted to uphold the honor of Japan until his death, but he didn't condone any and all violence against things foreign, and he increasingly seemed to be cured of that way of thinking. He'd gotten—"

"Softer with age," Fujita said, trying to make sense of it all.

"No, his sense of justice changed. At least, that is what I believe when I put the two notes together and stop ignoring my experience, especially with the two *dumb foreigners*." She read the note aloud to Fujita.

Fujita found all of this to be utterly fantastic, and she was clawing for anything to hold on to, anything that made sense of her heretofore sacredly held beliefs. "This doesn't make sense. Think of how our samurai heritage in our lineage has been handed down person to person. And, above you, that bag is about to break. Why should I not light you on fire? I'm not sure I care what you believe. You, too, have gone all soft as far as I can tell." Fujita's resolve still seemed aligned with the Samurai Clan.

There was a sudden shift in Suzuki. She next said what she heard in her mind as Jimmy's voice, what he might say. "Because lighting me on fire is not what will purify Japan." Suzuki was firm and was growing calmer, too. Was it a feeling associated with being compassionate? It was a new feeling, and although fleeting, it felt good.

"So, you want to find a kinder and gentler way to make Japan great again?" Fujita yelled. Both were going back and forth, looking for a place to metaphorically stand as the ground seemed to be shaking under them.

"I think that finding a way to promote the real brilliance of Japan is what will make a difference, not getting rid of all things that are perceived as *not Japanese*. Especially in the modern world." Continuing, Suzuki implored, "Give me a chance to make the case!" A drop of kerosene broke out of the bag and fell onto Suzuki's cheek. Out of habit from training for this moment all her life, Fujita reached for her lighter. She was totally focused. Suzuki remembered that Fujita was the most dedicated trainee of their group, next to herself. She had no doubt that Fujita would follow through on what she threatened to do if she had any reason to doubt Suzuki's story.

With Suzuki noticing the increasing smell of kerosene as more drops fell on her, the look of concern on her face was something Fujita was seeing for the first time. Something inside of her melted, and the connection between the two, albeit unstated, grew deeper. Both exchanged a knowing look and stopped any and all things they were doing as if suspended in air. There was nothing to say. They both realized in that instant, in part because of Jimmy's humane compassion, a mother's human love, and yes, the love and compassion of being friends, that they had been living a lie.

Neither one had the courage to confirm this understanding out loud. Because of the intensity with which each of the two women took to training, this was indeed a bitter pill to swallow.

"So, what do we do? Suzuki, I am, for the first time, in conflict about this. You were my idol."

"I know, Fujita. Me too. You know, I still admire you, and I definitely still love the Japan I have come to admire. That will never change—and there is no need for it to change."

Fujita looked up at the bag, and as she touched the lighter in her pocket, she blew out a breath of exasperation. She couldn't hold on to hate. Loosening its grip on her, even a little, made her feel better. A welling up of disbelief put her back on her heels, if only for an instant, as relief filled its place. She said weakly, "The modern world is leaving the beauty of Japan behind."

"Almost any place in the world could claim the loss of its culture, its *beauty*, as a victim of the modern world." While Fujita was too stunned to do more, she didn't untie Suzuki, but she took down the kerosene bag. It was time to talk this out. Both women were intense, intent, and in concord about getting to the bottom of this. The two of them discussed how the fear of loss makes anyone, indeed could make any *nation* cling to and glorify its past and wish to stop change of any kind.

"One thing I do know is that the two men are in trouble."

"One thing at a time. I need to understand more before I can risk *helping* you."

"Fujita, you know what the additional note says—"

"Hold it. Once again, tell me, just how did *you* get that note? You claim that it is from your great grandfather; however, I can't believe it existed without being uncovered all this time. Are you sure it isn't a fake?"

"Well, it's not that amazing and not likely a fake. We found it in an unusual place. Again, it was in the scabbard of my great grandfather's sword, stuck against the side on the inside."

"Eh? You did mention something about the scabbard before." Unlike her normal self, she had grown flustered, and details were not as black and white as when she had been taking only her own perspective into account.

"It wasn't even far down, but being dirty and flattened along the side of the casing, we had a hard time finding it even though we were looking for it. Come to think of it, being stuck to the side of the scabbard may have been because of blood. Ah, if Great Grandfather cut himself while pushing it into the scabbard, it would explain why it didn't fall all the way into the scabbard."

"You're serious, aren't you? And who is we?"

"Let's talk about it first?" Suzuki figured if she mentioned a foreigner, it might be the end of the discussion. Fujita's face crunched up, but her respect, deep down inside for Suzuki came to the fore, and she waited to see what her superior trainer would say next. Her human side was resurfacing, now in battle with her past self, created by the "training."

"Go on." Fujita wanted all the information before she made a decision. This too, had been part of their training. She realized suddenly that there had been many times in which, try as she might, she was not acting on all the information. *Could one truly have all the information?* Fujita asked herself.

The training stressed being informed, but ironically, in retrospect they often seemed to act on the looks of things. If something even seemed as if it was foreign, it was suspect even without proof. Things perceived as foreign were condemned first, and questions were only asked later.

"Explicitly, the note found in the scabbard completes the note found on his dead body, the note divulged by the Shinto priest. The two parts together give a very different impression than either half, if read separately. The note found on his body claiming for him to want to "live for the glory of Japan" is different than the one I have that claims he wanted to make amends for what he'd done in his life."

"He what? He has always been my hero."

"I know. Mine, too. Fujita, we may need to rethink our view on what it means to purify Japan and who we regard as a hero."

"Maybe, but what does this mean?"

Suzuki felt that there was no gentle way to say it, and so she continued. "It looks like we, and all members of the Samurai Clan, have been living a lie," she said with finality. This was a statement of the understanding they had both come to but didn't want to admit. Suzuki, while on her own, had wanted to dismiss what the two notes said when put together, but the human side, as noted by Fujita, even against Fujita's wishes as a sworn Samurai Clan member, convinced Suzuki to stop stubbornly holding on to her view. Suzuki would come to terms with this realization a little at a time.

Suzuki recalled Jimmy's kindness to her even when it wasn't warranted. It could no longer be seen as foolish, but more and more she came to believe that, on the contrary, it was quite wise. She was at a loss for the first time in a long, long time. She summoned her training to maintain calm and continued.

"My great grandfather started something that lived beyond him but ran out of time to live his final beliefs. His legacy was, unfortunately, based only on the anger and decisions of his youth."

"And don't forget the false impression given by the Shinto priest, albeit likely caused by misunderstanding. What can we do?" Fujita asked.

"I don't know if there is time…" Suzuki broke off, worried that it was too late. "The foreigners I mentioned, by all evidence, are two innocent men who were only taking a pilgrimage along the Sikoku route. They are now at the compound in the mountains simply because they are foreigners."

Fujita realized the seriousness of the problem. The group had been itching to make an example of foreigners for a long time.

"We were already on edge before the two men escaped, causing increased tension among the group," Suzuki Said.

"Suzuki, we've no choice but to act, although I wonder what we can do. They're only two of us," Fujita said.

"If there is anyone you trust, like I trust you, Fujita, we can ask for their help, but we need to try and break those two out of the compound and get them off Shikoku. They are being interrogated by Umura, the elder. As you can imagine, even if they are still okay—we have very little time."

"I get it."

Suzuki managed a smile. "Then would you please untie me."

"Of course," Fujita said, apologetically. Suzuki looked somewhat shaken. Fujita offered a word of reconciliation, "*Gambarimasho* or We're in this together. We'll figure it out, but time is of the essence."

"That's right." As they moved toward the door, Suzuki rubbed her wrists and arms where she'd been tied. "We have to put together a plan on the way to the compound."

Chapter 24
NOTEWORTHY MENTION

Several days later, after the give-and-take cat-and-mouse with Umura, Jimmy felt some movement in the floor below him. *What could it be?* A small note popped up through a crack made by elevating the tatami reed mat a little in the floor, something easily done since the mats are held in place only by their weight, which isn't much. The note read, "Will try to break you out, but this won't be easy. Return after reading." Then a copy of the note from the scabbard was passed up, and whoever was there was gone, taking the first message with them. Of course, Jimmy believed it had been Suzuki or someone put up to it by Suzuki, but there was no way to know. Just like that, the person was gone, and quietly, too. It seemed that she was changed after all.

Jimmy was holding a copy of the note that had been hidden for more than one hundred years in the scabbard of Great Grandfather Suzuki's sword. The main issue with the note having been hidden for so long became understandable to Bernd and Jimmy. He did not continue promoting a purge of foreigners in Japan all his life as was believed by his disciples. The note Jimmy held was in contrast to the one the Shinto priest used to promote the Samurai Clan so long ago.

The note, in conjunction with the message in the one found on his body and spread by the Shinto priest, demonstrated that either one of them alone was insufficient in explaining whether Mr. Suzuki's motives changed, remained unchanged, or otherwise. A fitful period of sleep, the two men waking now and then to try and figure out what to say, reluctantly brought the next morning. After a small breakfast, the interviewer started all over again for the third day.

"Get them out here!" The old man seemed grumpier than any of the previous days. This back-and-forth had been an obvious attempt by the Clan to wear the two foreigners down. *What was the reason for not killing us outright?* Jimmy wondered.

Jimmy confirmed what Bernd thought when he said, "The wearing us down is working." They had no way of knowing that the previous evening, Umura had met both his trusted advisors and had drank considerable amounts of *sake,* rice wine. He had not only told his men to be careful time and time again but also found the advisors to be persuasive. They wanted him to kill the foreigners outright and burn their bodies in a ceremonial manner, reminiscent of how the old Shinto rites would have it done, at least according to what had been instructed by *Suzuki's master* following the traditions from earlier in the Tokugawa period. The methods had come down to the current Clan members through word-of-mouth teachings in their lineage since the nineteenth century. The rituals emphasized the exceptional nature of Japan while diminishing that of foreign influence, especially highlighting *sakoku* — the exclusion of foreigners from Japan in the Tokugawa Period. Suzuki, however, because of his run in with the Christian samurai, was in life purported to be more extreme than even his master, resulting in the bloodlust in front of the two foreign men in the present day.

Roughly, and with an air of contempt, the guards pulled Jimmy and Bernd to their feet, mockingly saying "Get up," only after their arms had been nearly separated from their sockets, causing obvious tortured amusement for the other guards.

Jimmy winced while in the grip of one man but prayed for him nonetheless, realizing that his karma was linked to the man's, like it or not. He'd need to keep his wits about him either way, since he was most certainly to be tested again by the elder, as had been the format on the previous days. Thus far, it seemed, Jimmy had passed all the tests. His knowledge and experience in Japan had saved him each time. On one of the days, he'd been made to drink sake a second time in the morning. His unperturbed state was questioned, with him responding once more that *sake* "tied one to the gods," as his friend Akio had told him in Kyoto while conversing about trips to Shinto Shrines on New Year's Eve. He was so grateful for that friendship, which certainly had positively impacted Saori's integration.

Being compassionate toward all, Jimmy believed, could mean the difference between them both getting out of there or not. He prayed that Suzuki, the woman, would be able to return to somehow save them, perhaps with reinforcements—and he realized it could possibly have been only her working alone who passed the note through the floor.

Still, it seemed like a long shot, as deep as they were into the mountains. Jimmy did not feel that he could count on anything and increasingly matched his calm state to the intentional state building in him to be fully self-reliant in relation to others.

Jimmy thought more about the challenge to escape. Not only was travel hard on the steep slopes, but the Samurai Clan members would have guarded the place very carefully, as it seemed to be a kind of headquarters or base—and their escape a second time would not only put the entire Clan at risk but be a terrible embarrassment to them. He realized how good his karma must be, since he thought it was related, in part, to the good fortune that allowed for their previous escape. Now it was time to be fully present here and now. Counting on karma did not seem like a good idea.

"*Isoge!*" or hurry up! The elder was growing more impatient, if that were possible. When Bernd realized the elder's bad mood didn't bode well for their chances, he started to figure the odds of their getting out of there alive—and stopped quickly since the odds were depressingly low.

With no time to lament the humid summer weather, nor enjoy the nature that surrounded the compound, they were ushered out the door, half-pushed, half-dragged, to a place where they were made to kneel in front of the elder. It was the elder's turn to wipe the sleep out of his eyes. He was tired from the late-night debate over what to do with the foreigners, and he looked slightly hungover. However, his calmness was also apparent. He firmly held the leadership of this group, giving him a strong sense of presence. Jimmy wondered, *What has he done to gain such complete respect from this group, to hold such firm control over them?* His power over Jimmy and Bernd, through his influence over the group, was evident.

The elder's control over the group had several aspects to it. True, in a Confucian society, he was honored for being an older member of the group, even if he didn't want to acknowledge that *foreign* influence originated from China. It was more important that he'd undergone harsh training under the student of the "Master" who carried out that legacy. In fact, he was the last remaining member of a select group who had trained under the Master's lead student who was himself a master of their lineage. Others had not even met the master's student, being far younger than Umura.

Even now at his advanced age, he could stay up longer than most others without sleep and could do various tasks that required perseverance and strength that impressed even hale-and-hearty young men. Perhaps because of his martial arts practice, Jimmy had noticed the sinewy arms on the man, his apparent strength despite his age. He could only imagine the kinds of training he'd undergone in his life. Jimmy was among those who were impressed.

"So, you guys come to Japan with your crazy ideas of internationalism, is that it?" For some reason, he seemed to address this question to Bernd.

"Ah," Jimmy tried to answer but was pushed over backwards in one quick thrust that seemed to have come out of nowhere. Obviously, the man wanted to hear from Bernd before deciding what to do with them. It seemed that the previous days had been Jimmy's turn, and today was no longer his time for explaining.

"Out of respect for learning…" Bernd began, but didn't get far before the elder cut him off.

"Learning from books?"

"Well, yes."

The elder continued, "Then, I am stupid and foolish, according to your way of reckoning. I went to school to learn only the basics, believing that life in Japan, *real attendance in life,* was all that mattered for one to get the most out of life."

Jimmy took note. The Taoists were the same way, relying on experience over things learned from books; however, unlike the Samurai Clan, they didn't avoid books; they just didn't rely on them.

Umura, the elder, continued, "These days, the youth make such a big deal out of learning, but they can't even use a *soroban* or abacus. They're pitiful, and I think you most likely pity me, but I am the leader of this Clan precisely because of my ignorance of book knowledge. I took the time to tune my body and mind in other ways. That makes who the fool, eh?"

"No one is calling anyone a fool," Bernd managed to interject, at least trying to feign calm.

"So, which of you would like to challenge an old man to a fight?"

Jimmy and Bernd quickly looked back and forth at each other, and then the elder broke out in laughter. "I'm only messing with you. I'll let someone else take care of you. I've already had my share of purifying Japan." He continued to laugh as Jimmy visibly shrunk hearing these statements, making the members present think once again of his weakness as a foreigner—but they didn't recognize the compassion involved in his manner. He was concerned for all and especially the elder at that moment. He'd been taught that if you insult, you will be insulted; if you harm, you will meet one who will harm you. Jimmy took this literally at first, and then realized it could mean that in the future, you would reap what you sowed, not so different from what his Lutheran friend in Minnesota told him from the statement in Galatians Chapter Six in the Bible.

The elder got down to business. "So, what is your *real* purpose here in Japan? Whenever foreigners come to Japan, it has always been to take for their own advantage." He'd been holding this question back, thinking he'd have them answer it prior to their death. He needed to understand his enemy's intentions and motives. He was confirmed in his view that they were dangerous and had to be eliminated, although he realized they were still to be interrogated because of Jimmy's composure in the earlier interview.

This time, the elder looked squarely at Jimmy, as if he was daring him to come up with an adequate response—and was at the same time filled with the confidence that Jimmy couldn't respond in any way that would change their fate.

Jimmy prepared to respond. In his renewed sense of nervousness, it took time, but the note from the scabbard finally surfaced in his consciousness. "You know, sometimes things can change. Not all things seem as they might. Not all people stay who they were as a youth, and you yourself are a specimen of wonder it seems, since your youth."

"What? Are you mocking me? Trying to butter me up?"

"Not at all," Jimmy quickly and calmly replied, once again begrudgingly gaining the respect of the man and those nearby but by no means everyone. Some thought him ridiculous, no matter what he said or did. Jimmy went on.

"I honor that Mr. Suzuki grew as a person from his experiences, much as you have secured your strength of character with age." He could see the man was interested but also perturbed, so he hurriedly added, "Suzuki grew to regret some of his actions made in his life."

"How dare you talk of Suzuki. How dare you make any claims about him."

"Well, it is Suzuki who is talking, not me."

"*Nani!*" or What! the man shouted in angry disbelief. To this, Jimmy had to breathe first and then respond calmly for the most part, but now a little on edge. He revealed the note he had in his possession, the copy Suzuki had given him of Great Grandfather Suzuki's musings. After that, he quickly related what Saori had told him. He was careful not to divulge how he'd gotten either piece of information. Everyone stopped to think.

Naturally, this roused questions in the elder as to the authenticity, and whether to believe Jimmy's fantastic claims, even if he'd initially dismissed them outright. No matter how emphatically, calmly, or otherwise Jimmy made his claims, it all came to nothing. The elder wasn't buying the story Jimmy gave when pushed to admit how he'd come across the note—the place on Mount Kōya where Jimmy had held what he now believed was Suzuki's sword in his hands. Umura had lived too long under the belief that Suzuki had died *hating all things foreign*, which was felt to be the logical counterpart to the intense love of Japan that Suzuki felt and demonstrated. This, Umura believed, was a ploy, a last-ditch effort to gain the two men's safety. No way could they have known Suzuki as he knew of him. Umura ruminated in his thoughts for a moment:

I have the note from Suzuki. It was bequeathed to my family by the Shinto priest who was with him when he died. It is on our kamidana, our shrine to the gods within our home. He stopped short, thinking to himself, *It has a cut in it; could it be half of a note as this one has been described? Eh, what does this mean?* He was deep in thought about how to explain his own knowledge of Suzuki, which he firmly believed up to now superseded any other persons.

The elder believed Suzuki's love of homeland was equally as strong as his own. Jimmy sensed to remain quiet, hoping to have a chance to explain further in another meeting perhaps the next day, but as the moments went on, he became increasingly concerned that there would be no further opportunities. He realized that things had gotten worse rather than better as each day became the next. At present, things looked quite bleak. So, plucking up his courage, he gave it one last try.

"Thank you so much for taking the time to meet with me, I mean us." Jimmy drew from his experience in Japan to thank anyone, even a hostile enemy, for his time. He was also thinking compassionately about how fully and firmly Umura believed what he believed, right or wrong.

Jimmy's statement, an accurate and culturally poignant display of good manners made the elder pause for some time, and then, after more questioning, purposefully meant to present Japan as superior to all else, Jimmy and Bernd were again ushered back to their makeshift prison as the Clan members converged to discuss the import of the "supposed" note from Suzuki. Umura was stirred, but not moved.

That afternoon, Jimmy continued with one of the first meditation practices he'd been introduced to, *Chenrezi*, the deity of compassion, a common practice among those of Tibetan or Vajrayana lineages. It called to him on many levels: on behalf of Suzki, the woman, the Samrai Clan, and the world, and it even included his quest for being in a relationship.

Jimmy imagined himself and all people being mutually compassionate. He wasn't sure that it would improve his situation, but it most certainly made him feel better, as he hoped his caring would somehow impact the elder and the members of this group, even if only in a small way, and even if he and Bernd were harmed by the group. Bernd sighed, looking around the lattice-lined building, seeing bamboo here and there. No way out was coming to him, but he thought, *there must be a way*.

Jimmy continued the mantra. Truly, it seemed like the world's existence depended on the spreading of compassionate thoughts, words, and deeds.

Bernd didn't give up. He continued to devise ways of escaping their prison, only to find each time, each scenario would fail. For example, climbing the central pole to be out of sight would create a stir but get them no closer to being on the move and, even if on the move, likely to be dead soon. Calculations were made from his looking around the compound, its several bamboo buildings with thatched roofs. It seemed that the Clan favored these, considering modern buildings to be a foreign incursion. That people had been positioned on either side of the only entrance, the lone door he'd worn the ropes away on their last stay, reinforced the sense of hopelessness. As for the door, the ropes had not only been replaced but also strengthened. He continued to find fault in any plan he concocted.

Afternoon brought a small meal, almost insulting in its simplicity: rice and miso soup. Once again, it was emphasized that this was the food given to the Japanese by the gods. Jimmy smiled sardonically as he hoped that the Japanese didn't have to put up with it in such meager amounts.

In the evening, all they could do was to wait and hope that Suzuki or someone would arrive—and she or someone would be able to help. Jimmy began to meditate by following his breathing in and out, hoping to have an insight as to what their next action should be. He settled into the meditation fairly easily, considering how bad of a predicament they were in. He wondered: *How is Suzuki faring? Better than us, I hope.*

Chapter 25
ONE LAST CHANCE

Jimmy relaxed further into meditation and, after some minutes, had an insight. As he and Bernd were walking back to the cell, Jimmy had seen out of the corner of his eye Clan members practicing their strokes, parries, and stabs with *bokuto* or wooden swords. While meditating, he recalled the mental practice he'd done many times in his classroom. If anyone were to enter his room uninvited, intent on causing harm to his students, many times he'd rehearsed in his mind an approach to incapacitate them, related to his very real practice previously in aikido. His own *bokuto* was in the classroom closet and, if there were time to take it out, he'd be able in three strokes to take down or at least disarm an intruder. He hoped that this would never be necessary. Bernd shrugged when Jimmy told him this, mentioning that it didn't really matter—if they never got out of there.

A few moments later, Jimmy nudged Bernd, made eye contact, and urged him to look that way, but he was unsure Bernd understood what he was relaying. He'd have to clarify it in any brief opportunity when they could talk. Keeping his voice low, he began.

"Bernd, I know a little about using a wooden sword."

"Oh, I see. You were pointing out the practice area."

"Right. If only I could get my hands on one of the swords."

"I'm sure you could get us both killed. Jimmy, that's foolish. They have real swords."

"Of course, Bernd, but hear me out."

"Okay," Bernd said, like an unwilling participant in a tragic comedy.

"With only several people nearby, as in right outside the door to this cell, I may be able to incapacitate them long enough for us to run. It might not be a good plan, but if all else fails, I'll give it a try. I'm starting to feel a little desperate."

"Me too, Jimmy. I hope someone can find us soon. My organization won't give up." The guard decided they'd been talking too long, so he let them know this by the simple statement, "*Damare!*" "Shut up."

The guard then thought better of it and added smugly, "Get some sleep, guys. Tomorrow will be here soon, and you'll need rest. First, there will be a solemn time for prayer, and then it's your big day." This sounded ominous and was obviously intended to scare them, and it succeeded for a while until exhaustion took over, and both nodded off for an untold amount of time. Jimmy began dreaming:

He was outside the cell and had one of the practice swords. For the purpose of ridiculing him, they handed him the wooden sword to fend off their metal swords and then surrounded him. Of course, they believed that he didn't have a chance, and this was likely to be proven true.

Jimmy recalled all this when he woke up. The floor had moved again, causing him to wake up. Jimmy wasn't sure how long he'd been sleeping but felt somewhat rested. Suzuki was back with Fujita and a saw. After nearly a half hour of talking, they'd convinced Kinoshita to look out for them, but they were risking their lives the entire time they were in the compound. Jimmy found out later—per protocol, traitors would be hacked up and burned within minutes of being found out.

Jimmy feigned snoring, and the guards, probably thinking he needed to sleep before the morning's ordeal, seemed to smirk and think "weak foreigner" and go back to their watch. He took everything in while feigning sleep. Kameno, Suzuki and Fujita's man on the inside, had offered the two guards a dice game, which they'd begun after checking to see if the door remained securely fastened. This kept the two guards outside for the game. Kinoshita remained on watch for both the Samurai Clan *and* the women.

The hole in the floor became large enough to get one's leg through. Jimmy woke Bernd and after ensuring his silence, pointed out what was happening. They prepared themselves to move quickly.

Several minutes later, they slipped below the hut and moved along the corridor made by Suzuki several days earlier; then they got down on their stomachs and slipped out from underneath the building. As the guards turned to see they were gone, they then started to make a commotion. As planned, Kinoshita slipped out of the camp in another direction. The plan was to meet by the gnarled cedar tree at the base of the slope to the west of the compound. In the pretext of being the first one to go after them, after telling the others to secure the opposite direction, Kameno, one of their guards who had become part of the escape plan after clandestine contact from Ms. Suzuki, bolted out of the camp with full knowledge of the plan and where to meet.

All moved as quickly as they could, but Jimmy wasn't his usual nimble self since he was hungry, thirsty, and tired from the several days they'd spent in the compound cell. He was also mentally exhausted from the question-and-answer sessions. As they neared the cedar tree and the rendezvous with Kinoshita, they saw that he'd been captured along with Kameno behind them. Jimmy's group, too, were captured upon arrival at the cedar tree. The breeze, welcome after the stay in the small structure, lacked the usual characteristic of being refreshing. While Jimmy was initially grateful that the noise of the wind covered their movements, that cover had not been enough.

The plan had two fatal flaws. The lookout had noticed Suzuki, though didn't know who she was, as she was leaving the camp several days earlier. Also, there had been a human perimeter wall of Samurai Clan members posted just for this purpose. They didn't want to risk these two foreigners escaping once again.

All the captives were bound together one after another, and the delegation of Samurai Clan members led them up the narrow path to the compound. They walked right up to the area where he'd seen people practicing swordsmanship as the sunlight spilled over the horizon, causing Jimmy to squint. From his dream, Jimmy recognized his position, compared to those guarding him. He grew silent and started to breathe intentionally, moving ever so slightly to warm up his muscles, should he need to move quickly. He observed in semi-shock and semi-disbelief:

They untied him and *handed him a wooden sword*. He started to shake at first but then asked his mind to be calm with surprising success, considering the situation. His breathing slowed as meditative equipoise took over. The six of them were surrounded by five guards with real metal samurai swords. It looked like they were about to make an example out of Jimmy, just as in his dream.

Chapter 26
LUCK RUNS OUT

The five guards began to raise their swords, and as he was taught in *aikido*, Jimmy took the opportunity to enter his opponent's space, that of the man standing nearest him. This drew the others' attention as he poked the guy in the ribs, making him drop rather than complete the task of raising his sword. The element of surprise would hold for only a short moment, so he pushed through and began to run just after throwing the wooden sword to Suzuki.

"Traitor!" one yelled, but she held to her training and struck, crouched, and took out another one. Now there was room for them all to run. She'd gotten untied by using the anticipated swing of one of them to cut her free from the group. Disarming a fourth, she didn't bother to look back. The fifth, a soldier, was after them. She'd hoped he might follow. This, too, was part of her training.

After cresting the hill, she stepped to the side, and his eyes went to her while the wooden sword knocked him on the head. She'd always been the top of any of their group when it came to striking, staying calm under fire, and incapacitating an opponent. She made up with speed and skill what she lacked in size. Using the sword dropped by the fifth man, she cut the others free, but their troubles were far from over.

They got down to the cedar tree, collecting the stored materials that had been hidden just beyond it. Her sword had been among them, but her scabbard was missing. It looked like someone had picked up the scabbard but had not taken the time to go back and pick up the sword or didn't notice the missing item while they were leading the group back to the compound.

The sword had been a gift from her father, the one he'd used to train with the Japanese army. Her father had received it from Great Grandfather Suzuki. The Japanese army's stories from World War II had inspired her father to wield it wisely. Proud of his own lineage, he never lost his concentration—and pledged to never use it on civilians. In fact, he said, if that had been the case, he would not have given it to her. He would have been too *ashamed* to do so. She hadn't dared to take it into the camp, preferring that it be lost and rusted rather than having it be captured by the group that she no longer believed had as honorable a sense of justice as she once thought. The stories from her father's past suddenly filled her mind with awe. It was too bad that he'd died suddenly in his sleep several years earlier. He'd bequeathed the sword to her when he knew he was dying. Current needs brought her back to the present.

Leaving the cedar tree rendezvous spot, the fugitives split up into two groups of three. One of the women and men and one of the foreigners in each group. They were to meet at a spot that only Fujita and Suzuki knew. It was about a mile away. Little did they know that one of the Samurai Clan members was still following them. He was the outermost lookout, stationed just outside the perimeter. Unbeknownst to the renegade group, he had signaled, and others were on the way. They were especially after Suzuki's group. The blame for this entire fiasco would be placed on her.

Before they got to camp, they paused for a rest and something to drink. Jimmy, who was with Suzuki's group, wanted to push on to the camp, but she insisted that he eat something.

After about five minutes, the light reflecting off swords revealed they were surrounded by four Samurai Clan members. Additional Clan members had scooped up the other group in an instant in their dragnet operation.

Suzuki was flushed with anger but not surprised. She may have thought they had gotten away but remembered that being pursued was the normal protocol. Still, she thought it would take longer for them to catch up.

Kinoshita moved to pull out his sword but was cut down before he could unsheathe it. The others didn't move and mostly avoided breathing.

"Suzuki, you've gone mad," their leader insisted.

"Well, yes, but it is not in the way that you *think* I am crazy." Calmly, she shared with him a copy of the note from her great grandfather that she'd hastily made with Fujita before they set out. It was one of several for just this occasion, if they were caught.

"You're insolent."

"Maybe, but have you read that?"

"*Damare*—Shut up," he demanded. She nodded and urged him with her eyes to read it. The only thing keeping her alive was that the honor of the group had been tarnished. As a result, she'd have to be publicly humiliated in the middle of the compound to get the group's honor back.

"Eh, what is this?" he demanded again.

"It is a copy of a note my great grandfather wrote. It seems…"

"*Damare!*" This was too much for him to take in so quickly. He'd have to think it over while they walked back to the compound. Too much, too soon. *This is very strange. I know Suzuki,* he thought. *Her suddenly becoming rogue and insolent isn't like her. It only makes sense if what I just read is true. No wonder she's having second thoughts. Oh, I can't believe it.*

"I have my orders. Now walk up the path back to the compound. Suzuki, you know the way," he added with a touch of sarcasm. *I must follow orders, it's the only way*, he told himself.

The other group of Fujita, Bernd, and Kameno was brought alongside Suzuki's group by several Samurai Clan members who'd tied them all together.

The man scowled and said, "Any funny business and you all die. That, too, is part of my orders."

"I understand," Suzuki quickly said while looking to Fujita. Unfortunately, as far as Jimmy could tell, Fujita seemed to have no further ideas. Likely she would be killed for being an accomplice to Suzuki's unforgiveable behavior. Kameno tried to break to the left to get the sword of the man near him, but this time the element of surprise didn't work. He was stabbed in the stomach much like *hara kiri*—the samurai way of suicide. Bravely, he fell to the ground with a thud, and little sound came from him as he expired. They were all made to head back toward the compound, and because they had gotten farther away this time, it would take longer to get there. This set Bernd to thinking.

Bernd looked up to the trees, and Jimmy's eyes followed, both being on the same page. Jimmy wondered if the ropes they were tied up in would be of any use if they wrapped up someone to a tree by all of them running around a tree or two. He got this message to Bernd just as they had to go around two trees like those that had given him the idea. They inched nearer the compound; all the prisoners were tied together in one long rope. The verbal taunts were along the lines of taking a dog home on a leash and the like. Suzuki watched the others for a clue of any plan. Unlike her normal self, she had none.

Fujita caught Bernd's eye, and Bernd looked on both sides of the tree ahead of him and then at the rope. Fujita's nod was barely perceptible. Bernd hoped that she understood his plan. Fujita nodded to Suzkui and moved her head right and left.

How could this work? Jimmy thought with growing concern. It wasn't so straight-forward that anyone knew what to do or that they could coordinate. Bernd ran into Jimmy and started to argue. *Here we go*, Bernd thought. It did seem their only chance. They began to pretend to fight.

"It's your fault for dragging me on this stupid pilgrimage," Bernd said, starting an argument.

"Sure thing. Like you didn't bug me about going for the last three weeks, saying, We couldn't be on our way soon enough," Jimmy answered playing along.

"Shut up, you two."

Jimmy bowed deeply and moved to the right with Suzuki. Bernd and Fujita moved to the left. Jimmy feigned tripping and then wrapped the man he'd backed into around one of the trees. Suzuki grabbed his knife, cut the rope and used it to tie him up, all in a few seconds. It was stunning.

While the other guards were shocked into disbelief, Fujita and Bernd took the opportunity to wrap up the guard nearest them. The two others advanced. Suzuki was ready with her sword that she'd retrieved from the man who'd dared to touch it when he took it away from her. She unarmed one of them with expert technique, then parried with the other.

"You read the note. Let's talk," Suzuki said to the man leading the capture.

"Not a chance." The Clan member was obviously disgusted with her offer. He went to thrust and she blocked it, making him fall. He got up and raised his sword in an attempt to end this scuffle when the sound of officers calling out and hoisting their pistols stopped everyone in their tracks.

Hata emerged from the woods, and he and his men cuffed the one man and relieved the other guard of his weapon. "The rest of our party will crest the hill with men from my unit and the local police. I'm not sure we will catch all of them, but this will break up the Samurai Clan for the time being."

Suzkuki said, "How did you get here?"

"I followed *you*!"

Chapter 27

COMING TO TERMS WITH THE MODERN WORLD

Hata's troops had quite a scuffle with the Samurai Clan. The Clan had not seen the local police coming, and although they refused to use guns, they still fought hard to maintain the compound as the attack ensued. When it was all over, both sides had several losses. It took several hours until the compound was secured and a few days until the last few booby traps were discovered. Many Clan members escaped capture, causing concern about future reprisals; however, for now, the Samurai Clan was finished in the area. If it was possible at all, it would certainly take a long time to root them out and end their presence on the island. Hata had found a book of member names and group locations, which would aid in this endeavor. Fortunately, as Suzuki had confirmed, the Clan had not expanded beyond the island of Shikoku.

Hata explained how he had come upon the scene. He had decided to have Suzuki, and then Suzuki with Fujita, followed but at a distance. He'd used his best trackers, so he had an idea of where they might be going. He admitted that the two women had managed to lose his men several times because of Suzuki's honed skills. She was untraceable, but the trail was found because of the capture and being brought back to the compound prior to the dynamic escape. This was brought about, he now knew, by Jimmy's incapacitating one of the Samurai Clan with the wooden practice sword. He congratulated Jimmy, though Jimmy felt more relief than heroism. He hoped the others would be all right after their scare.

As for his two men who'd been taken out by members of the Clan, fortunately, the Clan thought the men were undercover police, not recognizing them as any kind of Secret Society members Hata told Bernd and Jimmy on the side. Bernd breathed a sigh of relief and exchanged a quick glance with Hata, who nodded slightly in return.

"Jimmy, I can tell you some permissible things about the Secret Society sometime, but for now, I'd like to focus on getting away from Shikoku," Bernd stated with sincerity.

"Bro, I am with you on that," Jimmy said with a smile. "There'll be time to swap stories later," Jimmy said, wondering how much he'd feel comfortable relaying about Saori, the Heian Period ghost.

Hata related to the group that the reason for coming out in force at the compound was his men had told him to be careful, something big was afoot. It had caused quite a stir when the front group of the search party reported seeing people scouring the countryside wearing swords. The local police did most of the work, as was fitting. The Secret Society seamlessly floated into the background of the whole matter—and Hata was the connection between both.

Bernd began breathing normally for the first time since the men were abducted a week earlier. Jimmy exchanged a high five and fist pump with Bernd, glad that they both made it through the ordeal, a good team if there ever was one. Jimmy maintained his state of calm and was grateful for it. He hoped all beings would be well and happy and was literally thrilled to think so, a chill running up his spine.

Next, Suzuki confirmed just how close the island had been to the precipice. "We were practicing our plan to move beyond Shikoku.

We'd been carefully planning it, a slow, painstaking process, for most of my life. Had to be slow to be undetected."

"Well done," Hata said. "We had absolutely no idea until the night of the maze." He explained further how he and his team had caught up with them.

"Eventually, I was personally involved, which happened as my men were closing in on the Samurai Clan. We often lost you and many others, not only because of your skills but also because I and my closest team hung back so far—not being sure whether you were in this for good or for bad." Bernd realized that he meant police officers who were also Secret Society members. Hata continued, "You know, if I hadn't stayed back so far, the Samurai Clan's multi-level protection plan would have scooped me up, too, I'm sure. As it was, they eliminated two of my best men who were the officers I sent out to meet you. They were killed and stuffed into a crevice in the mountains. If we hadn't found them, they would have been an eerie find for hikers at some point in the future. We found them only because of the tracing devices they were carrying. We went searching for them after we lost contact with them."

"Yah, the Samurai Clan is really professional," one of Hata's regular police officers mentioned and then stopped deep in thought. He followed up with, "I can't believe we've never heard of them until now." Hata nodded in agreement. Suzuki and Fujita exchanged looks and a high five.

"That was on purpose, of course," Suzuki said while Fujita smiled.

Bernd continued where Hata had left off, "That makes a lot of sense. So, since you hung back from us, it allowed you to scope out the place."

"Exactly. I was able to pick up the trail to follow you all back to the compound upon being captured. At that point, we had to fall back again to wait for reinforcements to arrive," Hata explained, and then addressed the two women. "What I don't understand is why you guys came back. Why did you defect from the Samurai Clan? It seems that loyalty to the Clan was nearly perfect and by the reactions the police have witnessed, remains so."

"It was," Fujita offered. "But the evidence led us to believe that we'd been living a lie. For someone with our training, once that message comes through, there's nothing else to do than to follow up and find out what the truth really is."

"What do you mean, *a lie*?" Hata's face scrunched up a little.

"Well, you see, my great grandfather is credited with founding the Samurai Clan, and I was the proudest member till only several days ago," Suzuki began to explain.

"What changed?"

"I still have mixed feelings about what we've found out. Unfortunately, my great grandfather, who has a legacy of being known for hating foreigners and anything foreign to Japan—likely did not, at the time he died, harbor those feelings. The problem was that almost no one knew that, and if anyone did, it would have been a Shinto priest who has long since passed, the secret dying with him, and even he likely did not correctly understand my great grandfather's dying wishes. As you can imagine, that jarring fact is very confusing for one who has taken the Samurai Clan's views to heart, such as myself. Things foreign were hated completely."

"Yes, that is what it seemed like when rounding up the Clan members," Hata confirmed. "They said some pretty awful things about having to take back our country, ridding it of foreigners, how the police got in the way of their work, and things like that."

"Well, we all believed that is what my great grandfather wanted as we carried on his legacy, but—" Suzuki choked up and couldn't go on. The recent shock was too raw, and the idea hadn't settled in yet. She walked out into the hall, turned around, and came back in to sit down and continue, noticeably distraught by what she'd found out about her great grandfather. Her strength of character shone in that moment.

"It seems that my great grandfather did hate all things foreign—or at least wanted to hold up the glory of Japan. And as Jimmy and Bernd accurately figured out, he did kill a Buddhist monk, along with his colleague killing another monk, but my great grandfather didn't die the way he lived. It seems likely that he would have wanted to change the Samurai Clan but died before he could do anything to make that happen. Another problem was that the Samurai Clan was already too far into the hype of purifying Japan so likely no one at the time, and perhaps even now, would have listened to him thinking that he had grown weak." She paused to collect her thoughts—and to collect herself.

"You did," Jimmy said encouragingly.

Jimmy instantly realized how important active compassion was. Talk was cheap, as was only thinking about being compassionate. He jumped in whole-heartedly. "Suzuki San, recognize that you have started, if not already completed, much of the change few people make even when trying hard to do so."

"No. I…"

"Don't sell yourself short. Your efforts as a human are beyond comparison. You've made strides most will never be able to achieve."

"But it was all for naught. For bad purposes."

"You really think so? Where are you now? Your humanity is intact. Besides, you're talking to two amazing foreign men. One who had the sense to get beyond his own culture and marry a Japanese woman. And the other is pretty cool himself." Jimmy had maintained a sense of humor through it all.

After a brief smile, Suzuki went on. "You may be right but—"

"No buts right now. Let it sink in."

All were silent for a while. Hata excused everyone for lunch. Suzuki insisted on eating alone; however, Fujita sat nearby as moral support, having been supported by Suzuki so many times before. As for Jimmy and Bernd, while eating lunch, they discussed the revelation about Great Grandfather Suzuki's colleague killing the apprentice monk as he ran out the back of the temple. Now it all finally made sense.

After lunch, Suzuki had pulled herself together enough to go on. "It was the last few lines of the note found in the scabbard that convinced us that he'd had a change of heart," *...I regret my misguided efforts and killing the monk, though done without my sword. I am glad now that I have no sword with which to commit more crimes. I must make amends, but how...?*

"Based on this, he likely would also have regretted his colleague killing the other monk on the steps of the temple building," Jimmy said.

"Makes sense," Bernd said, ever the logical one.

There was a pause, and then, Suzuki continued. "But there were two notes," she said still trying to make sense of everything.

"And what did the other note say?" Hata was enthralled. Suzuki was now in possession of them both, thanks to Jimmy writing down what Saori had told him she'd witnessed. She read from that note for Hata, for them all.

> *"It was a close call. I was stopped by the Christian. I vowed to make him pay if I was able to meet with him again. Alas, I did not. I wanted to go back to Mount Kōya, but after returning to Shikoku in one piece, I believed that it was a miracle. I lived for the glory of Japan ever after that."*

Fujita added clarification, "It seems evident that after he died, the Samurai Clan developed hyper-nationalism even more so than when he was alive. After all, the Clan during his lifetime, and this is true even in our time, wasn't and hasn't been organized enough to spread to Wakayama to kill the Christian samurai. Mr. Suzuki obviously feared the worst, being unable to reveal his change of heart to the Clan at his death. Too bad he died with the secret as his own."

"He did try to inform others through the notes, but the intervening of the conservative Shinto priest made them inaccessible until these two 'lazy' foreigners showed up." It seemed Suzuki was now developing a sense of humor.

"Hold on a moment." Hata had remembered something from the capture of the compound. He went away and returned with a copy of the note the police had found in Umura's belongings. Umura had retrieved the note to check for himself what was true, allowing the police to find it in his possessions.

"How did the Samurai Clan develop?" Hata inquired.

Suzuki replied, "The founders were followers of an ancient tradition, a mix of Shinto followers and martial arts specialists. Hence the training that was developed." Hata's look revealed a deep interest. "Briefly, I can tell you that Great Grandfather Suzuki himself had been taken under the wing of an extremely nationalistic Shinto priest."

"You mean that existed prior to the radicalizing force of Shinto in the build-up to World War II?" Hata said.

Suzuki said, "Definitely, although of course it must be hard to understand how we kept our Clan secret from all others." Bernd and Jimmy shared a knowing look but said nothing.

"In our case, it went something like this: the training was started only after the person demonstrated a strong love of Japan. For my great grandfather, that was through his proficiency with a sword, his commitment to the samurai tradition. Our family lineage is very, very old. Then the Samurai Clan pupil would undergo ancient austerities, practices that had become available to only a select few. For example, they would stand in waterfalls for hours, letting the water rush down upon them, or stay up practicing with wooden swords all night long. We are told there were various austerities, but recently less-severe practices have become the norm," Suzuki said, and Jimmy thought he detected a sense of nostalgia in her tone.

"Then you came along, Suzuki." It was Fujita joining in again, plainly enamored with her colleague's abilities. "Suzuki made us all look weak. She is truly blessed by the gods."

"Your *karma* seems good," Jimmy offered, intending to be supportive and positive, but the result was not what he'd anticipated. Suzuki seemed to shrink back on her sitting cushion. She breathed and then sat straight up once more.

"Sorry, Jimmy. We've been told to avoid talking in foreign terms for so long. It will take some time to get past that…aversion to anything foreign, such as concepts like *karma*." Having recovered, she added, "Thank you for your efforts. It seems your karma, uh, is pretty good yourself." He was growing to like her more and more, feeling they were kindred spirits, each striving to better his or herself. Looking around the group, Suzuki continued in the typical Japanese fashion of being humble.

"Oh, I am nothing special," she said and then looked away.

"I think all of us who have gone through this with you would disagree," Bernd offered while Jimmy and Fujita nodded in agreement. This was confirmed later by Hata when he made it a point to pause and bow respectfully in her direction just before they all left the precinct.

"I think I am very fortunate to have gotten out of the maze in one piece," Jimmy offered his review of their earlier bout in the maze.

"In the end, I am glad that I wasn't successful, but that is as they say a double-edged sword, a bittersweet understanding. Failure is unforgiveable in my lineage." Suzuki winced, having felt as if she'd failed then.

"You must accept both good and bad things," Jimmy said. "I learned that while studying about moving forward in life. After all, sometimes our best is far below what we may even consider acceptable. I have felt that way anyhow," he finished, trying to sound encouraging and non-judgmental at the same time.

"I'll try." The relief on Suzuki's face was evident. She obviously did not have much practice in cutting herself some slack. *We all could benefit from this way of thinking, being realistic with ourselves, in the twenty-first century*, Jimmy believed.

"I was coming over to help after downing the other man who was with you on my side of the maze, when that became unnecessary," Bernd said. Bernd was still trying to figure something out. "Who was that man who was with you?"

"His name is, ah, *was* Kinoshita. He was ready to leave the group, not as a coward, but to help Fujita and me rescue you both. He and I were a close team."

"Suzuki, you mean the man who…" Jimmy said.

"Yes, he is the Kinoshita who was killed in the scuffle."

"Wow, he underwent a transformation in a short period of time," Jimmy noted, stunned by the revelation.

"Jimmy, we all have. I was lucky that his loyalty to our duo was complete. It could have gone seriously wrong very quickly."

"After he tussled with Bernd, I thought he'd kill any foreigner he'd come in contact with."

"You know, Kinoshita was almost ninja like. From his hiding place in the rafters of the safehouse you were staying at, he observed you guys talking to Hata—in this very room—according to the description he'd given. We are all lucky that he didn't have a chance to divulge much. I guess he already felt he was in hot water for failing to overcome Bernd in the maze."

"How were you able to convince him?" Bernd asked.

"The same way you convinced me. I told him about your help after I'd rolled down the hill. It took a while, but first me, and then he came around in the end, though as you can tell the realization has come with some psychological pain."

"We are grateful for you," the two men replied almost in unison.

Suzuki said, "As for me, my head is in some ways still spinning, in no small way because of losing our colleagues, I mean, friends. You see, we were not allowed the luxury of calling each other friends in the Samurai Clan. It was—"

"Let me guess, part of the training."

"Right, Bernd." All smiled as their ability to summon humor was revived.

"It took me a lot of convincing, didn't it?" Fujita asked Suzuki with a sly look.

"Yah, my wrists still hurt from how you had me tied up." They joined hands, filled with joy that they were once more on the same team. "It is true joy to be together," Suzuki said. Jimmy almost spilled his coffee at this. It was one of the principles of Open Breeze, the meditation center to which he belonged.

"You've got that right," Jimmy noted encouragingly.

Jimmy and Bernd got up from the table, exchanged bows with the two women and the men, all shaking hands. After that, they split up into small groups for dinner. Suzuki and Fujita wanted some time alone to catch up. Jimmy and Bernd contacted family and friends after the recent enforced time away from the internet and phones. Hata needed rest after not sleeping for most of the past several days. The next morning, they got back together for breakfast.

"The training?" Hata wanted further explanation.

"Mr. Hata, that is for another time. Everyone here needs a rest from the story, and I am happy to stay in contact with you but really, *really* would like to leave Shikoku if only for a while," Jimmy implored.

As they sat down for a "morning set" of coffee, toast, and an egg, Hata called off the detectives who'd been assigned the overnight watch for these four people, told them to wait in the hall, wanting to be sure that extra help would be close. He told those watching the door and the perimeter of the building to remain. He wanted to allow the conversation to take place without more ears being present than necessary.

Sensing the connection of the group, Hata left them in conversation, sitting away from them but close enough to ensure their safety.

"What prompted Mr. Suzuki to be so aggressive against foreigners?" Jimmy had addressed his question to Suzuki but looked to both women. Suzuki took the lead.

"When he returned from Mount Kōya to Shikoku, after his close call with the Christian samurai, he wanted to work tirelessly for the glorification of Japan. He was angry about anything foreign, blaming things foreign for the loss of his sword—and any problems that Japan was experiencing as it met with the modern period. The other samurai on Mount Kōya, being Christian, really made him furious."

Fujita continued, "It was a bad time in Japan for our lineage. In the Meiji Restoration, the samurai were disbanded, and to him this was like tearing out the heart and soul of Japan. Since 1185, the samurai had been instrumental in the administration of Japan" (*Asia for Educators*).

"The violence and treachery of the Warring States Period is legendary," Bernd said.

Suzuki continued. "It is easy for me to acknowledge this now, having had a change of heart, but for him, he saw the Warring States Period as a necessary step on the way to the Tokugawa Period which, of course, was a time of relative stability in Japan. At least, that is what my father told me."

"Can you tell us more about your great grandfather? He sounds like a fascinating man," Jimmy said.

"He wanted to, as I have come to believe, gain for Japan what he considered was its rightful place in the world and purify it of foreign influence. He loved his country but perhaps, a little too much," Suzuki finished, looking distraught because of the shock of the truth, the losses, and the effort of the past few days.

Chapter 28
NEXT MOVES

"Hata already has a group of commandos surveilling the samurai compound," Fujita reminded everyone. "There's no way to get everyone, I suppose, but perhaps the police can get ahold of anyone who has come back to reconnoiter the place, find some clues, or snoop around. It will likely take time. The Samurai Clan is extremely resourceful."

"They are. Don't take them lightly, even for a moment. They still train very hard, even if it is not as intense as in the nineteenth century," Suzuki warned. "And there are branches all over Shikoku. Lucky for you, the Clan hadn't at this time launched the planned excursion onto the mainland—scheduled for next year and the years following."

"It seems like some of those plans may still happen," Bernd said.

"Probably. Many will be as shocked as I am that not only has the dream been delayed, if not ended, but their lives have been totally turned upside down. The energy to continue will be very strong," Fujita said, with Suzuki nodding.

Jimmy noted, "Not only is this true in extreme circumstances such as this—many people find it a challenge to give up their side of the story, even when it is apparent that they are wrong. Many of us are blinded by a perceived need to have it our way." He was expressing insights gained from the two teachers at Open Breeze over the years. Each year, the lessons resonated more and more deeply within him.

For the time being, he fell silent while the others continued to make sense of all that had happened. Finally, Jimmy said, "I'm grateful for becoming more compassionate. I've been fortunate to have received so many good teachings in my lifetime."

"I think we're all grateful for many things right now," said Bernd, to nods all around. Jimmy gave Bernd a hug, and Suzuki changed upon seeing this genuine behavior by the two men. Jimmy wondered how much his display of compassion had helped this change to come about.

"I'm glad that you two can show affection. We were told not to do that, even when not in public. It was one of our protocols. It was intended to keep the Clan tough and safe, and I now believe as a result, it has led to alienation more than anything else."

They all attended funeral services for Kinoshita and Kameno both men killed in the attempted escape were from the same small town. The families wondered why the foreigners were there but covered well any knowledge, if it existed, of the two men's nocturnal activities. To attend the funeral rites, Suzuki and Fujita agreed to be under heavy guard.

Hata said, "I can understand attending these funerals as they were so close to you when they perished; however, if you can manage, please avoid such public events for a while. It seems a miracle that you made it out of the service alive, based on what you've been saying, Ms. Suzuki." Hata was being extra careful, even though they were not in much danger, according to Suzuki and Fujita.

It was obvious that the Samurai Clan, because of their absence, was avoiding the services, as both men had fallen out of favor with the group, in addition to anticipated police presence. Suzuki wasn't positive, but she thought she saw the back of the man who led the Samurai Clan team who captured them the second time Jimmy's group was fleeing the compound that day. The team leader had gotten away as Hata and his men emerged from the woods. When he did that, he reminded

Suzuki of herself. She wondered if the note from her great grandfather, read to him prior to his parting, had made a difference for him. *Would he help get the word out, the truth about my great grandfather?* It was unlikely, but she held on to hope.

Suzuki and Fujita were held for trial along with the others but were given lighter sentences and parole since they agreed to help the Shikoku Police in convincing members of the Samurai Clan that Japan didn't need to purge itself of all foreign influence to be beautiful. Japan was inherently beautiful as it was. They would not only try to educate captured members of the Samurai Clan as to its founder's change of heart but also seek out other members to help them integrate back into society. Jimmy ensured that the latter would be a priority. His evening communication with Saori confirmed that, regardless of their separation, Saori believed her integration was a good thing. Jimmy was convinced more than ever that this was true.

Chapter 29
BYE FOR NOW

"I regret that I played a prominent part in the spreading and hysteria of the Samurai Clan. I've been such a fool taking after my great grandfather," Suzuki told those assembled: Jimmy, Bernd, Fujita, and Yuri, Bernd's wife, who'd come personally to pick up Bernd after his ordeal—Yuri wasn't taking any chances.

Fujita stepped forward. "Don't forget, Suzuki. Your great grandfather had come to realize that Japan is beautiful and that it hadn't lost any of its beauty. Japan's beauty only needs to be unveiled, not forced. That must live in you, too."

"Yes, it does, Fujita. Thank you. Like him, I think I will be happy to be rid of my sword. I think I know just the place for it."

"You're an amazing individual, Suzuki. Please keep going," Jimmy said with compassion and encouragement. After a brief silence, he continued. "You know, your great grandfather's sword was blessed by a Shinto priest to ensure that it would be used to uphold the beauty of Japan. It seems that even if it took a long time, the blessing is working. If I hadn't encountered it at Fukuchiin, then I wouldn't be here with you all having a deeper appreciation of Japan," Jimmy said.

"I'd hate to think what could have happened," Bernd added.

"But we *are* here," the women said in unison, demonstrating their collective wisdom.

Jimmy realized how much he had become attracted to and interested in Suzuki, something clearly beyond his *only being compassionate* with her. He really admired her intelligence and dedication to everything she did. As a woman, she was truly amazing.

When it came time to say goodbye, he pulled her aside and convinced her that she needed a hug, telling her that is what they did at Open Breeze. So, by the souvenir stand, which also served as a kiosk with newspapers, candies, soft drinks and sake, they shared their final farewells. Suzuki was flushed in a way she hadn't been expecting. Her brightly colored matching shirt and outfit was a nice change from the exclusively indigo garments she'd worn before. Much to Jimmy's liking and relief, she hugged him back, albeit awkwardly since it is not the Japanese custom. They also exchanged contact information.

The two shared a few uncomfortable attempts at kindness, in which Jimmy went for it by talking to a woman he was attracted to, and she deferred in a naturally Japanese way that she found intuitive, but not natural, since she was used to taking charge, striving to surpass others, and so on.

"Suzuki San, what is your first name?"

"Kaori," she said, blushing because someone was asking about her.

"That's a nice name. Perhaps you can come to Kyoto sometime, and we could meet up?"

"I like my world here on Shikoku…. Ah, you could visit?"

"Seems like a world away. Not sure if I want to come back anytime soon. This was a bit of a shock," Jimmy said awkwardly but sincerely.

"I understand. Perhaps, at least for now, we are too far apart in how we see the world."

"Perhaps."

Jimmy had tried and failed, but he felt really good. He looked forward to trying with another real woman again sometime. The calm he'd contacted during the ordeal at the compound remained with him, even if his stomach let him know he was a little nervous.

Together in the moment, they realized the cultural and societal chasm between them was too deep to traverse, at least so soon, so they parted. Suzuki was not fully in the present time, still subconsciously hating foreigners, and he was still getting use to the idea of dating—and her connection to the Clan made him uneasy.

Jimmy lovingly touched her hand in a way he'd never done before—and returned to simply being calm. Then, it was over, leaving an open space between them. Calm as he was, Jimmy had to hide the tear that flowed down his cheek. Suzuki held her emotions in check, a habit fully ingrained in her. Though they had exchanged contact information, neither thought that they'd get together anytime soon. Both settled uncomfortably into that understanding.

Jimmy realized the beauty of being attracted to a live human. While he did see her as physically attractive, he realized that Ms. Suzuki was appealing to him even more so for who she was, a dedicated, sincere, and determined human being.

Taking their leave of the two former Samurai Clan members, the three visitors prepared to leave Shikoku. Yuri smiled at being reunited with Bernd, which was undetected by the two men, each deep in thought about the ordeal they just went through.

"Shall we stop in at Temple Number Seventy-Five Zentsuji on the way off the island?" Yuri asked, having learned that Jimmy wanted to visit the place of Kobodaishi's birth.

"No way," both guys firmly said together. "We've had enough for now, Yuri," Bernd added. "Any other traveling or exploring of Shikoku will have to happen some other time." Jimmy nodded in agreement. She nodded in understanding but, being an avid explorer, couldn't help but feel a little let down. Yuri had not been to Shikoku since her middle-school class took a trip there.

Prior to leaving, Jimmy prayed at the temple nearest to where he and Suzuki parted. He wished her a long life and all the best, good health, and so on; then he was taken aback. He'd totally forgotten until then—it was the temple and him praying at it, the very image of his dream barely one week into this several-week journey. It felt like a lifetime ago.

After a short trip across the sea—as they got off the ferry in Wakayama City prior to making the trip to their respective homes on Honshu, the largest island of Japan—Jimmy noticed the usual looks from the Japanese, a mix of curiosity and wonder at foreigners, perhaps wondering why they were there. This was more poignant than before after the harrowing experiences on Shikoku, and Jimmy realized the looks were surely benign, the average Japanese person more interested than anything else. Any concern was simply his conditioned patterns projected onto the present moment, backed up by the recent experience and only *a feeling*. Jimmy was grateful at what seemed like an increased ease at dropping the pattern, thinking, *I feel confident and mentally strong as a result of this pilgrimage, which turned out to be quite a unique journey.* And then he was off to catch the trains back to Kyoto.

Chapter 30
SEVERAL DAYS LATER

Suzuki returned her great grandfather's red-and-orange scabbard to its new resting place above the shrine in her mother's home. Since she had no brothers, she'd be the one to inherit the home someday. The scabbard seemed heavier than the few times she'd held it, but that only made her laugh because the reason was so obvious. Her own sword hilt sparkled as the two rested together in a union of the nineteenth and twentieth centuries and because of her prayer for the benefit of all in Japan, the twenty-first century. She was impressed with how well the sword and scabbard fit together—as if made for each other. Was it the intervention of the gods?

Suzuki turned around on the tatami-woven reed-mat floor, walked past the *tokonoma,* the alcove that held the new scroll she'd purchased at the marketplace—it read "*Ichi go; Ichi e,*" meaning each meeting is a once in a lifetime meeting—and moved to leave the ancestral house on her way to her own home, her own life, and her renewed purpose in life. Suzuki would actively strive to recognize not only the beauty of Japan but also the beauty in all things. She was up to it. It would be her new training. It was wide open to her, whatever it would become.

Suzuki was grateful that Jimmy had saved her with his compassion. She knew they could not be together, being so far apart intellectually at this time, but she also knew that she would miss him terribly, even though he was only a "dumb foreigner." She smiled at this thought, a tear streaking down her cheek as she paused alone in the room.

"Everything okay?" Her mother expressed concern from the kitchen.

"No. But it will be," Suzuki said, wiping the moisture from the tear off her face. *I hope I can see him again sometime*, she thought, a surprising yet sincere sentiment. *Not likely*, she mused.

Suzuki's reply had caused her mother a moment of worry, and then the wisdom of age kicked in, and her mother resumed getting lunch ready. Her daughter was tough. *She'll be alright*. After all, she was the epitome of *Yamato damashi*, the soul of Japan. Her heart was beautiful, too. Mother was sure of that.

Epilogue
JIMMY'S RENEWED PURPOSE

From his experience with both Saori and now Suzuki, it was obvious to Jimmy that his purpose was to help others heal the lives that they'd lived to be fully present to their current purpose in life. He had been seeking peace for himself, and now he'd still be loving and kind to himself, but in a renewed sense—loving, kind, and above all else, compassionate with others, too. He was feeling ever more calm and very glad. He realized more deeply that his troubles came from being overly concerned with his own issues. In fact, that is how he would attain peace, by caring about others.

Jimmy said out loud, "I'll go to Open Breeze and settle into this calm that is building within me and continue learning so I can help others be calmer, too. To start with, I'll teach meditation, how to be present to the present moment. This is what the world needs, people who are present and calm."

Later that evening, Jimmy heard, *Way to go, Jimmy. We make quite a team, eh?*

Yeah, we sure do, he thought. Jimmy had figured out his purpose. Jimmy was glad that through his own connection to compassion, he could help others learn about themselves and, "in the process" make good on the Bodhisattva vow *to awaken speedily for the sake of all beings.* Jimmy thought as sleep overtook him, *May any efforts made benefit all beings.*

The End

SOURCES

- *Pilgrimage site: https://en.japantravel.com/tokushima/shikoku-88-temple-pilgrimage/67345*
- http://www.japanvisitor.com/japan-temples-shrines/kirihataji
- Asia for Educators https://afe.easia.columbia.edu/
- Book: *Shikoku Japan 88 Route Guide*, Buyodo Co. Ltd., 2023 (website: https://henro88map.com)

ABOUT THE AUTHOR

As an engaged member of the community, Daniel O'Brien, author of *Japanese Ghost in America*, supports others to be their best selves in community. Daniel lived in Japan for twelve years and has an MA in Advanced Japanese Studies. He teaches at Eagle Ridge Academy high school: medieval history and literature, as well as Eastern Studies—for which he was originally hired—as well as teaches meditation outside of school. He initiated and led an author's group and participated in a writer's group for many years until publishing his previous novel. He is excited about the course he is developing to teach mindfulness to teens to aid in calming the increasing anxiety of the modern world.

Daniel has two other books, *Star Points: Connections Old and New* as well as *Japanese Ghost in America*, the well-received book that features Jimmy of the current book as he begins his journey. Daniel looks forward to the third book in the trilogy, *Resolution*, as well as a book in the early stages about personal development through mindfulness and meditation. www.japanseries.com.